DeathWalker II

DeathWalker II

A Vampires Domain

Edwin F. Becker

authorHOUSE®

Photography by Kat Higdon

AuthorHouse™
1663 Liberty Drive
Bloomington, IN 47403
www.authorhouse.com
Phone: 1-800-839-8640

Published by AuthorHouse   01/27/2012

ISBN: 978-1-4685-3805-2 (sc)
ISBN: 978-1-4685-3804-5 (hc)
ISBN: 978-1-4685-3803-8 (ebk)

Library Of Congress Control Number: 2011918628

Contents

This Book Is Dedicated To
My Wife
A constant Inspiration

Chapter One

"**V**ampires my ass!" Don stated as they trudged through the wilderness in northern Minnesota.

"Hey, Professor Steiner is paying us good money to find this corpse. That is, if there even is one," John replied, reminding his friend that this was a paid excursion.

"Ah BS! That old guy is senile. First, who in the hell believes in vampires? Second, why would he possibly think the body of one is hidden in these woods? This ain't Transylvania!"

"Well, the story is that a good friend of his actually killed one. It was supposedly a female vampire, and her mate hunted down the Professor's friend and killed him in revenge. He believes that the remains of the female vampire are hidden out here somewhere. All I know is that he said they are likely not buried, and are possibly tucked away somewhere, protected from the sunlight . . . we should really start heading back soon . . . it's beginning to get dark."

"Come on, we can just camp out here. I'll protect you from the boogeyman. This way we will save a lot of time going back and forth," Don stated sarcastically.

Don was a hunter and tracker, and he felt very much at home sleeping in the wild. He was a big muscular man that looked like he belonged in the woods and could easily be mistaken for a lumberjack. John had taken him on as a guide, and to come along in helping search for the vampire's remains. John was skeptical of the whole purpose, but had a high respect for Professor Steiner, who had hired him. John was a smaller man, and appeared more the academic type—more of a bookworm or nerd. He had been told the story of a Ted Scott, who had accidentally met up with a female vampire and killed her with a crossbow. Supposedly, her mate hunted Ted down in Minneapolis and killed him in a gruesome manner. The Professor swore that he not only saw the vampire, he actually had words with him. John knew the Professor for over twenty years, and believed that there had to be "some" element of truth to the story. So there they were, following the Professor's directions, combing the wilderness in the northwest corner of the state searching caves, sink holes, and rock piles.

"I'm really not sure we should camp out here . . ." John was only reluctant because of the Professor's warnings.

"What? Afraid the boogeyman will get us?" Don laughed. "Look, we have to walk miles back to the car, and then search for a motel. Let's just stay out here."

"Maybe you're right. We would definitely save a lot of time and cover a lot more ground. I did promise the Professor that we would cover as much territory as possible in three days. I guess we should look for a small clearing and make camp."

Don led the way. They soon came upon a clearing which had a huge boulder the size of a house in the center. "Here is a great place; we can literally sleep with our back to the wall." He was pointing at the giant boulder. Don was an expert in the north woods and his instincts were finely tuned, so John agreed. Little did they realize that the body they were looking for was very close, and the boulder they chose to sleep next to was the favorite resting place of Christian, the hundred year old vampire, and his new mate, Katherine.

"Tell me about this professor guy," Don asked, getting comfortable.

"Professor Steiner is an expert in the field of anthropology and I studied under him. He has a brilliant mind, so I believe there must be some substance to his story. He has the courage to consider himself a vampire expert. Honestly, I'm not much for the vampire theory, but I'd like to believe he has some sound basis for this search."

"Well, you watch out for the killer vampires, and I'll keep an eye out for Bigfoot!" Don joked.

As they talked, darkness quickly fell. Being as there are no lights in the woods, they swiftly put a campfire together. Slowly, the silent woods became full of sounds, as crickets, frogs, and even owls began their songs of the night. They both carried MRE's in their backpacks—meals ready to eat—popular with hunters and survivalists. Outside of the glow of their campfire was utter darkness. It becomes so dark that people have been known to suffer from claustrophobia, being enveloped in darkness that seems to totally encase them.

"When you're done eating that, throw the tins in the fire. That will destroy the scent of food so a bear won't come sniffing around. I really don't want to have to shoot a bear. I am curious, if we do find some remains, how will you identify it as being those of a vampire?" Don questioned.

"Well, the Professor said firstly, not to move them, for he believes they will deteriorate should they be exposed to sunlight. He said that the jaws and teeth will make it obvious. It will have fangs that may be as long as four or five inches, and all of the teeth will appear as pointed and sharp as canines," John explained. "Should we find it, after we are done staring at it, I'm to leave a tracking device and get to a land line and call him immediately, as there is no cell phone coverage out here. However, he swears that if we find it we will be in dangerous territory, because her mate will definitely be in the area."

"You don't really believe all that vampire crap do you?"

"Let me ask you this; the FBI says over three quarter of a million people disappear every year. Where do you think they all go?" John asked.

"How many?"

"Over seven hundred fifty thousand."

"I have no clue. Given the way our government is going, maybe they all head for Canada. I would also guess that maybe there's a giant homeless camp in Area 51," Don joked.

As they bantered, they never noticed the woods becoming strangely silent, as the night creatures became quiet all at once. Just ten feet above them, on the flat top of the boulder, sat two vampires . . . listening.

"So you think that vampires are killing people and nobody is aware of them?"

"It's certainly possible. I mean, even if they find a mutilated body, who would have courage enough to attribute the killing to a vampire? Can you imagine what would happen to anyone in law enforcement that might even imply such a thing? They would be sent to the loony bin. The Professor says a detective he knows is very aware of the problem, but any word to the public would simply create chaos. Imagine how many of these kids wearing that 'Goth' make-up would get staked in the heart by a paranoid John Q. Public?"

Christian whispered to Katherine. "It seems they are hunting for us once again . . ."

"So? We'll just eat a little early tonight," she answered with a smile.

"No, you don't understand. They know this is my domain, and they will continue to come. The old man is obsessed with finding us. He is relentless. I'm afraid we must change our territory."

"So we cannot just eat them both?"

"We will only feed off one and leave the other to spread the word that we are here. That will guarantee that those who know of us will focus their energy on finding us here, while we will move elsewhere."

"Where will we go?"

"I'm not sure, but far, far away."

Meanwhile, below them, the conversation continued.

"So, the story is that this Ted guy killed a vampire with a crossbow?"

"If you believe in such things, it is a most effective weapon," John replied.

"Crossbow my ass! It's just a little too medieval for me. You should see what my .223 can do. As far as I'm concerned, you don't take a damned crossbow to a gun fight."

John just shrugged. "Hey, if you don't believe, there is nothing I can say with any authority to convince you. I myself have never seen a vampire, and other than Professor Steiner and his detective friend, I don't know of another soul that has."

"I will do my job, but I seriously think we are wasting our time and that old man's money. Who is afraid of a vampire anyway? Some of them sparkle like fairies, others sit down for an interview and cry like big babies. So they bite you—who cares? You want to see a good bite? I'll bring my Pit Bull out here and we'll see who bites who!" As Don smiled at the thought of his Pit Bull, he suddenly became aware of the sudden silence.

John began to speak. "Don . . ."

"SSHHH. Listen! There is no sound? Everything just went dead. Too quiet! It's a sure sign that a large predator is near . . ." Don immediately reached for his rifle and quickly chambered a shell. "I don't hear a darned thing moving?"

"What are you listening for?" John questioned.

"Any movement at all. A bear will make a lot of noise, so it's no bear, but even a big cat will step on dry leaves or a twig. I don't hear a thing, but whatever it is, must be near . . ."

In a whisper, Katherine stated, "Let's get this party started."

Christian frowned. "Your modern phrasing can be confusing. We want the one with the gun."

That said, Christian and Katherine descended silently, landing directly behind Don and John. Katherine thought she would have some fun. "Looking for us?" she said softly. Both being startled, the men turned in shock. Don immediately pointed and fired his rifle, in a complete reflex of fear.

Katherine smiled. "That was a mistake. Had I been human, you might have killed me!"

Before he could even pull the trigger a second time, Christian had a firm grip on his throat. Seeing Don overtaken and unarmed, John instantly realized they had no defense as they brought no crosses or weapons that might be effective, so he turned and ran blindly into the darkness in a hysterical fright.

As Christian inhaled the pleasant scent of pure fear, Katherine tormented their victim.

"So, we sparkle like fairies?"

"Do I sparkle?"

"We cry like babies?"

"Our bite is no worse than that of a dog?"

"Well, let's just find out," she taunted.

"Please! Let me go. I'll give you anything you want! Please!" Don begged.

Christian's eyes began to glow red and his human appearance instantly transformed to that which one never wants to see—a hungry nightmarish animal. "You have only one thing we want . . ."

As Don inhaled to scream, Christian bit a massive chunk of Don's throat. The result was a loud, sickening gurgle. As Don's blood flowed, Christian drank freely and offered his fountain of warm nourishment to Katherine. "Dinner is served!"

John was running blindly as fast as his legs could carry him. He was tripping on dead branches, and even ran smack dab into a tree. In the utter darkness, he did not know that the vampires could see him clearly and could have caught him easily in seconds, had they been so inclined. His mind was in a complete panic, and in the distance, he could see what appeared as a light, so he continued running toward it. John ran, stumbled, rolled, fell, and kept moving mindlessly toward a beacon that possibly held safety. The light he was traveling toward was a porch light on Ray Scott's home. It was Ray's son, Ted, who had been killed by Christian. Ray promised his son that he would never invite a stranger into his house, and he always wore a blessed cross. Even though he had never seen a vampire, he did believe. So when John reached the house and stumbled onto the porch out of breath, he found the front door locked.

"Help! Let me in!" John screamed.

Immediately, Brutus, Ray's Yorkshire terrier, began barking a warning. At this late hour, Ray immediately had flashbacks of all that he was told about vampires. '*No damned way,*' he thought. He immediately took his huge crucifix from the wall. Holding the crucifix with his arm extended, he yelled. "I am not inviting you in!"

"Open the door! Please help me!" John pleaded.

Having never seen a vampire, and not knowing what to say or how to act, Ray asked, "Are you a vampire?" He looked to Brutus, who was now wagging and not growling.

"Hell no! Please they are after me! Please open the door!"

Ray decided to open the door just a crack to have a look at this hysterical person. Even at his old age, Ray was a big man, and felt no one could force their way in. When he opened the door just a sliver, John came crashing through, knocking Ray to the floor. Before Ray could get up, John slammed the door, locked it, and leaned against it, as if he expected the vampires to force their way in. Ray just stared in awe. He realized that this was no vampire, as John had freely entered—but it was certainly the most frightened man he had ever seen in his life.

"What the hell is chasing you?" Ray asked as he picked his large frame off the floor.

"Vampires! I saw them. They got Don, but I got away! I ran for my life!"

"From what I have been told, if they wanted you, son, they would have had you already. You say you outran them?"

"All I saw is that they appeared out of nowhere and were right on us. It was a man and a woman. The whitest damn people I have ever seen. Plus, their eyes were glowing! Don shot one and she just stood there, smiling at him! That's when I took off . . ." John was babbling hysterically.

"Who beat you up? Was there a fight?"

"What? What do you mean?"

"Look at your face, son. Your cheek is bleeding and your eye is swollen."

John felt his face and could feel his swollen eye. When he looked at his hand, it was bloody. "I guess I ran into some trees, plus I fell down a number of times. I was running in darkness, as the crow flies. I must have bounced off of twenty trees and fell over a dozen more. I was running for my damned life!"

"Well, you're safe now. You say they're out there? How far away?"

"I . . . I don't know. I just ran. We were camped in a clearing,"

"The one with the big rock . . ." Ray assumed.

"Yeah! We were camped against the boulder."

"That is exactly where my son killed a female vampire and took over a hundred stitches in his torso afterward. In the end, they killed him," Ray stated sadly.

"You're Ted Scott's dad. Professor Steiner told me the whole story. That's why we were out here. We were searching for the vampire's remains. The Professor knew that the male vampire would be close. He warned us; I just really didn't believe, so we made the mistake of camping out there."

"That really was a mistake! Professor Steiner and Detective Evans are likely the only people in world that faced off with this vampire and are still breathing. I guess you now make it three. They educated me fairly well. Being an old man, I no longer have a need to do anything after dark, I wear this blessed crucifix my son gave me, and as you well know, I never invite a stranger into the house at night."

"Hope you know I ain't leaving until the sun comes up."

Ray handed him a large crucifix. "Here, hold on to this. It will make you feel better. Make yourself at home. You're safe here."

John studied Ray and had to ask. "If you know there are vampires out there, why the hell would you stay here?"

Ray smiled. "First, notice the crucifix you are holding is made of wood. Also, notice that the base has been carved to a point. I'm no good with a crossbow, but I would gladly risk my life to plunge that crucifix into that vampire bastard's heart. Son, I'm an old man. How could I sell this house to unsuspecting people, who may even have children, and not warn them? But, if I did warn them, word will be out that I'm an old lunatic, and nobody would believe me anyway. I assume you graduated college and you're a pretty smart fellow, and you obviously didn't believe in vampires. I built this house, my wife passed away in this house, and given I don't go dancing at night anyway, why should I leave?"

"If you saw what I saw tonight, it just might motivate you a bit."

"Where did you leave your car?"

"My car? I don't even know where the hell I am?"

"Well, if you did not see my house when you drove into the woods, then you must have entered on the other road, about five miles from here. We better call the police and report this."

"What the hell am I going to tell them?"

"Well, just give them a version of the truth. You and your buddy were out camping and were put upon by a couple maniacs, and you escaped into the woods. Your buddy fired a shot and likely missed. Having no defense, you ran for your life. There's no shame in that."

* * * *

Christian and Katherine were experts at making their kill appear as an animal attack. First, they scattered everything at the campsite, opening and emptying all the containers of food. Then, they clawed and mutilated the body, dragging it off and leaving it in the woods, hoping the other predators might finish the job. Afterward, they rested on the top of the huge rock, basking in the moonlight. Christian took in the sights, as he knew this would be his last visit to this place that he and his former mate of a hundred years loved so well.

"Where will we go?" Katherine asked.

Katherine was only concerned because as vampires were territorial, this meant that wherever they would go, it would likely become their home for possibly an eternity.

"We need to assume a new territory. I would prefer one that is near a substantial population, yet has wilderness."

"Well, to remain undiscovered and still enjoy human blood, we have many choices where humans can become missing and never be noticed. What do you think of New York?"

Christian scowled, "I refuse to live in a sewer. A hundred years ago it was a dung heap. I cannot imagine what it has become today."

"Well, Los Angeles is far too crowded, even in the woods, and Las Vegas is surrounded by desert."

They were a strange pair, as Christian was over a hundred years old, and Katherine had only been a vampire for a couple years. He had survived living outside the populated areas, and was very much at home in the deep woods, preferring caves as a resting place. Christian's first exposure to modern urban society was when he took his revenge on the man that had killed his beloved Anne. Katherine was actually the love interest of the man he had killed, Ted Scott. Taking her for a mate was his revenge.

Katherine had knowledge of all the modern ways, and at times, was amused by Christian's language and choice of words. Christian was learning of modern society, culture, and technology, but at times was confused by her manner of speech.

"What are our other choices?"

"Well, there is plenty of food in Miami, but nowhere but swamps for shelter. What would truly suit you?" she asked.

"We need to be near a city that has a population large enough to accommodate homeless, prostitutes, and undesirables that might never be missed. My choice would also have deep woods where animal predators are common, and caves. I relish large caves."

"Relish? Today relish is a condiment, it is something they put on hot dogs!" Katherine laughed.

"Hot dogs? Okay then, I enjoy, or I prefer, caves. Is that better?" Christian asked.

Katherine began thinking out loud. "We want a descent size city, with a substantial population that is surrounded by wilderness. Large caves will likely mean mountains. I know just the place—Branson, Missouri!"

"Missouri? I know not of Branson? I know of Kansas City."

"Branson has developed greatly in the last 20 years. It has a rather small residential population, but eight million visitors pass through there every year. It is in the Ozark Mountains, which are famous for their many caves. It is completely surrounded by wilderness. I once read that almost half of the twenty thousand people that work there are transients from the surrounding states. Plus, hunters, fishermen, and outdoor sportsmen from all over the world wander the woods and lakes year around. It would be wonderful. We could even travel the town at night, because it has a very active nightlife."

"We would not be obvious walking amongst the humans?"

Katherine laughed. "Are you kidding? Today, they cover their bodies in tattoos, pierce their faces, dye their hair outrageous colors, and even put on white make-up to look like us. All we need to do is to get a good spray tan and we would appear as middle class normal."

"Spray tan? What is this spray tan?"

"We can easily go to a tanning salon and they will spray our skin to look as if we have spent time in the sun. We can even go to the theater and enjoy the entertainment."

"It sounds perfect. We may only have one problem," Christian stated most seriously.

"What would that be?"

"A place so perfect must already be the domain of one of our kind. They would view us as intruders and a threat. Likely, there will be conflict."

"Are there many of our kind?"

"Being most honest, I don't really know. I was amazed that there was a number of our kind in Minneapolis. I came upon one, and felt an instant pending conflict. As you know, sharing is not our strong suit. I would assume we are not many, as there seems no broad knowledge of our kind amongst humans. By and large, we are considered to be mythological, which is much to our advantage. Tell me more about this spray tan?"

* * * *

Having called the state police, they were now at Ray's house taking the report. Violence was very uncommon in this part of the state, so there was great concern as to whether this would be the beginning of a crime spree.

"Tell me about these two people." The state trooper was an old veteran of the force. "How were they dressed? What were they wearing?"

John, taking Ray's advice, told the absolute truth. "He was wearing a suit . . . a dark suit, very tailored and well fit, and she was wearing what appeared to be a dark evening dress, like one a woman might wear going out to a dinner."

The old trooper scratched his head. "So a man in a suit and woman dressed for dinner are out wandering in the wilderness at night? And they just appeared out of the darkness? That certainly does not in itself sound threatening, so let me ask you, why did you run?"

"When the man attacked my companion and had control of his rifle, I felt I might be his next target, and I was unarmed. So I panicked and ran."

The trooper understood that John, being a small man, could easily choose flight over fight, given the situation. "Was there a scuffle? What happened to your face?"

"I was running in complete darkness in a state of panic. It was pitch black out there and I ran into everything in my path."

"Do you have any idea where in the woods this occurred?"

"I just know we were in a clearing with a huge rock formation. I think I began running east. That's all I know."

"What kind of vehicle did you travel up here in?"

"An Escalade. A white Cadillac Escalade."

` "Well, I'll put out an APB on the vehicle and find it for you, if these suspects didn't take it." The trooper reviewed his report and asked, "Were you men doing drugs or drinking?"

"No!" John stated indignantly.

"Well, you must understand, with you looking like you've been in a fight or struggle, if we find a body out there, you initially may be considered a suspect. Unfortunately, it is rather common for two hunters to be out in woods, have a few too many beers, and get into a fight."

"Then do me a favor. Administer the alcohol test. I have no trace of anything in my system."

"If you have no objection, it might be good for you to establish that on the record. I'll go get the kit." The trooper left for his car to retrieve his breathalyzer.

"What do you think they're going to find out there, son?" Ray asked.

"I have no idea, but I'm pretty sure whatever they find will not be good. There is no way Don survived. Did you see how that cop looked at me? He already thinks I'm crazy or on drugs."

"Nah, that's just their procedure, especially in this part of the state. Rarely do we experience random violence or crime. Out here, most people die a ripe old age, and other than a drunken bar brawl on New Year's Eve or a rare animal attack, we don't see things like this. Other than Hawaii, the people in Minnesota enjoy the longest life span in America. I would place a call to the Professor. Tell him what happened and that his instincts were correct. I believe he will create a plan to finally get this son-of-a-bitch. Mike Evans, the Minneapolis detective, has been practicing his skills with crossbows and would like a crack at this vampire. Now that we know that this is his stomping ground, it's only a matter of time before they get him."

*　*　*　*

In the faint glow of the moon, Christian and Katherine reclined, simply enjoying the view of the night sky. Other than to feed, a vampire is a most docile being. Aside from their mate, vampires have no need to socialize, including with their own kind. The only driving force for a vampire is hunger. Other than a mate, vampires feel no need to create other vampires, for all that would do is create more competition for their food source, plus it would increase the risk of becoming known to the public. It was that awareness that sparked vampires to be hunted down and killed in Europe in the 19th century. Christian had always enjoyed his life outside the general population. As the population grew, there was always a hitchhiker, runaway, and even an occasional hunter that he could feed on without being discovered. With his last trip to the city, he found the homeless, prostitutes, and gang members to be an abundant food source. It seemed no one took notice should they just 'disappear.' In the wilderness, Christian was not above feeding off of a large mammal, should human blood not be available. From his first days as a vampire, Christian found caves to be a perfect place to rest and hide from the sun. Most of the state parks prohibit the public from exploration, because of the danger and need to preserve natural resources. It was the ideal place for a vampire to reside, being large, dark, and protected.

"What are you thinking?" Katherine asked.

"I am saying farewell, in my own fashion."

"Are you sad?"

"No. It is best that you and I establish our own domain and it is time for me to let my memories of Anne fade."

"Is that possible?"

"Yes. It is time for us to create our own memories."

"When will we leave?"

"We will begin our journey with the next nightfall. The few humans that know of us will begin searching within days. They will likely spend weeks, if not months, searching before they realize that we are gone. After that, they will have no indication as to our whereabouts."

"You will like Branson."

"Tell me why millions of people would visit there?"

Katherine had only been a vampire for a few years, and had been an attorney in her human life. She had traveled, and was educated on all modern technology. Slowly, she was educating Christian to modern culture.

"Branson is in the center of the country, geographically, and easy for people to travel to by automobile. It actually has more theater seats than New York City, as well as hotel rooms. Unlike Las Vegas, which is marketed as a sinful city, Branson's attractions are for the whole family. Many famous celebrities appear there, and it offers a wealth of recreation. You might enjoy seeing their old fashioned paddle wheeled riverboat," she explained.

"I haven't seen a riverboat in more decades than I can remember," Christian sighed.

"You don't believe we can negotiate our existence with those of our kind?"

"I think you will find that your natural instincts may not be to negotiate when faced with one of our kind. I am not an expert, but it is my assumption that you will bristle and become aggressive beyond that which you can control. I am not sure whether it is unique to gender or not. I do know that once, when facing another male, my instincts were to end his existence. It was the Professor that is hunting me that stated a fact that was very profound. When I threatened to end his life, he said he had little fear, as he is old and had led a full life, by warm blooded standards. He responded that it is I that should be afraid, for if he ends my existence, I have eternity to lose. He was quite correct, for we must protect our eternity. More vampires only create a competition for food, and a greater chance of discovery."

"I guess that is an example where less is more . . ." Katherine stated wisely.

Christian had never heard the phrase, and he smiled. "That is very good. Less actually equates to more in a true sense."

"Professor Steiner is an intelligent man, but his remaining years are few . . ." Katherine was assuring Christian that the Professor's pursuit would not be long lived.

"I never underestimate any man guided by purpose, regardless of age."

"Well, Branson will solve our dilemma. Unlike Minneapolis, the most undesirable element of the population lives outside the city proper. We will never want for food."

*   *   *   *

The trooper administered the breathalyzer, and was slightly surprised that John had no alcohol in his system. As veteran state trooper, he knew that rarely does the average citizen understand what the years of experience have thrown in his path. Most people view a law enforcement officer as one who spends his day giving out speeding tickets. In reality, they address the bizarre human behavior that most are never aware of. He had seen men attacked by bears that swore it was Bigfoot. He had seen far too many hunting trips turn into drunken brawls. He has seen hunters climb trees to get a better shot, and fall and break their necks, or wind up falling on their gun and shooting themselves. All too common were naïve people entering the deep woods with no respect or knowledge of the dangers. Now, hearing the story of two attackers wearing formal wear deep in the woods seemed to be a new one. He now knew that John had not been drinking, but could not rule out drugs of some kind. Other than being hysterical, John seemed normal, but as a person unfamiliar with the wilderness, the trooper also knew what tricks the mind could play in the dark woods, once fear and panic have set in.

"They already located your vehicle. In fact, it has been under surveillance all day. We don't often see Escalades left abandoned on the side of the road. Obviously, we will wait until morning to determine the location of your camp. We'll come get you in the morning and we can start the search for your buddy. Get some sleep! And put something on that eye!"

The trooper left and Ray threw a pillow and a blanket on the sofa. "Here, take these. The bathroom is over there. In the medicine cabinet, you can find some antiseptic and bandages. Make yourself at home, son. Kitchen is that way. I would call the Professor even at this late hour, as he may want to come out here and get an early start, with it being a five hour drive. I'm turning in. You try and get some sleep." As Brutus led Ray to the bedroom, Ray left John alone with his thoughts. His first thought was to dial Professor Steiner.

* * * *

Christian began imagining the pleasures of walking amongst the population. "I would so enjoy attending the theater."

"I guarantee we will, and it will be no problem."

"We will not appear odd?"

"The only thing odd about you is that you are so lean and fit. The average American is now considered obese."

"Obese?"

"When you were in Minneapolis, you did not notice?"

"No, as I was obsessed with finding my prey, and also amazed that I was viewed and put upon as being prey by many warm blooded predators myself."

"You will enjoy modern society. Food is abundant. Humans seek isolation in the woods to manufacture drugs. All will become food. We can exist forever just feeding on society's undesirables."

"Tell me more of modern society?" Christian asked.

"You will be pleased. Unlike when you were alive, today there are many types of undesirables that can easily become food. There is an overwhelming number of homeless and a huge population of illegal citizens that, on record, do not even exist. There is a whole society of drug users and manufacturers that are ours for the choosing. There are gangs and prostitutes, both female and male. There are a growing number of survivalists that shun society and live in the wilderness. Sustenance will be of no problem. A missing adult in modern society does not raise an eyebrow, unless they are of prominence. If I can acquire a computer, they even have a thing called 'Craig's List,' where lonely people advertise. You merely call them and they will come to us for 'dinner.' The only thing we must avoid, however, is children. They have what is called an 'Amber Alert,' which initiates immediate action by authorities, who will search relentlessly."

"I have never had reason to harm a child . . ." Christian responded.

"Tell me, how will we recognize our kind?" Katherine wondered.

"You will know immediately. You will feel confrontational or feel avoidance."

"Why avoidance?"

"With our kind, it will likely be confrontational, but there are other beings that are not human which you will be able sense and know without question to avoid."

"What type of beings?"

"I am not entirely sure. My one experience was many years ago. I came upon a man in the wilderness that I viewed as prey. As I approached, my senses told me he was not human. What manner of being was a mystery, but I knew to avoid him and not engage contact. We never have need of confrontation for the sake of confrontation in itself."

"Your senses are stronger than mine. You will protect me?"

"I will defend you to my death."

*   *   *   *

It was 7 A.M., and Professor Steiner was banging on Ray Scott's door. This initiated Brutus into his 'alarm' bark. Both Ray and John met him at the door. Brutus was familiar with the Professor, and demanded attention by pawing at his leg.

"Hello, my little fellow. Good morning, Ray. Thank you for accommodating John here." The Professor started his journey at 2 A.M.

after talking with John and realizing he would not be able to sleep. "So, our vampire is here. From John's description, it is definitely Christian, and he has Katherine, as we originally theorized."

"I was lucky to escape with my life. I don't know what the police will find, but Don surely did not survive," John stated.

The Professor, being highly intelligent with an analytical mind, knew exactly of Christian's ploy. "John, if there were two vampires, they simply allowed you to escape. You could never have gotten away from a vampire, especially in open ground. If you are here, it is for a reason, and there could only be two. One, he is declaring war, and is luring us into his territory, or two, he is leaving, and this will put us on a wild goose chase while he relocates. Either way, you are most fortunate that he needed you as a messenger."

Unaware that the police and forest rangers had begun their search at dawn, a police car pulled into Ray's drive. The state trooper approached and announced that they had located the campsite. He explained that the site was actually closer to Ray's house than where John had parked and entered the woods. It was suggested that they proceed to the campsite immediately. Both John and the Professor decided to make the hike through the woods. No sooner than walking in the direction, John realized there was actually a path going in that direction that he had never seen while running hysterically in the dark. He looked at Professor Steiner, concerned about his age.

"It's at least a mile. Are you sure you want to walk this?"

"Youngster, I cover six miles a day on campus going back and forth. I'll be fine." Steiner appeared a miniature version of a well groomed Santa Claus, with his stout build, white hair, and beard.

The trooper led the way. As they walked the path, they could actually see places where John had ran and disturbed foliage along the way. It was almost a mile when they entered the clearing. Immediately, they saw yellow police tape marking off areas near the huge boulder. Forest rangers had arrived riding ATV's which were parked around the site. Based on the different uniforms, it appeared three agencies seemed to be involved. They walked to the Captain, and the trooper introduced them.

"So you're John Hudson?"

John nodded. "Yes, sir."

"And you claim, from your statement, that two people did this—a man in a dark suit, and a woman in an evening gown?"

"Yes, sir."

The Captain just grinned. "Son, there is nothing about this scene that shows another human was anywhere near here. We have no footprints, other than two sets. One is likely yours, and the other is that of the deceased. Look at the site; it is all too obvious that an animal—most likely a bear—did this. All the food tins have been opened, and the random scattering of your gear is an all too familiar sight. I saw from his driver's license that your friend was six foot four, and 250 pounds. Looking at you, unofficially, I would rule you out because unless you clubbed him when he was sleeping, he would have swatted you like a fly. I'm not sure why you ran off, and judging by your face, it looks like there was some kind of fight, but without confirmation by forensics, it looks like your friend was killed by a large predator. I would not advise viewing the body unless you have a very strong stomach. I'm hoping you might want to tell us what really happened."

John was shocked, looking around at the gear scattered over a fifty yard area. "I saw exactly what I told the state trooper last night."

"Mr. Hudson. If a bear came at you and you became frightened and ran, just say that. No one will judge you for being afraid of what could have been a five hundred pound animal."

"No! It was a man about 6'3" and rather slender, and a woman with dark hair and an evening dress maybe 5'4"."

"So this man who is 6'3" and slender, overpowers your friend, who is built like a wrestler and is bigger and outweighs him by fifty pounds? Plus, your friend has a weapon?"

John could not believe that he was facing doubt. "Did you find bear prints anywhere?"

The Captain paused. "Well, no, but these claw marks and the manner in which this campsite has been violated tells a pretty clear story."

"Well, I have nothing else to add," John stated in agitation.

"Son, pending forensics and lab results, I'm afraid you are not going to be a very credible witness. Look, I have no idea whether it was hysteria, or some kind of hallucination, but I can state with authority that there is no trace of anyone but you, your companion, and some large predator, that have been in this clearing."

The Professor interrupted. "Was he bitten in the neck?"

The Captain grimaced. "Sir, it is pretty damn gruesome. The only way we even knew what he looked like was from the picture on his driver's license. He was torn to pieces and it is obvious that other animals devoured various parts of the body. The only way we could possibly identify him is a fingerprint, DNA, or dental records. So my answer is yes, he was bitten on the neck, plus a few hundred other places. The body is actually about a hundred yards from here and it is pretty clear it was dragged. So would you like to change your story any?"

"No, sir. I don't think you'll find any beer cans or drugs, so if you want to label me as being hysterical, that's fine with me."

The Professor pulled John aside. "John, let it be. They will never learn the truth. Better they blame an animal than consider you a murderer. In a way, this vampire did you a favor. Given this evidence, there is absolutely no way to prove otherwise. Let it go. Just let it go."

"Mr. Hudson, you're going to have to come with us. We'll take you to your vehicle, and you'll have to follow us to the station. We are going to need your fingerprints and some additional information."

The Professor let him know he was okay on his own and he could walk back to Ray Scott's following the path with no problem. As he walked, his mind wandered back to his confrontation with Christian. He never saw Christian's transformed face, but his steely eyes would never be forgotten. As he looked at the tall pines and dense foliage, he wondered just how many deaths were attributed to people becoming 'lost' in these woods, or attacked by animals? He also wondered why fate had sent Ted Scott down this path that fateful night to uncover the existence of this creature that nightmares are made of. As he walked, he kept one hand in his pocket, where he gripped a wooden envelope opener. It was a 'stake' that he kept with him at all times. As he came to the end of the trail, he could see Ray sitting on the porch with Brutus sleeping in his lap.

"So? What's the verdict?" Ray asked.

"Well, John will most likely be labeled as being hysterical, and the killing will be attributed to an animal. Likely, the forest department will shoot the closest bear to the scene and close the file."

"You know better?"

"Unfortunately, yes. This vampire is very cunning."

"Do you think he is luring you into hunting for him?"

"Honestly, I believe he is gone. I cannot imagine him wanting us to hunt for him in the daytime and possibly finding him when he is completely vulnerable. He is far too intelligent for that. I believe he wants us hunting him here, while he is relocating far from us. We will likely never see or hear of him again."

"Well, I will keep my pointed crucifix close at hand anyway," Ray stated with conviction.

The professor smiled and produced his wooden envelope opener. "And I will always have this in my pocket."

The Professor felt defeated. Although he would continue hiring searchers, his only hope was to find the remains of Christian's former mate, Anne. In his heart, he knew that Christian and his new mate, Katherine, were long gone. All hopes of finding Christian and confronting—possibly destroying him—were also gone. Finding a lone night creature in a country of three hundred million people, during the hours of darkness, is literally an impossibility. *'Where would a vampire go?'* the professor wondered. *'Likely not to the Sunshine State.'* He knew he would be continuously searching national news for any deaths appearing suspicious, but in a country where hundreds of thousands of people simply disappear, the Professor knew that in spite of his future effort, the search was likely over. He sat quietly with Ray, resigned to his failure. Little did he know that fate can take amazing twists.

Chapter Two

Branson is the jewel of the Ozark Mountains, and it is a destination known for conservative family values and patriotism, as well as being a wholesome, crime free oasis from this eroding modern culture. It boasts entertainment fit for the whole family from children to grandparents. It has water slides, theme parks, and even an old fashioned paddle wheeled riverboat. Although it has a small population of 6000, it employs 18,000 additional workers to accommodate the 8 million yearly visitors from all over the world. The residents of Branson know they live in a special place, where they have nearly 400 eateries, more golf courses than you can count on one hand, and a lake so clear you can see 30 feet down. They enjoy over 100 shows that run morning through night and a Christmas season that is considered the 'fifth' season, but they also know there is a dark side. They know that crime, regardless of how heinous, is rarely reported and that the police, though well trained, have more than they can handle. They also know that sometimes there are unexplained happenings that no one ever wants publicized.

With the 18,000 nonresident workers and 8 million tourists passing through, it can also bring a very bad element; plus, with a daily population that is 99% temporary, it is easy for a traveler to just 'disappear' without anyone noticing or becoming alarmed. If a waitress originally from Oklahoma doesn't show up for work the next day, it is assumed that she went back to her home town. If a housekeeper from Mexico doesn't come into work, it is assumed she returned to her home country, and was possibly even illegal. No one really knows how many have come to Branson for work or pleasure and have just simply never returned home. The only indicator that this might be a problem, is now and then when a fisherman snags something he never planned on, or a hiker exploring the woods trips across some unidentifiable remains. Yes, Branson has problems that you will never see on the colorful billboards lining the highway that lead to the city of God, family, country, mom, and apple pie!

Away from the bright lights on the south side of Table Rock Lake, an area was being taped off. With only the light of the full moon, flood lights were being pointed at an area where a partial rib cage was discovered by a man hiking with his dog. Detective Wayne Higdon was waiting for a forensic specialist as he examined the surrounding area. With a spotlight focused on the partial rib cage, he could see it was clean as a whistle and could also see the marks of powerful teeth that had chewed on the bones. *'Likely a big cat,'* he assumed. Although new to Branson, Higdon had already learned that south of Branson there were two animal preserves that were home to large cats. The Ozarks did have its share of mountain lions, but the preserves were home to lions, tigers, leopards, and various large cats that were taken from carnivals and attractions, or from private citizens who realized that these huge predators were not 'house pets.'

Higdon had also learned that the animal zoo just a few miles away also housed big cats and a variety of wolves, with cages that at times were no stronger than chicken wire. The only thing keeping some of these animals caged was the promise of a daily meal. He had learned that now and then a large cat or wolf would escape. Most times, these predators were semi-tame and no threat to humans unless frightened or hungry, and were easily tracked and captured. He also knew that a human tripping across one of these animals and reacting by screaming and running immediately triggered their primal instincts and could instantly become 'prey.' Rarely was any incident publicized, for Branson could never afford the negative publicity. This was further complicated by the fact that these preserves generally did not report these types of problems, and would track and recapture these escapees on their own, so as to not have their licenses revoked. This partial rib cage certainly appeared on the surface to be the work of large predator.

Higdon was made aware that homeless, campers, and even runaways would sometimes imagine these woods as a large park, rather than the wilderness that it really is. The Ozarks are a natural home to mountain lions, black bears, bobcats, and an assortment of venomous snakes—so mistaking these woods as a campground might be a fatal mistake. Wayne Higdon had moved to Branson after 12 years with the Springfield PD. He wanted a safer environment for his wife and child, and to escape the urban jungle that Springfield was slowly becoming. His partner was Jerry Cunningham, an older veteran of Branson. Tall and dark haired, Higdon was conditioned to the problems of a city bursting with population, and as far as crime went, he was conditioned to the gangs, shootings, and armed robberies that Springfield had become plagued with. Jerry, on the other hand, was born and bred in Branson, a town that, until recently, had rarely ever recorded a murder—although finding humans remains from time to time was almost routine. Jerry had been on the force for 25 years and knew Branson and the surrounding area like the back of his hand. He had brown hair littered with gray. He stood at 6 foot and was slightly overweight. He had a nervous habit of biting his thumbnail, which made it appear at times as though he was sucking his thumb.

Branson, having no crime lab, would forward these remains to Jefferson City, where the possible gender and age might be determined and DNA would be matched to a national database. However, any success in identifying them was actually near impossible. If they belonged to someone from another state that had come there for work and had no DNA on file, there could only be a search amongst missing persons of the approximate age and gender. Had this person never been reported missing, it would be a dead end. Unlike the CSI television programs that can do this within minutes, in reality, this might actually take months, if not over a year. Most recently, this had been complicated by the economy, as foreclosures had caused whole families to relocate, sometimes without leaving any forwarding address, thus, disappearing. Plus, just outside the city limits was a substantial homeless camp, with transients coming and going daily.

"Other than the initial paperwork, will we have any more work to do on this?" Wayne wondered.

"Nah, the only recent missing person was an old guy with Alzheimer's who went off wandering and got lost in the woods. We eventually found him, no worse for the wear. Check out the full moon . . . it always brings out the crazies."

Wayne looked off across the lake, and in the distance was an island. "How big is that island?"

"I don't know. It might be 20 acres or so. Why?"

"Well these bones are so clean . . . it's like they were possibly washed up from the lake."

"Well, I don't think they came from that island, as the water is pretty deep between here and there. These bones would have sunk some 60 feet down."

For some reason, this island that Wayne had seen so many times during the daytime suddenly looked ominous, as it was surrounded by the foggy mist rolling off the lake.

"It's just kind of strange. We have a clean set of bones setting on the surface, as if someone just tossed them here for us to find."

Jerry thought for a second. "Well, the guy who called us said that his dog found them. Could be that the dog found them elsewhere and brought them here. I guess we'll have some men canvas the area in the daylight."

As they watched the forensic specialist bag the evidence, a distinct howl echoed the mountains. It caused everyone to stop for a moment to just listen, as it seemed surreal.

'*Wolves?*' Wayne wondered. "Is that what I think it is?"

"Could be a wolf. A pair escaped the Branson West animal attraction last year, and as I recall, only the female was ever captured."

"Doesn't that worry anyone?"

"Nah! A wolf has plenty to eat around here on just the possums, raccoons, rabbits and squirrels. It's not likely that it will approach a human. That's why some of our best trackers and hunters in the area can't seem to catch him."

Wayne still was concerned. "That howl made a coyote howl sound like a chipmunk. How friggin' big is that wolf?"

"They said it was a large Timber Wolf. Apparently he has a good set of lungs on him!" Jerry laughed. "Hey, full moon, a wolf howling, and here we are, staring at some human bones. Now this would make a great commercial for Branson! Come to Branson, we'll scare the shit out of you!"

"Well, you have to admit that it's a bit weird . . ." Wayne mumbled.

"Things really have gotten weird. The whole county is searching for that missing couple from Forsyth. Here, a clean cut local couple with a web of family ties, just go missing? All they find is an empty house with all their belongings and personal items; no missing vehicles, and not a single clue. Now that's weird! I talked to a friend working on the case and they have zilch! This couple was working, attending school, church going, and not a hint of anything that might contribute to their disappearance. They have no fingerprints, no witnesses, no sign of struggle, or even anything that appears to be taken or misplaced. Their investigation is dead in the water. One day, I should brief you on some of the Ozark folklore. The Ozark history has everything from vigilante groups, to vampires and werewolves, to Hell Hounds and Sasquatch! Better yet, I'll take you to meet old Jonah."

"Who is old Jonah?"

"Old Jonah knows more about the mysteries of the Ozarks than anyone living."

"Jesus Christ! I thought the biggest problem in these parts was shoplifting . . ." Wayne muttered, shaking his head.

Jerry laughed. "Hey, look around. What is missing from this picture?"

"I don't know? What?"

"Press! You see any press out here? I always laugh when I watch that Las Vegas commercial that states, 'What happens in Vegas stays in Vegas . . . 'because just going to Vegas taints the reputation of anyone traveling there. It basically telegraphs that you are going there for the vice. Now, Branson has it perfected. What happens in Branson really does stay in Branson. Our press knows not to stick their nose where it doesn't belong. The Branson press only comes when they're called, or unless something will be picked up nationally, like the flooding—and then they will put a positive spin on it! Taney county was declared a disaster area, but not a word about Branson, other than we opened our dam. Probably the only other city with as much control of the press is New York. My brother lives there, and the stories he tells me are unbelievable; yet all we see is Central Park, Wall Street, and Donald Trump."

"Yeah, certainly not like Springfield. Even a simple fender bender can make it to the local news. Any major crime and we were always dodging reporters. You say, someone thought they saw Bigfoot? You're pulling my chain, right?" Wayne questioned.

"No, just little southwest of here an old guy swears he saw Bigfoot grab a fish out of the river just before dawn, a few years ago. Likely, he was three sheets to the wind . . . but every now and then some super hunter comes down here searching for Bigfoot. Again, you'll never hear that one, because Branson would not seem so 'family friendly' with a Bigfoot romping around. Just the rumor would kill the business of the mom and pop campgrounds."

A loud call broke their conversation. "Detectives? You better come look at this."

A patrolman canvassing the area had shined his flashlight on a strange sight. It was a huge footprint, but unlike any he had ever seen. Cunningham and Higdon both squatted to have a closer look.

"This has to be a joke?" Cunningham scratched his head in wonder.

"No way could this be real." Higdon put his foot over it, measuring. "It has to be a size 24? This thing would be as big as Shaq! This had to come from some Halloween store, like the huge costumes where you put something like this over your feet . . . clown shoes or something."

Cunningham was familiar with all the possible animal tracks. "If this is real, this ain't no cat. Given what I have heard about Bigfoot, this doesn't fit that description either. Look at the toes and pads; fake or not, this is a canine print of some kind. These claws alone are two to three inches."

Higdon, in searching, found another partial print. "Check this out. If that is a real print, and this is the direction it was going, it has a stride of about six feet and walks on two legs!"

Cunningham called for a camera. "Take a picture of this," he ordered.

"This must be a joke . . . although you did mention vampires and werewolves!" Wayne chuckled.

"Werewolves my ass!" Cunningham replied as he studied the print, biting at his thumbnail.

The sight of men gathering in the darkness in this wilderness area attracted the attention of the resident vampires, Aaron and Rebecca. High in the trees and shielded by darkness, they watched and listened from a distance.

"That Howler will be the death of us. There must be a way to eliminate him," she hissed.

"Well, we know we must avoid him. When he is in form, he is far more powerful than we are. If only we could locate him when he is in human form, then we could rid our territory of his presence," Aaron reasoned.

"Look! That animal just leaves body parts scattered all over the mountain. Discreet, he is not! Without him, we would have the perfect existence. I want that werewolf dead!"

Aaron and Rebecca dominated this territory. As far as they were aware, Southwest Missouri and Northern Arkansas were exclusively theirs. Their favorite place was the Branson area and the Ozarks, as transients and stragglers in the Mark Twain woods were common, and feeding was easy and rarely noticed with deep dark caves being plentiful to hide in from the sun's rays. The only exception was the werewolf, named the Howler. During the phase of the full moon, for three nights, he wreaked havoc in the wilderness. In Ozarks folklore, he dated back over a century. He was huge, ferocious, and mindless in his quest for food. Aaron and Rebecca were smart, in that they always chose their prey intelligently. It might be a homeless person sleeping in the woods, or a drug dealer out in the wilderness cooking meth or growing marijuana. They found it easy to target people who might never be missed. Either they hid their kills or mutilated them to resemble something animals might do, but the Howler had no such intelligence. Whomever or whatever he encountered met an immediate grizzly fate.

Aaron had become a vampire in 1967. He was 21 years old, and after dropping out of college, he went to live in a "hippie" commune in southern Oklahoma. It was there on one dark night that he was attacked as food. Somehow, the vampire that attacked him, did not drain enough of his life's blood to completely stop his heart. He awoke a vampire. Rebecca was a member of the same commune and he had always fancied her, so it was pure instinct to choose her for his mate. They would both be in their 60's by now, but instead, appeared as a pale twenty something's. Trial and error over the years had taught them the skills to remain undiscovered and lead a safe, satisfying existence. The Howler was their one curse. His indiscriminate killing often led to search parties canvassing the woods and searching the caves, which threatened their existence. Fortunately, the Howler's rampages only lasted during the cycle of the full moon.

Aaron was tall and athletic, with dark hair and features, and Rebecca was barely 5 foot tall with raven hair. However, Rebecca had a temper and a rage twice her size. Both had dark piercing eyes. Other than their pale appearance, they resembled the modern grunge youth of today.

Vampires have no knowledge of other nonhuman beings unless educated or exposed to them, so although they had overheard the name "Howler" and "werewolf" in human conversations, they were confused as to the manner of being and method of killing it. They had one confrontation with the Howler which had ended badly, so their instinct was to simply avoid contact during the cycle of the full moon.

"I'd like to kill him!" Rebecca snarled. "Look what he has done. They will be searching this whole area now and it is unsafe to rest anywhere near here!"

"I'd like him dead too, but if you remember, our last confrontation ended with him tossing us around like rag dolls and we were lucky to escape with all our limbs intact."

"Fire! That may be the answer," she suggested.

"Fire? Sorry, vampires and fire don't go together. Why risk our own existence? Let the humans deal with him. It is best we avoid him. Should he realize who we are and what our intentions are, he will be hunting us, and his advantage is that he can walk in the daytime. So, as I said, let the humans deal with him."

"Like they have done for a hundred years, if their tales are correct? Their track record is utter failure. This huge beast thrashes around 3 nights a month, leaving body parts lying around at whim, and apparently they blame some poor mammal and kill it, only to face the problem again and again. They are complete idiots!"

"Well, fortunately, the Howler enjoys the taste of idiots . . . as do we."

Rebecca smiled. "I agree. Better them . . . let's eat. There is a big man guarding a marijuana field outside of Harrison. No one meaningful will miss him. It will be as if he was never there."

Off into the night they flew, leaving the detectives to finish their work, which no longer interested them. They knew better than to rest anywhere near this area, as likely police, searchers, and cadaver dogs would soon flood the area looking for more remains once the sun comes up.

So, with the vampires fleeing the area, and the detectives about finished with this first phase of this investigation, the woods would soon be silent from activity. About six miles away, along the shoreline, rested the Howler. As a werewolf for three nights during the full moon, he had to eat and he ate whatever he encountered. Tonight, it was a deer that made the mistake of crossing his path. He was at rest feeling full and satisfied, staring at this bright full moon that controlled his life. He was actually an old man, and in human form, lived as a hermit. Having been through this cycle hundreds of times, he was also smart enough to leave clothes tucked away and hidden throughout the area, so when he awoke stark naked, he could easily become clothed. As a werewolf, he was a mindless animal—however, a cunning mindless animal. He avoided the general population, and always made sure he was in the deep woods when he 'turned.' He had been named the "Howler," as his calls echoed the mountains for all to hear. At one time, a small town, now long gone, was named after him because of his eerie howls.

As a man, he was older and not one that would stand out in crowd. In fact, he was rather ordinary. As a werewolf, he was enormous, standing seven foot tall and with jaws large enough to snap off one's head. He had the speed to catch a deer, the vision to see clearly at night, and the ability to smell the scent of prey over long distances. There was no method to his killing other than hunger and opportunity. Most cycles of the full moon normally presented a danger to only the local wildlife, but every now and then, it would be a man that would have the misfortune of crossing his path. As a man, he no longer faced the dangers he once faced a hundred years ago, when people did believe in werewolves and actively hunted them. Today, he lived as a myth and as something that people no longer believed in. He was safe to live his cycle of life uncontested and undiscovered—at least, for the time being. He had been shot a number of times in his years, but never by the one thing that would end his life—a silver bullet to the heart.

He loved the environment of Branson. Over the years, he changed his name and appearance and continued to reside in the city where the population rotates daily. Branson is a city where he could move from motel to motel without ever raising an eyebrow, with its 22,000 rooms. A city where stealing an overstuffed wallet or pocketbook from an unsuspecting tourist was child's play. Most of all, it was a city where he could disappear for three days without notice. His name never mattered. Today it was Bill Smith, and tomorrow it might be John Doe, as it held no meaning. He made no friends, and he mildly altered his appearance from time to time. Glasses, no glasses; beard, clean shaven; mustache, and even hair dye when he wanted to shed the all too common gray that Branson was famous for. As a human, he did possess a higher level of all senses, including that 'sixth' sense. He had no knowledge of vampires, other than what he had seen in movies, and only a fragmented memory of two human-like creatures he encountered as a wolf, which he quickly sent on their way. How he became a werewolf, he really didn't know or remember, as his encounters with wolves were numerous a century ago. At this point in history, he was no longer viewed as the tortured soul being hunted, and instead, he was imagined as an almost romantic mythological being. He found being a werewolf in the 21st century to be no problem, but was also careful not to create competition. Any human crossing his path when he was in form was certain not to survive.

So, as the vampires headed south to drain some poor soul who may never be found or remembered, the Howler reclined on the shores of Table Rock Lake. After having his fill of deer meat, he was about to rest for the night. As the river boat passed, little did the tourists know that in this oasis of shows, theme parks, golfing and waterslides, that they were being watched by a werewolf!

* * * *

Detectives Higdon and Cunningham decided to have a late bite to eat, so a stop at Elmer's pub was just the place. It was a popular local hangout where tourists rarely went, and they served the best pizza in town.

"So? You think that rib cage is a dead end?" Higdon asked.

"Yeah, pretty much."

"This is not that unusual out here?"

"Nah. Last month, in an old closed up motel, they found a whole body. It was a male, thirty-something, no ID and no obvious cause of death. He had likely had been there a year or so. They still don't know who he is . . . or was? Things like that never hit the news here in Branson. News like that is far too scary. We can't have little old ladies running around worried about running into skeletons."

As they ordered their pizza and a couple Cokes, a young man entered looking their way. Higdon caught him staring and said to Cunningham, "We have a clean-cut male, early twenties, wearing a hoodie, looking in our direction." Cunningham turned, and waved him over.

"Wayne, this is Danny. Danny delivers food all over Branson. Danny, this is my new partner, Detective Wayne Higdon. So, what do have for me?"

Danny slid into the booth and spoke softly. "Jerry, we have a whole new cat house that set up in a condo at Mountain Falls. They have at least four girls that look really young. Unit 414. Aside from their trade, you'll likely find a half pound of cocaine and a brick of weed. There were no weapons that I could see, but then you never know. There is a guy at the door that looks like he was breast fed on steroids. He is huge. Lots of activity after dark."

Wayne watched as Jerry folded a hundred dollar bill and slid it to Danny. "Thanks Danny."

Danny quickly rose and with a quiet, "See you guys," was gone.

"Informant?" Wayne asked.

"The best," Cunningham replied. "In Branson, the true pipeline to everything going on is the food delivery people. They deliver food to the hookers, gamblers, and even the dope dealers. A look inside a place will show them vice, stolen goods, firearms, and even possible violence and teen drinking. Danny is invaluable. In one night he may visit 30 motels and 20 condos, and does nothing but drive around town, all the while observing anything suspicious. He's a goldmine. It is actually a strange thing, as people regard a food delivery guy as their 'friend.' They invite him in, talk about their problems, even offer him tips in 'trade.' The crimes he has eliminated are far too many to even remember. Someday, I will have the department do something special for Danny. I have a few other sources in the food pipeline, but none equal Danny."

"Twelve years on the job in a much larger city, and I just learned something very valuable. Who knew? It makes so much sense, that it is almost too obvious."

"Let's leave it our little obvious secret," Cunningham advised. "Just reporting teen drinking, Danny likely saved over a dozen lives keeping those teenagers off the road. Everyone loves the guy and no one ever puts it together. He's my best weapon." Cunningham continued educating Higdon to the ways of Branson. Soon, they were discussing Ozark folklore, some of which was very dark.

* * * *

Outside of Harrison, Arkansas, only thirty miles away, was a field of marijuana growing freely, only guarded by a single man armed with an AK47. He was sitting on a wooden crate with his rifle on the ground, and was sampling some of the precious plants that he was guarding. This was a routine night that would normally be entirely uneventful, so getting a little high seemed no problem, even if he nodded out.

Silently, Aaron and Rebecca landed lightly and slowly approached. When the guard finally saw them, he rubbed his eyes, thinking it was a hallucination. Realizing it was not, he stood and picked up his gun. '*Two damn kids snooping where they shouldn't be,*' he thought.

His finger was off the trigger, as he felt the sight of the rifle and stern words would quickly send them on their way. "Kids, if you're looking for a private place to do the nasty, this ain't it. Get your asses moving away from here." He held the rifle out. "I won't tell you twice."

Aaron smiled. "You would kill us for just walking in your field of Mary Jane?"

"Mary Jane? What did you do, walk out of the sixties?"

Aaron and Rebecca both laughed. "As matter of fact, we did!"

"Look, I don't want to hurt you kids, so just turn around and go somewhere else. If you're both too high to understand, my method of sobering you up isn't pretty . . . so I am asking you for the last time . . . leave!"

He was not above shooting them both and burying the bodies out in the wilderness, but their appearance was unthreatening and deceiving, and he decided a mild beating would suffice. He set the rifle down, and since little Rebecca seemed no threat whatsoever, he went for Aaron and threw a punch that did nothing but sail through air, as Aaron dodged it easily. He quickly threw another with the same result. For an instant, he stood confused as Rebecca asked, "Are you done playing?"

The guard looked at her and replied, "Lady, I ain't playing."

She laughed. "Ha! I'm not talking to you . . . idiot!"

When he turned to take another swing at Aaron, he stopped instantly, for he was now facing a vision out of his nightmares. Aaron's eyes were glowing bright red and his teeth protruded to the sharpened tools of death that they really were.

"My turn," Aaron growled.

As the guard turned to run, he faced Rebecca, who had also transformed to her vampire appearance. He found himself screaming in horror. His scream was cut short, however, as Aaron grabbed his throat, cutting off his breathing, silencing him. "Dinner time!" He bit into the man's neck, as Rebecca bit into his thigh and femoral artery. Less than a minute, with his blood literally being suctioned out, the guard passed out and would soon be dead. After having gorged themselves, they laid back in satisfaction.

"Should we shred him?" she asked.

"No, let's just make him disappear. What can anyone do; report that the guy guarding their dope disappeared? No one will report it and no one will care. In a few weeks, we can return and do it again. Even the people that hired him will think he stole some plants and left. Perfect!"

They would easily transport the body and rifle to a mountainous area and dump it in a cave or sink hole, likely never to be found. This was typical of their method. Feeding off the fringe of the population and disguising or hiding their kills, allowed them to exist in complete secrecy. It was this reason that they hated the Howler, who might encounter a human and literally tear him apart, leaving remains and evidence scattered for all to find. More than once they were forced to leave their territory because of hunters or searchers looking for the wild animal they held responsible.

"Where do we go now?" Rebecca asked.

"Well, we know the Howler will be roaming, so I suggest we stay away from resting near here for a few days."

"I wish we could do away with him. I hate that dog!" she hissed.

"Well, according to local folklore, he is far older than we are, so I imagine many have tried and failed. Our best strategy is to avoid the area during the full moon's cycle and a few days after, should he have created any disturbances."

"I want him dead!" she screamed.

"I do too, but for now, we will rest elsewhere, just to be safe."

* * * *

Outside the glowing lights of Minneapolis, Christian and Katherine set down. They had decided on feeding and resting there on their way to Branson. To Katherine, it was like coming home, as this was the last place she was a human, before being turned into a vampire by Christian.

"Ah, the city," Katherine sighed. Christian did not quite understand her fondness for the urban surroundings, as he had avoided it for a century.

"So many things confuse me about this populated society. I did enjoy the food, as so many different types of people seemed to come at me like predators. There was actually no hunting involved with my last visit. I was actually confused by their aggression."

"Take my hand. Show me the things you find confusing," Katherine offered.

"Let me take you to where I first entered this city."

Christian remembered entering a neglected area near the Mississippi. Here, they set down, Christian wearing his tailored suit and she in a slim evening dress.

"This is not the best area to travel if you are human," she commented. "It is considered dangerous at night."

"Well, let us walk, for it was near here where I was set upon by negroes. I did not understand them."

"You mean, blacks," she corrected.

"Blacks? Does that not insult them?"

"No. At this moment in history, it is their preference. However, it is confusing, as some prefer being called African Americans—yet if you call some of them African Americans, they get angry, claiming they are not African. However, the word negro always makes them angry."

As they talked, they never realized that they were not only being watched, they were strategically being surrounded by three black gang members. They appeared as prime victims. All the gang members observed were two of the whitest middle class people on earth, who made the mistake of wandering into their hood. One gang member appeared in front of them and swaggered toward them in his hip-hop swagger. Christian pointed.

"There! Look at how he is walking. He seems to intentionally drag his feet? Watch . . . there! Look; he is grabbing at his crotch and holding his privates?"

Katherine explained. "This is part of their culture. It shows he is unafraid, and possibly even aggressive."

"The grabbing of one's crotch is aggressive?" Christian's confusion continued. "Did Lincoln not free the slaves?" he asked.

"Yes, they are free men."

"Why then, do they wear those enormous chains?"

"That is considered jewelry."

"But . . . the huge oversized jewelry he wears? Is that not considered feminine?"

Katherine chuckled. "No my dear, it is what they call 'bling.' The larger and more obnoxious it is, the more important his believes he is within his culture."

"His culture? Are they still like tribes?" Christian was now very confused.

At this point, the gang member blocked their path, holding his arms out. "Yo, yo, yo. You crackers lost?"

Christian and Katherine just ignored him and continued their conversation. It was, to them, like visiting a zoo.

"Did you understand that?" Christian asked.

"The Yo-Yo, was to get our attention. He is calling us 'crackers' because we are white, like Saltines," she explained.

"It is complimentary or insulting?" Christian wondered.

The gang member just stood there, also in confusion, as he had never been totally ignored. He raised his hockey jersey, flashing the gun under his shirt. Still, these two naïve white people continued, as if he wasn't even there.

"It is insulting and meant to be intimidating," she explained.

"So, his funny walk and feminine jewelry should intimidate me? Do you find it intimidating?"

"No, my dear. Even when I was human, I only wondered why the black people wear a hockey jersey when they actually rarely ever play hockey? They seem to shun water and ice."

As they conversed, they were being surrounded. Even as they talked, they could hear two people coming from behind.

"Look, you is pissing me off! Gimme yo green!" he demanded.

"Do the blacks not become educated? Why does he speak in incomplete phrases?" Christian asked.

"It's their language, dear."

This seemed so unusual that the gang member began looking around, thinking this was much too strange and could be some kind of set-up. Meanwhile, Christian and Katherine stood there as relaxed as if they were strolling through the park. Knowing there were gang members behind them, Katherine turned and smiled at them.

"Come join us," she offered.

Now, all three gang members each shared looks of confusion, and watched them both while thinking that if this was not a set-up, then possibly they were armed and would produce weapons. The leader who had approached them began to think that they were just crazy.

"Do you know where you is?"

Christian laughed. "No, the proper English phrasing is, 'do you know where you are?'"

"Are you crazy? You see this nine I gots? It got a cap with your name on it." He began waving his arms, in a motion that was meant to be threatening.

"See?" Christian pointed and looked to Katherine. "Is that not ritualistic?"

Finally, the gang leader had enough. "Look, you two crazy ass mutha fuckas, give us all your stuff and we just might let you go back to the crazy house you escaped from."

Katherine smiled. "Christian, there are three of them."

Christian replied, "Waste not, want not. We will let one escape."

The gang leader became furious and drew his 9mm gun. "Escape? Escape? Now I'm gonna cap your ass!"

Before his could point and pull the trigger, Christian had him by the throat. Just as swiftly, Katherine turned and grabbed one of the gang members who were standing behind them. Seeing their transformed faces, their bravado immediately turned to pure fear. The third gang member simply screamed, "Oh shit!" and began running in blind fear. Both Christian and Katherine savagely bit into their throats and began feeding. Their hunger was not to be controlled. Within a few minutes, both were satisfied, and they let the bodies drop to the concrete.

As Christian licked his lips, he looked to Katherine, perplexed. "What exactly is the meaning of 'cap your ass?'" As he spoke, Christian knew from his last visit that it was likely that this 'negro,' with his huge jewelry, also carried a fair sum of money. Rifling through his pockets, he produced a large roll of bills, which he put in his jacket.

She smiled. "He was intending to shoot you, dear."

"Does everyone speak this way, or just the black people?"

"Actually, it is not exclusively racial. It is a culture within our society. In fact, we have many cultures within our society. This society is very divided; more so than when you were human. They even have a black president now."

Christian looked perplexed. "Does he speak like these people do? If so, how do educated people understand him?"

Katherine laughed. "Dear, he is very educated and he likely does not understand their language, either."

Christian shook his head, changing the topic. "I must take you to where I saw men dancing with men! In public yet!"

"Christian, it is called a 'Gay bar.'"

"Yes! That is what he called it!"

"Who, dear?"

"The man I ate."

"They now have what is called 'alternative lifestyles.' This is where people of the same sex choose to live together."

"I understand, but to what purpose? They can have no family or heirs? A hundred years ago, this was considered a mental affliction."

Katherine laughed. "Today they can allow them to be married and even let them serve in the army."

"Insanity! Who would want to be in the Army with an afflicted man that may find another man attractive? This would only make the army weak and cause mistrust."

"Trust me, it far easier to feed off these people than apply reason to their society. It is one of the many things I will never miss."

"Shall I take you to see this Gay bar?" Christian was asking, thinking that Katherine was unfamiliar with this anomaly.

"Christian, this modern society is filled with confusion. Men can dress as women and women can dress as men. Some will even have medical surgeries to attempt to change gender."

"They are not treated as being mentally ill?"

"No, they are considered as a valid minority population."

"So you do not wish to see men dance with each other?" he asked, as if he thought she might find this amusing.

"No, my love. Let us fly high and enjoy the lights of this city before finding a place to retire."

* * * *

Up in the Northwest corner of the state, Ray Scott and Professor Steiner sat out on the porch swing, enjoying conversation. They had maintained a friendship after Ray's son had been killed by the vampire Christian.

"I am glad you could stay with me, as I get tired of talking to Brutus."

The little Yorkshire, hearing his name, perked up his ears.

"Well, I always travel with an overnight case, so this was a nice opportunity for us to get to know each other a little better and for me to enjoy this remote area."

"Professor, do you really think he is gone for good?" Ray asked.

"Absolutely. He is a cunning beast, this Christian. You don't exist for as long as he has and remain undiscovered without being very, very intelligent. He has no respect for us warm blooded beings, except as a preferred food source. His little diversion was only to draw us into focusing on this area of the country, while he relocates—this I am sure. I will still have students or colleagues search this area, but if we are lucky, we will only locate the remains of his previous mate."

"Where do you think he went?"

"Well, given that the population north of here does not have much to offer long term, and west has a higher degree of sunny days, I would guess due south or southeast somewhere. My best guess would be near St. Louis. There he would have a huge population of undesirables and homeless, and also have wilderness close by. He could merely follow the Mississippi River. Outside a city like that, he could possibly live his next 100 years without detection. The only sign of his victims might be the pictures of missing people on the back side of milk cartons."

"Aside from us, Mike Evans, and now John, is anybody aware of this?"

"I suspect not. Who would believe? As far as the public is concerned, they have enough human monsters to deal with, like serial killers and pedophiles. On the way out in the morning, I will pay my respects to the Baker family, but do you think I could possibly tell them that their daughter isn't missing and instead, has become the mate of a vampire? There is no way! I would not attempt to do that, so Kathy Baker will always remain on the FBI's missing person's list . . . forever."

"How did you develop this interest in something that no one believes in?"

"You mean, no one believes in *today*. If you step back a hundred years or so, you will find that there were many believers. When our population was sparse, a missing person was immediately noticed. Finding a body completed exsanguinated was like the vampire leaving its calling card. They even sold hunting kits, equipped with everything one would need to hunt these creatures down."

"You're kidding me!" Ray shook his head in disbelief.

"No, I am not. In fact, werewolves were also a concern a century ago. I admit that they were more common in Europe, but they were said to have migrated here, as well."

"Werewolves?"

"Honestly, I know little of them, but they are the perfect creature to exist in a country like ours, with hundreds of thousands of acres of wilderness. However, should they have existed, it is likely that they were easily hunted and killed, as a silver bullet is a lot easier to deliver than a stake through the heart."

"No one would believe that!"

"Actually, Ray, this society really doesn't believe in anything anymore. Our belief system, in general, has been severely compromised. Whether God, angels, demons, heaven, hell, and you name it, believers are dwindling. From my perspective, we have come to worship money, Wall Street, and celebrities."

Ray thought for a moment. "Professor, what did coming face to face with a vampire do to your belief system?"

"It strengthened my belief in God, Ray. It strengthened my belief in God."

"How so?"

"By meeting this demon, it provided confirmation that God and his heaven also exists."

"So, you won't stay one more day? Old Brutus here would love it."

"I would love to stay, but I really must get back. I am booked into a short vacation. I'll be taking a break from all this and I am just going to enjoy myself. It will be a week of entertainment, great food, and relaxation."

"Well, since you didn't mention gambling, I know you're not going to Vegas."

"No, Ray, I'm heading for a peaceful place known for clean entertainment and family values . . . Branson, Missouri!"

Chapter Three

The Professor wasn't home in Minneapolis an hour before his phone rang.

"Professor, this is Mike Evans. I think our vampire is back," Mike began.

"Mike, it is certainly possible. I just returned from up north, and he was there, but I'm sure he left and is likely never to return. I'm certain he is relocating."

"Well he is—or was—here in Minneapolis, because we have two gangbangers with their throats torn to shreds, completely drained of blood."

"Ah, it is just as I thought. He is heading south, likely to a populated area like St. Louis."

It was Detective Mike Evans that also faced Christian and found the body of his good friend, Ted Scott, after his unsuccessful confrontation. Mike not only believed in vampires, he was always looking for evidence that they were present in his city. He had actually killed a vampire in his search for Christian, who fled Minneapolis after killing Ted Scott and making Katherine his mate. Christian had only been in Minneapolis a few days, but he left a trail of bodies that Mike would never forget. He actually looked forward to having another chance to kill this vampire that had murdered his good friend.

"So you think he possibly only stopped here on his way to St. Louis?"

"Are you sure it was he?" the Professor asked.

"Yes, positively. We had one eye witness that identified Christian and Katherine to the tee. The witness even described his proper manner of speech, and the fact that he did not understand street talk."

The Professor described what Christian had done up near Roseau at the Canadian border in attempting to create a diversion that would allow him to safely change territories. The Professor explained that it was likely they would never hear of Christian again. As he talked on his speaker phone, he was gathering his clothes to pack for his trip to Branson.

"I think searching for him is futile. Since we are the only two people that know who and what he is, he will likely distance himself from us. The odds that he will remain anywhere near here is just not logical. I, myself, am taking a vacation for a week."

"Where are you going?"

"Branson. Branson, Missouri."

Mike was surprised. "I went to Drury College in Springfield to get my degree in law enforcement. It has one of the best programs in the nation. I have a friend down there who was a former classmate of mine, Wayne Higdon. Are you going alone?"

Mike Evans was recently divorced. Aside from his demanding job as a detective, his obsession with vampire hunting became too much for his wife to cope with. She was convinced he had become obsessed to the point of insanity. Only a few years before, he watched helplessly as his good friend, Ted Scott, bled to death—compliments of the vampire Christian. He also became a bit of joke within his department, as he carried a crossbow pistol in his car. As a detective, he was exposed to the worst of human behaviors, but knowing vampires existed added a whole new dimension of evil for his mind to cope with. Suddenly, he saw an opportunity to take a break from his job and from his obsession, and just relax.

"Would you like a companion?"

The Professor was both surprised and pleased. "Certainly, if you think this old man would be good company. There is plenty of room left on the tour bus."

"When do we leave?"

"In two hours. We will be in Branson at about eight this evening."

"Let me come and get you. I have weeks of vacation time stored up, and this sounds like fun. Plus, maybe I could see how ol' Higdon is doing down there. One question; we have these two bodies that, no doubt, were killed by vampires . . . are you positive Christian is still not here?"

"I am positive. He may have stopped here, but I would bet anything that he is headed further south. I would make a fair bet that they are on their way to St. Louis."

"I trust your opinion. Let's go relax in Branson."

Once on the tour bus, Mike and Professor Steiner caught up on what had occurred northwest and how Christian had disguised his kill as being from an animal. Cruising the highway, the hours passed quickly and soon Mike Evans was on his cell phone locating his old friend, Wayne Higdon. Calling Springfield Police, he found it coincidental that Higdon had relocated to Branson. Mike was happy that he could enjoy Branson and also reunite with an old friend. Aside from the necessary legal education, the law enforcement course at Drury College also required a rigorous physical curriculum, plus weapons training. Evans and Higdon seemed to always be competing for that top position. Both had earned detective status in a relatively short time, and both had curious instincts and perception that made them excellent investigators. So Mike looked forward to seeing his old friend. It was a quick phone call and Wayne was anxious to meet them when they arrived. Having napped a portion of the ten hour trip, both were well rested when they arrived at the hotel. Wayne was happily waiting in the lobby. After unpacking and introductions, they found themselves in the bar catching up on old times. Since the entertainment street in Branson is route 76, which almost always is bumper to bumper, Mike was making light of the fact that Branson would never have a 'drive-by' shooting problem. Wayne was absorbing the humor, as certainly Minneapolis had much more crime than Branson, so Mike had the bragging rights.

"Okay, tell me; how many of these seniors have you used your taser on when catching them cutting into the buffet lines? How many walker collisions have you cleaned up?"

Wayne Higdon laughed. "Okay, but you must be here for the wheelchair races. We call it the Branson 500 . . . that's 500 feet!"

As they laughed at the thought, Higdon's cell phone rang. All Mike and the Professor heard was, "Not again. You're kidding me? No, it's okay. Tell Cunningham I'll meet him there." He turned to Mike. "Sorry, I have to go visit a crime scene."

Mike was interested. "What is it?"

Wayne spoke quietly. "We had found a partial human rib cage last night on the other side of the lake in the woods. Tonight, they possibly found some more remains. I need to view the scene."

Professor Steiner and Mike instantly shared a curious glance and Mike jumped at the chance to be involved. "Hey, you have a professor of anthropology here and another set of trained eyes. Can we go along?"

"Why not? As long as the Professor here understands the rules and does not contaminate any of the crime scene."

As they began driving to the scene, both Evans and Steiner were surprised at how quickly their surroundings went from glitz and bright lights to darkness and wilderness. Taking short cuts to get on the opposite side of the lake, it was also surprising how fast it went from a very populated area to empty, ominous woods. There is very little level ground outside the town, so when Higdon pulled over on a narrow shoulder of the road, the car tilted a bit. Off in the distance they could see lights, but it was downhill and through dense brush. Higdon looked to the old professor. "Are you sure you're up to this terrain?"

"I'll give it a try, young man."

Higdon explained, "Here in Branson, we are almost always walking up or down hill. Believe me this is not as bad as some of the parking lots at the theaters."

They walked silently and carefully down to an area that was widely taped off as a crime scene. As an officer went about examining the area, they could clearly see a scattering of what appeared to human bones, including a detached arm. Evans and Steiner shared looks of concern that only they understood. They knew it did not appear as the work of a vampire, but their instincts told them that something was just not right. Even from a distance, the Professor could see groves in the bones that could have only been made by very sharp, strong teeth. Higdon saw his partner, Cunningham, leaning against a tree.

"What do we have?"

Cunningham stopped from biting his thumb nail and scratched his head. "I sure hope these will match up with what we found last night. If they don't and we have multiple victims, that could, unfortunately, become newsworthy. Who are your friends?"

"I'll introduce you. Mike Evans is an old classmate from Drury, and Professor Steiner is a professor of anthropology."

Cunningham laughed. "What? Is he looking for the missing link?"

"Nah, just vacationing."

"Let's see if we can find anything before forensics gets here and bags this stuff up."

* * * *

Only a few miles away, the Howler was stalking. He had made his transformation to a werewolf and was combing the woods, looking for prey. He was hungry—very hungry. Typically, it would be wildlife that would cross his path and become his dinner, but tonight there was a new scent in the air and the Howler followed it. As a werewolf, he dominated the wilderness, as even a bear could not defend itself from this huge ferocious beast. He moved toward the attractive scent quietly, as any skilled nocturnal predator would do.

Loaded down with camera equipment was an old man. He was out in the wilderness attempting to photograph the area's night creatures. He hoped to get an owl or a fox, never thinking of the dangers of a cougar or bear. He sat still beside a well balanced tripod, which his camera sat on top of, and his vision was only that which the lens viewer provided. His expensive Nikon was set to take a perfect picture in the dim night glow. As he sat listening for any faint noise or movement, he heard the distinct sound of leaves being crushed under foot, so he instinctively pointed the camera in that direction.

Regardless of how skilled the Howler was as a predator, his weight crushed anything under foot. He moved slowly and cautiously. With sight equivalent to night vision, he could clearly see his potential victim, who appeared to be looking directly toward him. He could see that the human was holding an apparatus, but as a mindless predator, it was of no consequence. He moved closer and closer, hidden by the foliage and darkness. The unknowing photographer kept his lens pointed in the direction of the sound he was hearing, possibly anticipating a fox, or even a razorback pig. When the Howler came to the last layer of foliage that kept him hidden from sight, he prepared to strike. The photographer, thinking his subject would soon come into view, began snapping off photos. He anticipated getting a unique special image . . . and he did! What he saw next through the viewfinder sent him into hysterics, and he instantly began screaming for help. As the Howler struck, screams echoed through the mountains, but the photographer's finger kept snapping off photos as the tripod and camera fell to the ground. The attack was over in a split second. The poor photographer never even felt the full extent of his own fear before he was literally torn apart. The Howler went into a feeding frenzy until his hunger was well satisfied. There, in the wilderness, he left the remains scattered about without a care, as any wild animal would do. Now, he was off to find a place to rest for the night.

It was Higdon that heard the distant echo. "Was that a scream?"

"Sounded like it. It came from the west," Cunningham replied.

"We're at an end here. I'm going to take a drive west and see what I can find."

Higdon flagged Mike Evans and the Professor, and they trudged uphill to his car. "Come on, we're going to investigate. It's likely just a stranded motorist or some kids out drinking. People sometimes make the mistake of thinking these woods are a giant playground."

They drove the dark road slowly with the windows open, so as to hear any sounds. "We thought we heard a scream echoing from this direction, but the sounds bouncing around in these mountains can really play tricks on you."

As the road followed the lake, which was in the valley below, they all looked into the darkness searching for anything unusual. Less than a few miles down the road, Higdon spotted a car pulled off to the side. "This certainly doesn't belong here. Hopefully all we have is a stranded motorist. The only problem is the hood isn't up." He pulled his car over and they all got out. The Professor just gazed at the distant glow of the city and the full moon shining over the lake. He remarked, "My, what a heavenly place."

Higdon didn't like what he saw. The car was locked, with the hood down and no flashing lights. In his mind, this meant the driver intentionally went their way on foot. Walking around in this part of the Ozarks at night could be dangerous, even if only for the rugged terrain. He began calling.

"HELLO? ANYONE CALL FOR HELP? HELLO, BRANSON POLICE. HELLO? BRANSON POLICE, CALL OUT SO WE CAN FIND YOU!"

There was no answer. "What do you want to do?" Mike asked, as his police instincts took over.

Wayne retrieved a flashlight. "Here, see if you can spot where someone might have entered these woods."

They began searching the edge of woods, and soon, Mike spotted some obvious broken branches and crushed leaves and foliage. "Here!" he yelled.

The Professor tagged along as Higdon and Evans followed the path of disrupted branches and leaves. The path became clearer as they headed downhill. Then, Higdon caught a glimpse beyond his worst imagined outcome. "Jesus Christ! Be careful, this is a real mess!"

Mike could only mutter, "Oh my God!" Scattered about was the photographer's equipment, along with parts of his body. He had also been decapitated, and his head was laying in clear view.

"What the hell did this?" Mike gasped.

The Professor just whispered, "The poor man . . . what could have done this?"

"I have no clue, other than it was certainly not human." With that comment, Mike Evans and the professor once more exchanged knowing glances. It was the Professor that spotted the camera a few yards away. "That camera over there may give you a clue."

Higdon produced latex gloves from his pocket and then walked over and picked it up. "Look at this thing! It's a top of the line Nikon."

"Is it film or digital?" Mike asked.

"Digital. Let's have a look." They quickly huddled together as Wayne turned it on and began reviewing the photos going backwards from last photo taken to first. The initial images were of random photos taken as the photographer was moving in panic. Then, the camera displayed the image that made them all gasp at once. The man had captured the blurry face of the werewolf. A hazy image of red glowing eyes, massive jaws, and teeth that made the jaws of an alligator appear almost harmless.

"What the hell is that?" Evans stammered in confusion.

"I have no idea?"

"It appears as though it's part of the canine family," the Professor suggested.

"We have no idea of the distance, but using that leaf in the photo as an indicator of size, that thing is enormous! I'm calling this in. Cunningham is going to shit!"

As he talked on his cell phone to his partner on his way to the car, he left Evans and the Professor alone, sharing a single flashlight. In the dark by themselves, they could talk freely. "So what do you think, young man?"

"Professor, I have never seen anything like this, other than what we ran into in that drain system . . . but this is no vampire."

The professor took a deep breath. "Michael, I believe what we just observed on that camera is the clear image of a werewolf."

"A werewolf? Come on," he replied, skeptically.

"Michael, that is the same tone I heard when you first heard the word vampire."

"Are you saying you believe werewolves really exist?"

"Well, I can't say that I did until now . . . but there is no doubt this image is that of a werewolf. Records of lycanthropic behavior originate back to biblical writing. Modern psychiatrists write the condition off to being a type of chronic pseudo-neurotic schizophrenia. Lycanthropy is a fact, Michael. I just don't know if any psychiatrist has ever seen an example such as this, but that is most definitely the image of a werewolf!"

Mike shined the flashlight about the scene and easily found the point which the werewolf exited. "It looks like he went that way," Mike pointed.

"Young man, don't expect me to follow. All I have as a weapon is the wooden envelope opener in my jacket pocket."

"And my sidearm is at the hotel. There is no way I want to face that thing empty handed."

"If folklore is correct, you will need silver bullets."

"That's just great! I take a damned vacation from vampires and what do I get? Werewolves! I just can't wait to explain all this to Higdon."

Wayne came running back. "Cunningham is on the way. He is not going to believe this crime scene, nor the image in that camera."

As he spoke, the Professor looked around and became serious. Mike Evans noticed his look of concern. "What is it, Professor?"

"The silence. Suddenly these woods are completely silent. You could hear a pin drop. Do you know what that could mean?"

Evans scoffed. "No way. No damn way. Not them too? What the hell have walked into?"

"Son, I don't know much, but this is a sure warning sign. When the woods that are normally full of sound go silent, a large predator or vampire is present."

As Wayne Higdon began taping off the area, Jerry Cunningham arrived. "Holy shit! What happened here?"

Higdon produced the camera. "Take a look at this! This is the last thing the victim saw before he was torn to pieces." He took the Nikon and showed Cunningham the display. One glance, and Cunningham shook his head.

"This is distorted. For all we know, he pressed the macro zoom, which enlarged the whole image."

"What if this is the real image?"

Cunningham studied it, and to Higdon's surprise, he simply stated, "We must go see Jonah. Jonah will know what that is. Jonah is ninety years old, and is an expert at Ozark history. Whether real or folklore, Jonah is a walking history book. When backup and forensics arrive, we're heading off to see Jonah."

The Professor's instincts about the silence were correct, for off in the distance, high in the trees, sat Aaron and Rebecca. The resident vampires were furious at what the werewolf had done to bring attention to their personal domain.

"We should try killing him again. He will force us to relocate, and where will we go?"

As he watched the warm blooded glow of the humans, Aaron observed. "Two of them are different. I sense their curiosity, and one of them is projecting anger. I feel we should avoid them."

"I think we should just go down there and silence them all!" Rebecca's temper was flaring.

"No! We will just take great care until this passes."

"I say kill them! Maybe more carnage will bring an end to the Howler."

"No!" Aaron stated again. "We will keep our distance for now."

As the Professor listened intently, the crickets began singing and frogs began croaking and the sounds of the wilderness returned. What he did not know was that it was because Aaron and Rebecca had fled the area and had taken to the night sky.

* * * *

East Branson is like most any other rural Missouri town. Far from the busy 76 strip and over the bridge and up Mount Branson, away from the commercial area of town, is a barren 76 highway scattered with random businesses and no method to the zoning. Set in the middle of a gravel parking lot was a huge metal building, with a homemade sign reading 'Tami's Tanning salon.' Arriving in Branson, this deserted business became the first stop for Christian and Katherine. They could see the lights were on and business was open, but the parking lot was empty, as it was near closing time. Christian followed Katherine as she led the way.

"Here! Here is where we will become tanned, as if being in the sun," she announced.

Christian was skeptical. "This is not dangerous to us?"

"No, they will merely paint our skin. It is a type of dye, and it will eventually fade."

"Then let us proceed."

When they entered, the attendant was behind the counter with her feet up, watching television. As she heard the door bell, without even looking their way, she yelled, "Hey, we're about to close!" Christian and Katherine walked silently to the counter. Katherine spoke sweetly.

"We would like to be tan, please. A spray tan?"

The girl looked up to see two of the whitest people she had ever seen. Along with watching television, she had been drinking beer, and her senses were not at their sharpest. "Well, I said I was closing. We only have a few minutes."

Christian produced the roll of bills. "Can we convince you to accommodate us?" Christian peeled off two, one hundred dollar bills. The attendant flashed a hundred dollar smile.

"Not a problem. We only have one booth. Step behind the curtain. Remove your clothes or put on a bathing suit, and just step into the booth and close the door. I'll tell you what to do after you enter. How dark would you like to be?"

"I would like us quite dark. Make us as if we have been to the Caribbean," Katherine explained, while Christian watched in wonder.

The girl picked up a musty odor from Katherine and suggested, "We also can add a scent, so your skin will maintain a fragrance. Coconut is most popular."

"Yes, lots of coconut!" Katherine ordered.

The girl continued. "When you are inside, make one body rotation slowly with your arms down at your side, then a second one with your arms raised up in the air. Once we are done, just lightly dab yourself dry with the towel." Being half drunk, the girl was slurring her words and, incredibly, took no notice whatsoever that her customers were strange in any way. Christian watched Katherine as she stepped behind the curtain, and with vampires having no inhibitions, removed all her clothes. Once inside the booth, the attendant asked, "ready?"

She then directed Katherine as she pushed the controls. "Okay, slowly turn completely around. Remember, arms at your side." About thirty seconds later, she ordered, "Arms in the air now. Please turn slowly, again." Another thirty seconds and she said, "Okay, now just dab very lightly and you can get dressed. The full color will develop in the next twenty minutes or so."

All the while, Christian watched in amazement. When Katherine came out, he was surprised at the healthy glow her skin had already taken, combined with the fragrance of coconut that filled the air.

"Next!"

Christian also had no inhibitions, but felt it very strange removing his clothes in a public place, even if he was in a private setting, yet he followed the instructions. Within minutes, he was putting his clothes back on and admiring his hands, as they began turning a dark tan. *'Amazing,'* he thought. As he exited from behind the curtain, he was astonished at Katherine's new appearance. She looked human, as her tan had become a bit darker. Then, Katherine made a huge mistake. With the attendant watching, without being aware, she walked in front of a full length mirror. The girl sobered up immediately, and knew something was horribly wrong, as she saw no reflection. Trying not to draw attention to herself, as Christian and Katherine admired their new look, she moved to her cell phone and dialed 911. Forgetting it was set to speaker, the dispatcher answered, "911, how can we help you?"

As soon as Christian heard it, he moved like a flash to silence her, while Katherine, being aware of what a cell phone was, smashed it to the floor. As Christian held his hand over her mouth, he asked. "What shall we do with her?"

Katherine smiled. "Well, we are both hungry. I guess we will eat!"

No sooner than she uttered the words, Christian bite savagely into the attendants neck, holding his hand over her mouth so that any screams were futile. He then offered her to Katherine, who drained the balance of her life's fluid. When done, Katherine dropped the body to the floor. Christian stood in silence before asking, "What shall we do?"

"We should leave. She dialed 911, and the police will track her cell phone signal. They will be here within minutes."

Christian looked at the slight blood splatters on the counter and wall. "It will be evident that violence had occurred, but we will take the body. If we leave it, it is evidence that we were here." He picked up the body with one hand and they exited quickly into the night sky. In the Ozarks, they could easily find an isolated part of the wilderness where it might never be found. Within a few minutes, Branson police were on the scene. Immediately, they were puzzled. They saw the blood, and could not find anyone in the salon, but knew that it was not a robbery, as the two, one hundred dollar bills were still laying on the counter, and the cash register was untouched.

"Call it in. We need the detectives on this," the officer determined.

"What do you think?" his partner asked.

"Well, maybe they'll get prints. We know there is no video, as it's prohibited in these tanning salons, after so many recordings showed up on you-tube. There's not really very much blood, so for all we know, they might have gotten a bloody nose and headed for the ER. Could be a domestic thing, like a pissed off spouse. I didn't see a car out there. I guess it could be a possible abduction."

* * * *

On a state highway that runs on the outskirts of Branson was an old rundown log cabin. It had some antique advertising signs nailed on the outside, and appeared as possibly an old roadside attraction of years gone by. The men pulled into the gravel drive and gathered outside. Cunningham explained, "This is one cantankerous old man, so whatever you do, try not to piss him off in any way." That being said, he knocked on the wooden door. It opened slowly, and a short, rather stocky old man with long white hair and a beard greeted then curtly.

"What do you want?" he asked, as if being bothered.

"Mister Blevins, we need your help. I don't know if you remember me, but I'm Detective Cunningham with the Branson police department." Jerry flashed his badge as he introduced himself.

"All right. Come on in."

They looked around, and it was the definition of rustic. There was homemade wooden furniture everywhere. In the dining room was a huge wooden table where they all sat. They noticed that Jonah moved rather spryly for a 90 year old. "All I got is water or some sweet tea, and you're welcome to it," he offered.

Cunningham produced the camera. "Jonah, would you take a look at this and give me your opinion?" The old man moved over to Jerry's shoulder, and looked into the camera's display.

"Where did you come by that?" he asked.

"It was found on the south end of Table Rock, with what was left of a man. He was torn to pieces. He captured this image before he died," Jerry explained.

They all sat anticipating his response, as he walked slowly to the head of the table and took a seat. "Now, if any one of you laughs at what I am about to tell you, I'm kicking your ass out! What you captured there—no doubt—is the Howler. He is likely the last of the werewolves that once plagued this area of the mountains. I never have seen him myself, but my grandfather did, and that is exactly what he described. My grandfather actually put a bullet in him. Unfortunately, it was just a lead ball, and not silver."

Mike Evans was dumbfounded. "You have to be kidding me?"

"No, sonny. I don't joke. Have you never heard his howls echoing these mountains?"

"I was told it was a male wolf that escaped from Branson West game preserve," Higdon replied.

The old man chuckled. "And you never noticed that he only howls during the full moon? Or, that our best hunters and trackers can't find him? There never was a male wolf that escaped. In fact, they never even had a male wolf. It was all a tale made up to explain the howls."

Higdon asked, "You mentioned silver. Is it like the movies, silver bullet and all?"

"Exactly." The old man rose, and going to a drawer, produced what looked to be a box of modern ammunition. "Here! This is what you need. These are .38 specials, but they will also chamber a .357."

Cunningham was stunned. "Where the hell did you get silver bullets?"

"Young man, these are common. Anyone that has a western holster and rig wants these for dress up—you know, looks. Rarely does anyone fire them. They want their gun belt to look pretty. Should I need to go out at night in the full moon, my .38 is loaded with them. Take the box. Replace them when you can."

The old man then told stories that he had been handed down through family and friends over the years, of how people decades ago made a habit of not going out during the cycle of the full moon. He explained that Branson was not more than a speck on the map until only a few decades ago, when it exploded into an entertainment Mecca. He told of how the dam had created Lake Taneycomo, which is one of the most unorthodox bodies of water in the nation, closely shaped like a fish skeleton. Hardly more than 100 yards wide at any point, it has almost 900 miles of shoreline. All this contributes to the thick mists and fog that haunt the valleys. He then told of werewolves being hunted down, with only one thought to still exist . . . the Howler.

"He's smarter than the rest were. You can only catch him during the full moon, unless you wound him. That is how they caught many of them in the old days. They finally figured out that if they could wound them while in animal form, when they turned human they could look for the wounded man, which was safer than facing off with what you see in the camera. However, that does not work with those damn vampires."

"Vampires?" the Professor gasped.

"Oh yeah, we once had them too. I haven't heard of any in decades, but they're sneaky devils, they are. They were here around 100 years ago, but unlike werewolves, they were easier to find. During the daylight hours, they sent search parties into the caves and I believe that they pretty much wiped them out. My late brother always went hunting, hoping to find one so he could try his new weapon. I was kind of glad he never faced off with one, because if it didn't work, he would have been dead."

"Tell me of the weapon," the Professor asked.

"Well, his theory was that sticking a vampire in the heart with a pointy stick was a little too dangerous, so he thought making a wooden bullet might be the answer. Well, to put enough powder in the bullet to make it lethal, made an explosion that destroyed the wooden bullet, turning it into splinters. It would be like attacking a vampire with toothpicks. Then, it occurred to him that petrified wood was still wood by definition, but harder and stronger than lead. So he machined a box of bullets himself." The old man went to a drawer and produced a box, tossing it on the table. "Here, these are .38 Special also." He produced a second box. "These are 12 gauge shotgun shells, and instead of a deer slug, they have a hunk of petrified wood. Don't know if they will work or not, but it made sense to him, and he was ready to risk his life trying them. He passed on about 20 years ago."

As Higdon and Cunningham sat in awe of the whole conversation, the Professor and Mike Evans continued their questions, as if the topic was not unusual in the least. "May I ask, where did he find petrified wood?"

Everyone smiled as Jonah answered the old Professor. "Youngster, there was a time about fifty years ago when petrified wood was a popular fad. They made commercial statues, and most common were huge ashtrays. My brother had one of those ashtrays, and now, here it is in these bullets. Will they work? Personally, I don't care to try them myself."

Higdon was just amazed. "You're actually saying you have or had vampires and that you likely have a werewolf, roaming these woods?"

"Wayne, believe it or not, both the Professor and I have seen a vampire. We know they exist." Evans interrupted.

Cunningham just seemed as if he were muttering to himself. "Sweet Jesus, all the stories I've heard are true." He began biting at his thumbnail.

Old Jonah laughed. "Oh yes, but you won't want the Branson Chamber of Commerce hearing you talk about it. You'll find yourself out of a job real quick. This is our little secret. When I think of all those ignorant tourists running around here, I cringe. None of you ever wondered why the Branson outdoor attractions shut down so early, yet the indoor shows can run late? You have never noticed that all the outdoor attractions close even earlier in the fall because the sun sets earlier? You boys really think that any business with good sense might have a reason to kick out 15 to 20 thousand people, who are having fun and spending money, so early in the evening? It's all in front of your face—that is, if you want to see it!"

Cunningham muttered again, while biting at his thumb. "I need to think this out."

Higdon just stared at Evans. "You saw a real vampire?"

"Yeah. I actually saw more than one, and killed one. No, I didn't believe either, until I emptied my 9mm into one and it stood there, smiling at me. I have a crossbow pistol in my suitcase at the hotel."

"You're kidding me?" Higdon replied. "How do we get rid of them?"

Old Jonah spoke seriously. "You arm yourself well and go out in the woods. You won't have to hunt them, because soon they'll be hunting you. You have a day, maybe two, to catch that Howler, or you have to wait until the next full moon. However, if there are still vampires out there, they like to eat every night—so I'm told."

Mike Evans picked up the boxes of shells. Cunningham thanked the old man, and they gathered outside. "Obviously, we mention this to no one, nor do we mention any of our suspicions. If Jonah is correct, a rumor like this could cost us our jobs and Branson would become a ghost town."

* * * *

Katherine was anxious to walk amongst the population. "Let us try out our new appearance and go to the theater!"

"Are you not reluctant?" Christian questioned, hesitant to go against his instincts of staying hidden.

"Why would you have any fear? You walked amongst the humans in Minneapolis?"

"Yes, but I was blinded by revenge. I had no concern for my existence."

"Well, trust me, there is nothing to be concerned about. You will appear a lot more normal than many of these warm bloods," she assured.

"Shall we appear as formal?" Christian wondered.

"No dear, you are fine. I want to see Andy Williams. His voice is beautiful."

They took to the air and set down in the woods near the theater. They walked out and across the street, behind the theater and into the parking lot. They walked uphill, hand and hand. The first people they encountered were exiting their car. Christian became a bit anxious, but when they were merely greeted with a smile, he relaxed. Person after person smiled at them, as if they were completely normal. Christian observed every detail. "Why are they dressed this way for the theater?" he asked, for in his day, the theater was a formal event, and he was observing men in tee shirts and even shorts.

"Things are more casual here. In fact, the whole culture is much more casual."

"So it is not in bad taste or disrespect?"

"No. Just try not to stare, dear." She cautioned him, because his look of confusion was blatantly obvious. "You can wait outside and I will get the tickets. Have no fear; with your new tanned appearance, you look very handsome."

He handed her the roll of bills and waited outside the main door, in what was a designated smoking area. Katherine proceeded to the ticket counter and asked for two tickets in the rear of the theater, away from the main body of people. After paying, she waved the tickets as she returned to Christian. "We'll enter the theater after the crowd is seated."

With only minutes before show time, they entered and were ushered to their seats. Christian was amazed that no one took notice of them, as their new tanned appearance made them look normal and healthy—plus, they emitted the wonderful scent of coconut oil. Christian was in awe of the whole experience. The stage and lighting was like that which he had never before seen. When the music began, the sounds he heard were overwhelming. Then, when Andy Williams began to sing, he thought how he had never heard a voice so wonderful.

"Is he very popular?" Christian whispered.

"He is a legend. He was an icon before I was even born. He is ageless." Katherine saw the expression of concern on Christian's face. "No dear, don't even think it. I have watched him age very gracefully."

Christian found the evening a revelation of enjoyment. Having fed earlier, the interaction with humans offered no temptations. He watched and followed Katherine's examples, as she was familiar with all these things. During the break, it amused him when a tourist couple asked where they were from and Katherine answered that they just flew in from Minneapolis! It also gave him great comfort that as long as he did not enter the men's room, there were no mirrors or reflections to worry about. When the show finished, no one took notice as they walked through the theater parking lot, across the street, through a hotel parking lot to the edge of the woods, and took flight . . . except for one confused young man. He was in the hotel parking lot smoking marijuana in a van, facing the edge of the woods. He watched the well dressed couple, paying little attention until they left the ground and disappeared into the air. He sat for a few seconds in complete disbelief, before calling 911.

"911, how can we help you?"

"Like, I just saw a man and woman take off. Like, flying?"

"Ummm, as in flying in a plane, or helicopter?"

"No. Like, Superman. They rose off the ground and took off like a super hero. They were here and poof, now they're gone!"

"Sir, have you been drinking?"

"No."

"Are you on any substance?"

"Well, I smoked a joint if you consider that a substance, but I'm not wasted. I saw them take off. It was like they defied gravity or something."

"Where are you located, sir?"

"I'm in a white van in the parking lot at Restful Inn."

"I will dispatch someone to take your statement."

Cunningham, Higdon, Evans, and the Professor were on their way back to the earlier crime scene when a call came over the radio.

"Unit 700, can you get over to the Restful Inn? We have a guy in a white van who claims he saw a couple flying in the air. I'm pretty sure this is a substance situation."

All Evans had to hear was 'couple flying in the air' and asked, "How fast can you get there?"

Higdon immediately grabbed the radio. "Dispatch, hold that guy until we get there. This is Detective Higdon at Unit 688, we are en route." He turned to Evans. "We're on our way."

Making a U-turn, they sped to the scene. The officers had the man against the van and were searching the van. The man was complaining.

"Hey, like I called you man! Me! I didn't do nothing."

Higdon asked, "What do you have, officers?"

"This guy admits he smoked some pot. There is no doubt he is a little high. He insists he saw a couple in their thirties take off flying from about over there." He pointed toward the woods.

"Let me talk with him," Higdon ordered. He waved Evans over and told the man to relax.

"Now, tell me exactly what you witnessed."

The young man about twenty, looked frightened and immediately stated, "It was medical marijuana man. Like, I got a touch of the Glock-O-Ma."

"So you have glaucoma and you can't see?"

"No man, I can see great."

It was obvious that the kid had no idea what glaucoma even was. "Look, kid. We don't care what you did, as long as you're not selling, holding, or driving. So you don't have to worry. I want to know every single detail about that couple. Can you tell me that?"

"Yeah. I was sitting here facing the woods. They were about thirty or so. He was kind of tall, maybe six foot something, and he had longish brown hair. She was shorter, maybe five foot something, and had long black hair. They were holding hands, and I thought maybe they were going into the woods to . . . you know. Instead, they took off like in Smallville! I swear!"

"What were they wearing?"

"He had on a dark suit and she had a nice dress, as if she was going out clubbing or something."

Evans had to ask. "Were they pale? Like really white skin?"

"No. In fact they were so tan they could have been Mexicans."

"Mexicans? Are you sure?"

"Positive. The woman was really hot. I noticed her the most. She looked like she belonged in a thong, if you know what I mean. No, they were really tan."

Evans shook his head, whispering to Higdon. "This makes no sense. The vampires we were chasing fit this description, but they are nearly as white as mimes. They can't be tan, because the sun destroys them."

The officer was listening to Higdon question the stoner, and decided to mention what seemed pure coincidence. "Detectives? We had a call earlier in East Branson. We had a missing girl at Tami's Tanning Salon. There were traces of blood, and no sign of the attendant. Two other detectives are on that case."

The Professor wondered, "I don't think vampires could use a tanning bed?"

"No, Tami's is for spray tans. They simply paint you, like a car. It's the latest thing." Higdon explained.

"So you think they got a spray tan? Great, they got a damned spray tan! They can now walk around Branson without being conspicuous. They very well could be here! Son-of-a-bitch! Christian and Katherine could be here . . ." Evans looked at Higdon. "Can you get me a .357 or a 12 gauge?"

"Sure. What's your preference?"

"Both! We're going hunting!"

Chapter Four

Wayne Higdon had no problem giving his friend his back-up .357 snub-nose, and the short barreled 12 gauge he kept in his trunk. It had been a long night when he dropped off his friend, Mike Evans, and Professor Steiner. He left thinking he would pick them up in the morning, but Mike had other ideas. He and the Professor had slept on the bus, and his adrenaline was flowing in high gear. He knew Christian was near and he wanted him badly. Once Wayne had left, Mike was at the front desk renting a car. Although he clearly saw the image of what was identified as a werewolf, he wanted to believe the carnage of the photographer was vampire related. "Let's go, sir!" Mike ordered.

"Where?" asked the Professor, who was ready to retire.

"I've rented a car and we can revisit that crime scene. I'm not all that tired, and given the bullets and shells, we have the weapons to confront whatever we encounter."

"What of your friend?"

"I'm not sure he can truly understand what it is they are dealing with, but we do."

"Okay, then; what is your plan?"

"We will revisit the crime scene and follow the path where it looks like whatever the hell it was exited. Either we will find it, or it will find us. We will put silver bullets in the revolver and the petrified wood shells in the shotgun. Whatever we run into, we will kill."

"Michael, I am not ashamed to tell you that this frightens me a great deal."

"I'll tell you what; you hold the revolver with the silver bullets, and I'll carry the 12 gauge."

"I know nothing of guns."

"Professor, it's like pointing your finger. You point and pull the trigger."

The Professor reluctantly agreed and they took off in their car as Mike followed the route taken by Higdon earlier. Slowly, the lights faded and they were on a dark highway searching for the yellow police tape that marked the trail. Although the Professor had the snub-nosed revolver in his jacket pocket, he was almost afraid to touch it. He had his hand over his pocket, for fear that just a jostle might make it explode. They didn't have to look all that hard for the trail, as a Branson police squad car was stationed near the path going to the crime scene. Evans pulled over and parked. Being in full view of the officer in the squad, he held out his badge, hoping from a distance it would not be questioned. Seeing what appeared to be a detective and with the Professor looking easily like a forensic expert, the officer stayed in his car. Evans walked to the patrol car confidently and asked the officer to borrow his flashlight, which he did without question. Walking to the path leading down to the crime scene, Mike turned to the Professor. "You don't have to do this. You can wait here if you like." The Professor shook his head.

"No, Michael. I'm coming with you."

Mike carried the shotgun, hoping to test the petrified wood shell on a vampire. In his mind, the werewolf story just didn't register. The carnage he witnessed was not much different than that he had seen in a vampire's lair in Minneapolis. He had no expectations of encountering a werewolf, which is why he left the Professor with the security of holding the gun with the silver bullets. The remains had been removed, but blood splatters were everywhere as Mike shined the flashlight about the scene. With the Professor following behind, Mike began following the crushed foliage that was indicating the path of an exit. Slowly and as quietly as they could be, they moved through the dark woods downhill toward the lake. Gripping the shotgun tightly and flinching at every strange sound, they cautiously moved forward. The trail was obvious, so their anticipation was at a peak. Soon, they were at the lake's shore. The shore on the south side of Table Rock was not like the sandy beaches built for tourists on the north side, as it was all rocky edges. Off in the distance was the dark island, only 100 yards away. As the cool night air breezed over the warm lake water, a mist began to rise. The path led to the lake, and they both stood there looking about, as if to find any indication of whether 'it' could have gone left or right.

Only a few hundred feet from where they were standing, and laying on a huge rock along the shore, was the Howler. The scent of man began to awaken him as he sniffed the air. Silently, he turned and faced the direction from where the human scent originated. He was not hungry, but the smell of man always presented a threat. He rose to his feet. Mike could barely see in the distance, but did observe movement.

"Professor, I think I saw something move," Mike whispered.

The Howler could see clearly in the dark and "in his mindless instinct" would react to anyone violating his territory. He began moving toward them. Mike could barely make out anything except a dark image, but could tell it was coming in their direction. As Mike focused on the hazy image, it started to become clear and Mike knew instantly that they were in trouble. It was huge, growling, and traveling at an inhuman speed.

"Holy shit! Professor, can you swim?"

"Son, I do ten laps in the college pool every single day."

"You are not going to believe the size of what is coming this way. I may get one shot off, but get ready to swim to that island and pray this thing hates water!"

The Professor took off his woolen sport coat, forgetting that the revolver with the silver bullets was in his pocket. He laid the jacket at the shore. The Howler, realizing he had been seen, began running at an incredible speed. Mike aimed and pulled the trigger. As he heard the roar of the 12 gauge, he yelled, "Dive!" and dropped the shotgun at the shore. The water was a warm 70 degrees as they swam for their lives. The werewolf stood at the water's edge, roaring. About half way to the island, Mike called out, "Are you okay Professor?"

The Professor called back, "I'm fine!"

As they swam frantically, they could not see the Howler's rage as he paced back and forth, kicking the sport coat and shotgun into the water. Although easily able to swim, being in deep water made the werewolf feel vulnerable, so he avoided it. Had he been hungry, it may have been a much different situation. Mike and the Professor did not realize how fortunate they were, as no one in decades had ever faced the Howler and lived to tell the tale. It was the fastest hundred yards that they had both ever swam. Mike reached the island first and immediately searched for the Professor, who was lagging behind but moving at a strong and steady pace. He watched and could see the werewolf disappear into the woods. As his adrenaline level began to lower, he realized the night air had become colder than the water, and being soaked, he began to shiver. As the Professor reached the shore, Mike helped him to his feet. It was then that he saw that the Professor had shed his jacket. "You left your coat?"

"Yes, it was heavy and wool and I did not think I could have made it with it weighing me down."

"The revolver?"

"Oh! It was in my jacket . . ."

"I'm guessing it's between 1:00 and 2:00 a.m., and here we are on an island in this wilderness, defenseless."

"Why would you worry? We are alone here. I'm sure once it becomes light, someone will rescue us."

Mike always anticipated the worst case scenario. "How do you know we are alone here?"

"Well, whatever might be on this island could never match what we just witnessed. That almost makes facing a vampire seem rather tame. Did you see the size of that thing?"

"I certainly did! One glimpse is all I needed."

The Professor watched as Mike began searching about, and knew he was looking for anything he could use as a weapon. From where they landed, he could see the other side of the lake and could see the riverboat docked and the lights. "Michael, if we swim another hundred yards, we will reach the riverboat dock. It is well lit and likely has a night watchman."

As Mike searched, he looked in that direction. "Professor, I believe the distance is a bit further and this water is deep, or so I'm told. Are you really up to it?" As he talked, he picked up a tree branch and snapped it over his knee, leaving a jagged, sharp edge. From his pocket he produced a pen knife, and began sharpening the branch to a spear-like point.

"What are you expecting?" The Professor asked, as he was feeling safe, having just escaped certain death.

"I don't know. But this island is pretty large, and have you ever seen what a razor back pig can do to a human leg? Plus, this is home to the cotton mouth and copperhead. Unlike a rattle snake, the cotton mouth has a mean offensive disposition, and a copperhead will actually come after you."

They had no way of knowing that their whole misadventure was observed by Aaron and Rebecca, the two resident vampires.

"Humans are so pitiful," Rebecca scoffed.

"They did better with the Howler than we did. They had the sense enough to flee. If you remember, I almost lost my arm and you almost lost your head. "

"I want that animal dead. Likely they are police, and they will alert more police, and this whole area will become unsafe for us. They will soon be searching through every cave and crevice."

"What can we do? We are helpless. That beast runs rampant with no one to stop him. Even if this passes, he will do it again and again," Aaron reasoned.

"We should follow him and attack him while he sleeps . . ." Rebecca suggested.

"He would smell us coming long before we could even get close, and would greet us with the same fury as he did in our last encounter."

Rebecca thought for a moment. "Well, the other solution is to keep these two police from telling of their encounter. I'm hungry anyway. So? Two of them disappear. Or, if we drain them carefully, they could be found in the water and will appear as having drowned."

Even from hundreds of yards away, Aaron could see the two walking the shore, looking toward the opposite shore and the riverboat dock. "Yes, that might be the thing to do. I sense they are thinking of escaping to the tourist area."

"Good! I at least can feel like we stole them away from that werewolf."

"Though . . . I am conflicted about this, for if he creates all this carnage, maybe the police will bring enough resource to finally end his life. All we need do is go away until this whole thing blows over," Aaron suggested.

"Where would we go? Unfamiliar territory always frightens me. Let's just kill them and be done with it. We should attack without warning."

"No, we must control how they are drained, for we want no signs of attack. A simple bite into their femoral artery, and let the water do the rest of the damage. We need not surprise them, because where will they go? We should land in the woods."

Mike and the Professor never heard a thing as they discussed their dilemma. Mike had decided it was best for them to stay put on the shore of the north side of the island, where they would be visible to tourists and various state park workers. They had only a few hours until the sunrise, and this seemed the most logical and safe decision. It was with a start that the Professor became aware of two images silently watching them from only a few yards away.

"Michael, we have company." The Professor instinctively reached for his pocket and his wooden envelope opener, but remembered it was in the jacket that he had discarded, so he stood empty handed.

"Identify yourself," Mike ordered, as any cop might do.

Aaron stepped forward. "We were amused by your brief encounter with that beast."

"You are vampires . . ." Mike replied, trying to appear brave.

"Correct. You know of us?" Aaron was surprised.

Defiantly Mike stated, "I have killed a few of your kind."

As they talked, the Professor was shivering. It was caused by the combination of being wet in cool night air, and the fear of knowing they were completely vulnerable. He slowly moved back and closer to Mike, keeping his eyes on the female vampire, who was nearly hidden in the shadows.

"Where did you find our kind?" Aaron was curious.

"North. North in Minnesota. There was a number of your kind. Needless to say, there are a lot fewer now." Mike grabbed his spear with both hands. He knew there was only one possible way to survive, and that was to take his best shot with the spear. Should he miss, he would dive into the water. As they traded comments, he was planning in his mind that he would jab at this vampire without warning, and yell to the Professor to dive. His assumption was that if he missed the vampire's heart, his only hope was that it was possible that vampires also shunned water. Mike glanced toward the Professor and could see the fear in his eyes. The Professor was beyond understanding what Mike was trying to communicate with his eyes and body language. What Mike didn't know, was that the Professor was paralyzed by fear. Mike decided to try and negotiate their lives. "We are not the ones you should kill."

Aaron smiled, for he could smell the Professor's fear. "Why might you think that?"

"I am a cop, and the Professor is a prominent expert. Should we be killed, the hunt for you will be relentless."

Again Aaron smiled. "That would be only if the officials know that you are truly dead. There are ways to make things appear deceiving."

Rebecca was tired of all the talk. "Let's just kill them!" That said, her face began its metamorphosis to that of a hideous beast. Mike knew he only had seconds, and he thrust his spear, actually missing the heart and stabbing Aaron in the side. He never heard Aaron scream as immediately he turned and yelled "Dive!" and dove into the water. Though the Professor anticipated the series of actions, he was frozen in fear and as Aaron screamed, Rebecca pushed the Professor to the ground and bit into his thigh. Aaron removed the spear, which had missed his heart, and watched as Mike disappeared under water. Aaron then held the Professor down as Rebecca drank her fill. Afterward, she offered the balance of the Professors blood to Aaron. The Professor felt no pain in his state of shock, and slipped into a lethal sleep. Meanwhile, Mike would attempt to swim below the surface, only coming up for a breath of air. His desire to survive gave him motivation to hold his breath and remain invisible from the surface for much longer than normal. The only thing he knew was to swim in the direction of the riverboat dock.

"What shall we do?" Rebecca questioned.

"Let him go. We might be seen if we pursue him."

"What of the old man's body?"

"Let's just take him and go," Aaron replied, frustrated.

"Take him where?"

"To where he can never be found."

Mike was swimming for his life, not knowing that with every breath he surfaced for, whether the face of a vampire might be there to greet him. It seemed like he was swimming for an eternity before the huge riverboat was looming over him. Not knowing if the vampires were above him, he surfaced under the dock. There, he could remain hidden, and he could stand in the waist deep water and rest. He desperately watched for any signs that the Professor was following, but did not see a ripple, and he knew Professor Steiner was gone. He just stood there, looking at the dark still water with the island in the background, and cupped his face in his hands, wondering how everything went so wrong. He knew it was a mistake, putting the Professor in harm's way; for although knowledgeable, he was untrained and unskilled for hunting down much of anything. He was standing completely still when a beam of light shined upon him. "You! Come out with your hands in the air!" Mike slowly moved from under the dock to see a security guard holding a taser and a flashlight. As he slowly walked to shore, Mike could see from the look on the guard's face that he was actually frightened.

"I'm going to reach for my wallet very slowly. I am a detective. Don't you dare let that taser go off with me being as wet as I am. Understand?" Mike ordered with authority. He produced his badge and identification.

"I'm with the riverboat security. What were you doing under there?"

There was no way Mike was going to tell the true story. "Actually, I'm working with Homeland Security. We had a tip and I was doing surveillance. I really can't discuss it." Mike saw the security guard's eyes widen, and knew he was dealing with what was likely an untrained civilian who was no more than a watchman. "Now that I possibly have been seen, can you get me to my hotel so I can do my reports?"

The guard was immediately curious. "Terrorism?"

Mike knew better than to feed any rumors. "I can't say much, but it has to do with illegal drugs. Now, can you get me to my hotel?"

"Sure. We have a car that drives the property. He can take you. It will be light soon anyway."

*   *   *   *

As Mike was racing for the riverboat, Aaron picked up the Professor's limp body. "Let's go home." They raced across the sky and when Aaron observed a wilderness area with no roads and no paths, he merely dropped the Professor's body into the woods, where it might never be found. They then proceeded to their resting place. Their cave was large and ran deep. It was in an area of protected caves that were prohibited from the public for safety and to protect their natural state. Deep within and protected from the sun, they relaxed.

"What of that other human?" Rebecca asked.

"Nothing. What will he say? No one will believe him. In fact, he, himself, may be held responsible for the missing man."

"I think we should kill them all. We should make them all appear as being torn apart by that beast. Let them finally decide to hunt him down and do away with him," she snarled.

"Humans are a curious lot. Should he return to that area tonight, you can do as you like. As far as the Howler, he rarely attacks humans and mostly feeds off of the abundant wildlife. We should not add to this attention he brings. My instincts tell me that unless he has developed a taste for human flesh, we should avoid him. If he becomes true competition for our food, then we must make a choice. Either a fight to the death, or we must relocate."

"I say a fight to the death," Rebecca replied. Aaron thought aloud.

"The last time we fought him, it was you that attacked him and I only became involved to save you."

"Next time we should attack simultaneously and without warning. He cannot be that strong."

"Well, Rebecca, tonight is the last night of the full moon cycle, so hopefully we will not have to worry about him for a while. I'm tired, my dear." Aaron closed his eyes and fell into a day's rest.

On the opposite side of the mountain, Christian and Katherine chose their own huge cave to make home. It was inaccessible by road, and far from any human access on foot.

"I love our new appearance," Katherine stated.

"I only await our competition to surface," Christian replied.

"What if there is none?"

"We have only been here one night, and I sense this territory could be paradise. It seems unlikely it has been overlooked. Do you think other vampires appear painted as we are?"

"Most likely not. I only had knowledge because I was human in the recent past. It had just become a fad."

"A fad?" Christian questioned.

"A fad. It is when a certain action or item becomes overwhelmingly popular for a brief period. Will we attend a theater again this night?" she asked.

"No. I believe it would be wise for us to explore the area. If we face conflict in staying here, we should confront those whose domain we share."

"Must it be violent?"

Christian paused, as if in doubt. "Unfortunately, as I have told you, I don't believe sharing is in our nature. However, negotiations are not completely out of the realm of possibility. In my brief stay in Minneapolis, I found more than one vampire sharing that territory. I found this unusual, so I guess a compromise could be achieved."

"I must rest." Katherine closed her eyes and fell into a relaxed state.

* * * *

As he entered his hotel room, he could see the sun begin to rise. He knew Wayne Higdon would be coming to get him within a few hours, so he showered and changed into clean, dry clothes. Mike decided that he would tell Wayne exactly what happened before deciding what to do next. He sat, wondering what they would find left of the Professor on the shore of that island. *'More damn vampires!'* he thought, as the two he had escaped from were not Christian and Katherine. *'How many of these damned things are out there?'* Mike had now lost two friends to these monsters, and was only thinking of how to get even. He opened his suitcase and produced his crossbow pistol. *'Next time I'll be ready.'* He sat in a daze, imagining the vampire standing before him, and firing an arrow directly into its heart. *'Die, you bastard!'* As he daydreamed, a knock at his door broke his imaginary confrontation.

"They said you just got in a little while ago, and I have a report of an abandoned rental car. What were you up to?" Wayne asked.

"I screwed up," Mike mumbled, hanging his head low.

"What happened?"

"Well, after you dropped us off, we . . . er . . . I decided to revisit the crime scene."

"Oh God!" Wayne responded and sat down. "What happened?"

"Well, the Professor and I followed the trail of whatever the hell it was that was left for us to follow. We ended up on the banks of the lake. He had the revolver with the silver bullets and I had a 12 gauge with the petrified wood slugs. It was only because I had a gut feeling that it was vampires we were really dealing with. Then we saw it . . . or it saw us! This damned thing was huge! It moved like a cheetah. I got one shot off, and we both hit the water and swam to the island."

Wayne interrupted. "So you shot at a werewolf with petrified wood? You saw it up close?"

"Too close. That thing is nearly 8 foot tall. That old man Jonah was right. Once it saw us, it came after us as though we were rabbits. Unfortunately, the revolver with the silver bullets was in the Professor's jacket pocket, which was left on the shore. I completely screwed up. Had I had the revolver, I could have emptied it into that thing."

"So you guys got away?"

"No. When we got to the island, the vampires soon descended. There were two of them, and me with no shotgun or wood shells."

Wayne interrupted again. "They were useless anyway. I researched petrified wood. It has no wood properties. It is a fossil type of quartz. If vampires must be killed by wood, those shells would have only given you a false security, and would have likely gotten you killed. How the hell did you both survive?"

"We didn't. The Professor froze up, and with the speed of vampires, it was likely fatal. I'm guessing we will find his body on that island. I barely made it into the lake and swam to the riverboat dock."

"Did anyone see anything?"

"Yeah. I owe a patrolman a flashlight. He was stationed at the scene. Plus, I was spotted by a watchman at the riverboat. They actually gave me a ride back here. I told them it was a Homeland Security issue and they seemed happy to help me. They know nothing."

"Okay . . . as far as I'm reporting, we have a possible missing person. He was last seen at the south shore of Table Rock. This will give us access to a boat and to search the island. Jesus Christ! What do we do now?"

Mike lifted his crossbow pistol. "I want another crack at them."

"What do they look like?" Wayne asked.

"Depends. When they appear, they just look like pale humans. However, when they decide to eat, they change into monsters. Yes, they can fly. It's like they just defy gravity and move fast. They move very, very fast. I only know of what seems to be their one weakness, and that is that they seem to come directly at you. At least, that has been my experience. The other possible weakness is that at times they become talkative. It was that weakness that allowed me time to dive into the lake. Will you tell Cunningham?"

"He's my partner. If I'm in this, so is he. I have had a slight exposure to the supernatural, so I have no doubt these things exist, but Jerry? I think he will have difficulty grasping the situation until he actually confronts one of these creatures and sees for himself."

As if on cue, there was a knock at the door, and Cunningham entered. Mike and Wayne decided to brief him on the night's events. He sat and listened, and although he believed what he was hearing, he felt that is was nothing that traditional efforts could not overcome. All the talk of silver bullets and wooden stakes and crossbows seemed ridiculous in his mind. Although so many things in the Ozarks were unexplained, talking of werewolves and vampires was beyond his grasp. "So in the end, we have a missing Professor. How do we know he is not just sitting there on the island? I suggest we follow this up. All I want mentioned is that we have a lost man, and no more. Already forensics is attributing the death of that photographer to an animal attack. No mention of anything else. Let's go!"

Cunningham had no problem getting the state park to lend them a boat. Arriving at the island, all three detectives examined the scene. "All I see is a lot of footprints." Cunningham concluded.

Mike found the spear he used, but it was clean with no traces of blood. There was no trace of footprints beyond those at the shoreline.

Back in the boat, they went to the south shoreline and looking down into the clear water, they could see that not far from shore was the Professor's jacket, which they retrieved. Close to it was the shotgun. As Mike had stated, it had one discharged shell still in the chamber. As Jerry and Wayne examined the shotgun, Mike sat silently, contemplating the Professor's fate. "It was all my fault. What the hell was I thinking? That old man never had a chance."

"Did you have any idea what was going to happen or what you were walking into? I don't think so. Sure, if you knew how it was going to unfold you never would have brought him along, but that wasn't the case. You can't look back. We need to set a trap. We need to have the right weapons."

Surprisingly, Jerry Cunningham agreed. "If that is possible, we should set up a trap and end this before it goes any further. So far we have an old photographer who was out at night and attacked by a large cat. As far as the Professor, he will become a missing person in another 48 hours. If we have these creatures out there at night, let's be out here tonight and do our own meet and greet."

The three detectives sat in their car after finding the jacket and shotgun, and began planning. They all started reviewing all that they had been told. Cunningham looked to Mike. "The only one that has seen these creatures is you. What are we really facing?"

"With vampires, they are night creatures. They move fast and can descend on you from the sky. It's like they have some kind of night vision or thermal vision. The Professor believed that they could see warm blooded beings from the air."

"Thermal vision? That is interesting . . ." Cunningham replied.

"Why?" Mike wondered.

"Well, if that were the case, we have thermal suits. The water patrol uses them to prevent hypothermia. They are light weight, and insulate the body, sealing the heat in. If that is the case, these suits would make us invisible from the sky. Actually, the Armed Forces use a version of these for that specific purpose."

"If we are invisible, what good would that do?" Higdon asked.

"Let's say two of us were invisible and wearing these suits and one of us remained visible as bait. They might descend thinking they have a single victim, and instead, we could ambush them."

"Now that is interesting . . . the only problem is that we need more weapons. I only have one crossbow pistol. However, I have enough arrows," Mike stated.

"How many arrows?"

"Six."

"Six?" Cunningham repeated in disbelief.

Mike just smiled. "Yeah, six. Believe me, you will only get one good shot, and that's if you're lucky. It might be possible to get two, but the last time I needed two shots, I nearly lost my arm, as it was torn to shreds. Your idea is a good one. If we can fool them into thinking there is one person alone in those woods, they may come to get him. Depending how we set this up, two of us may get a clear shot, and the 'bait' may also get one off. It could work."

As they tossed ideas around, the plan was developed. They would go to the deserted south side of Table Rock and venture deep into the woods. Two of them would wear the light weight thermal suits and hope that it makes them invisible from the air. One would wait in the open and act as warm blooded bait. Cunningham volunteered to be the bait. Higdon would have to go to a sport shop and buy another crossbow pistol and a dozen wooden arrows to be crafted to fit. It was planned that Cunningham would also carry the revolver that was loaded with silver bullets, just in case the werewolf showed up. They would prepare and meet at sundown. Mike decided that he would get a few hours sleep, as he was exhausted. So after dropping him off at his hotel, Cunningham, the old veteran, had time to talk with his partner, Higdon.

"How well do you really know this Mike Evans?"

"Pretty well. Well enough to know that if he says he faced off with one of these things, that he is not lying. Besides, I saw his scars and more stitch marks than I can count. He is obsessed with killing these creatures. He watched as a vampire killed one of his best friends. His obsession cost him his marriage," Higdon explained.

"I know what everyone thinks the image was in that camera, and I know the tales old Jonah told us, but I just can't wrap my head around this thing. Do you really think this so-called trap will work? I mean, do we really have these things roaming the Ozarks?"

"You know Branson, but look what gets reported in this county. Just in the last month, a young couple with strong family ties just vanishes. Then we have a 36 year old woman found in the Mark Twain woods and they label it as 'natural causes.' Only a week ago, they find the body of a 40 year old man in a deserted hotel who has been dead for a year. No cause of death and no ID. This weird shit is obvious. Okay, granted, it's not all within Branson City limits, but it is all around us."

"So you really think we will draw these things into the open?"

"Who knows?" Higdon shrugged.

"And as far as using a crossbow pistol, can that really be the weapon you want to be armed with in a life or death situation?"

"Mike says it has worked for him."

"I can't see it. I think I'll borrow an AR15 from SWAT. I mean, think about it. What can possibly stand up to an AR15? You're talking 12 rounds per second if set on automatic."

"You may only have a second."

"Well? 12 rounds, or a little bitty arrow? Sounds like a no brainer."

"Evans seems to know his stuff."

Cunningham smiled. "Yeah, but did Evans ever try an AR15? It will cut anything at close range in half."

"Myself, I'm going to the sport shop and getting the strongest crossbow pistol money can buy. Then, I'm getting some wooden arrows and cutting them down. I'll have my Glock handy, but I have to heed Mike's advice."

"Well, you do what you got to do. I'll pick up a couple of thermal suits and I'll meet you at his hotel about seven."

Wayne watched as Cunningham walked away biting at his thumbnail and knew he was worried.

* * * *

That same morning a little old man awoke stark naked in the woods. This was nothing new for him, because he was known in Ozark folklore as the Howler. He felt the pain immediately, and realized his shoulder had been wounded. He had no memory of the event that caused the wound. It was not the first time this had occurred, as he had been wounded many times in his life as a werewolf. He looked around to determine his location, and quickly realized where he had clothes hidden. He proceeded towards that spot. Moving a large rock, he exposed a plastic bag containing everything he needed, including shoes. He quickly dressed. Also in his bag was a pair of binoculars. His disguises were honed to a fine science. In this case, he would walk out of the woods a bird watcher, like so many other common tourists. He knew exactly where to exit the woods where the public would be present, and he could weave his way amongst the people and disappear, returning to his motel room. Every move he made was perfect and precise as he had done this so many, many times. His shoulder was in pain, but he had bandages in his room and knew it could never be fatal, as these wounds never were. He had no memory of anything but staring at the full moon as it rose in the sky and the pain and torment of transformation. As he walked, he appeared no different than any one of the thousands of old men moving about Branson.

He was tired of living, but knew he could not be killed. At least, not any longer, for no one believed in werewolves . . . therefore no one carried a weapon that would end his life—or so he thought. At one time in his existence, he fought for survival, as werewolves were hunted down in masse. Now, being the last of his kind, he was alone. A werewolf's survival instinct is overpowering, otherwise suicide might be his answer. Instead, he looked forward to another full moon and a blind rampage as a nightmarish monster. As he walked a brisk pace for his age, no one noticed him in the least. He had learned to become almost so plain that he was invisible to one's memory. Yet he was the Howler. He was a creature famous in Ozark's Folklore. You could find tales of the Howler in any gift shop. There was even a town named after his haunting howls in the mountains, although Howler, Missouri, had long since shut down. In his time, he had killed men, women, children, and most any animal found in the Ozarks. As decades passed, he chose to remain a myth, as he learned to go deep in the woods and attempted to exile himself during his three days of torment. Most times, he survived on wildlife, but now and then a human would cross his path, to their misfortune.

As a human, he maintained certain abilities, regardless of his age. He had boundless energy and cat-like reflexes. His vision was far sharper than the average man. His sense of smell was intense, as he could identify scents and even smell fear. He could also heal very quickly. When he reached his motel room, he bandaged his shoulder. Turning on the local cable channel, there was nothing on the news, so his assumption was that nothing had likely occurred the previous night, and his wound may have been from a fall or maybe a feisty bear that fought back futilely. He had no memory of tearing a photographer literally into pieces. The only way he learned of his possible killings was from watching the news and making assumptions. If they announced remains were found, he assumed it was something he may have done. He was tired of his life, but knew he was doomed to continue for all eternity. He found himself hungry, for it had been twelve hours since he had eaten. He picked up the phone and called for some food to be delivered. Branson is one town where most anything can be delivered, as it caters to its tourists.

The call came into Elmer's, and it was an odd order. At a time of day when their most popular item was a huge breakfast burrito, a man ordered two plain rare steak sandwiches. As the cook prepared them, he recognized that this was not an unusual order, as he had prepared it many times. In his reasoning, this must be a popular meal up north, where a lot of the tourists come from. An order of rare steaks in the morning didn't raise an eyebrow. He bagged it up and placed it on the counter for delivery. It was strange that Danny was working, but he had an early morning dentist appointment and decided to put in some extra hours. Everyone loved Danny. He was young, ambitious, and very clean cut. His blonde hair and boyish good looks gave him a trusting and innocent appearance. Unlike the youth his age, he was well groomed and had no piercings or tattoos. No one was ever reluctant to open their door to him. As an unofficial informant, this worked to his complete advantage. With Danny, it wasn't only the money given to him by Cunningham, as he had a strong moral compass and hated to see some of the corruption seep into a home town he was proud of.

"Gimme the tickets for these, boss! I'm working a long day today."

Danny knew most daytime deliveries were pretty much boring. So as he drove the Branson streets, he was not as vigilant as he normally was at night. He was always looking for something to be reported to Detective Cunningham. His first delivery was to an old Branson motel almost around the corner from Elmer's. Danny knocked on the door and an old man answered. "Just put it on the table," the old man ordered. Since the old man was in a tee shirt, Danny took notice that his shoulder was bandaged. He wondered how this old man hurt himself, for the bandage was rather large. Danny also thought it strange, as this man appeared very old, yet his arms were buff and toned. '*Weird*,' he thought. Danny was almost compulsive about observing anything unusual, and the next thing was curious. The old man asked, "How much?"

"$12.50," Danny answered. He then watched as the old man went to the dresser and on the top were not one, but three wallets. He scanned the room for signs of anyone else staying there and there were none. '*Who has three wallets?*' Then, he watched as the old man opened one, and it only had a few singles, so he tossed it down and opened the second wallet, producing more bills. '*He doesn't seem to know how much is in each wallet?*' He handed Danny $15.00. "Thanks," the old man mumbled.

"No, thank you sir!" Danny replied.

As Danny left, he never saw the old man throw the bread away and tear at the rare steak like an animal. However, the whole situation seemed curious to Danny. Was the old guy a pickpocket? The bandaged shoulder, the buff arms, and the multiple wallets just cataloged in his mind as a possible mention to Cunningham.

* * * *

While Higdon was shopping for a crossbow and arrows, Cunningham had his idea of what he wanted for protection. He just could not imagine facing something that was intending to kill him and not having the most powerful weapon in his hands to defend himself. If he was to be the bait, so to speak, he wanted fire power. Being a respected veteran, it only took a phone call to have an AR15 put into his trunk. In his mind, if there were such things as vampires and werewolves, they would be no match for a fully automatic AR15. He had the thermal suits and as far as he was concerned, he was good to go.

Wayne Higdon was at the local sports shop buying the most powerful and accurate hand held crossbow pistol he could find. Designed to shoot metal arrows, the clerk thought it strange that Higdon only wanted full sized wooden arrows that did not match. Wayne saw that it would be easy to cut them down, as pistol sized arrows had no feathers and were only meant to travel a short distance at high velocity. The one thought going through his mind was that to use this effectively, his target had to be very, very, close. If this was meant to kill a vampire, he knew that he would soon be forced to stare one in the face. Higdon was a good Christian, so his last stop was the church. As he walked in, it was empty, and he slid into a pew and fell to his knees. "Oh, God, protect all of us," he prayed. "If there are such creatures, this evil must be destroyed and not allowed to walk in your world. Father, protect us, as our intentions are as acting as your humble servants. Amen." Higdon slowly left and hoped that God had heard his prayer. He knew that if Evans was correct, they would need all the help they could get!

Chapter Five

Jerry Cunningham had his own theories, regardless of the Ozark folklore. In his twenty-five years on the police force, he learned there was a huge difference between a gun in the hands of a private citizen, opposed to a trained law enforcement officer or professional hunter. Regardless of old Jonah's tales, the silver bullet theory just wasn't believable. In his mind, the silver bullets were likely used simply by trained hunters who were conditioned to staring down wild animals. In his thinking, training and accuracy had to be the difference—not the bullet. No way was he going to rely on a revolver with six shots, versus an automatic assault rifle with 30 rounds. He understood the folklore, but he reasoned that all these tales came long before modern weapons.

So as he loaded his gear, which would make him appear as a common hunter in the woods, under his Flak jacket would be an AR15 with a collapsible stock that would allow it to hang under his arm, hidden from view. In facing a wild animal, this was his weapon of choice. He loaded the thermal suits and had spray painted them black, which would make Higdon and Evans literally invisible in the dark woods. He decided to carry the snub nosed revolver with the silver bullets, but tucked it into his ankle holster. If he was to be the bait, he wanted the most powerful weapon possible. At 12 rounds per second, the AR15 gave him the most comfort, but he would keep it his little secret.

As the sun began to set, he drove to the hotel to meet Evans and Higdon. Evans and Higdon dressed in casual clothes and tee shirts knowing that they would be wearing the insulated thermal suits. Each carried their regulation side arm, but also the crossbow pistols and a supply of arrows.

Once Cunningham arrived, they were soon on the road moving toward an area deep in the woods south of Table Rock Lake and far from the tourists and population. After parking away from the road, they began their trek into the wilderness. In single file, they marched, weaving their way through the trees and foliage. In the dense forest, it seemed as though they walked miles before coming upon a small clearing which was only about 20 feet square. They decided this is where Cunningham would make camp.

"You guys get out of the clearing and put on those thermal suits. I'm going to make a small fire. Then I'm climbing into a sleeping bag, but I'll have my weapon ready."

As Cunningham began piling up wood and branches for his fire, Higdon and Evans found a place in the brush close by. Cunningham did everything he could to appear as a camper alone in the wild. From a distance they were being watched by Christian and Katherine, sitting comfortably high in a tree.

"Did you see that? Two of them disappeared?" Katherine was stunned as the three warm blooded figures suddenly became only one, once they put on the thermal suits, which made their warm blooded appearance invisible.

"This is some kind of a trap. They have use of something that cloaks their warm blooded presence. They have a plan of some sort. I believe the one that is uncloaked is baiting some of our kind."

"So you believe they are vampire hunters?"

"For what other reason would they cloak their warm blooded presence?"

"We should leave," Katherine suggested.

"No. We will observe and see how this unfolds. I don't believe this involves us."

Christian and Katherine watched as Cunningham sat in the open, appearing as a vulnerable meal and an open invitation to any vampire. There he was, deep in the wilderness, unarmed and beyond a call for help. With their night vision and ability to see thermal images, something else got their attention.

"Look west," Christian ordered.

Katherine could see a warm blooded being that was huge in size. It was much larger than a human, and moving in the direction of Cunningham. "What is that?"

"Heed your senses. It is not human, nor is it a common mammal."

"Then what is it?" Katherine asked.

"I feel it is something we should definitely avoid."

The Howler was hungry and had picked up a scent. Unfortunately, the scent was human. He proceeded following the smell, moving quickly toward Cunningham. With his nose to the air, he moved with speed and silence, and soon saw the glow of the campfire in the distance. Now, he began stalking his prey. As he moved closer to the glow of the fire, the smell of human became stronger and stronger as his lips and teeth began dripping with saliva, anticipating his soon-to-be meal. As the Howler reached a point where he could see into the clearing, he paused long enough to see only one man lying near the campfire, rolled up in sleeping bag. Almost opposite of the Howler, Higdon thought he heard a rustle of leaves.

"Did you hear that?" Higdon asked.

Evans put his ear to the air. Both their hearing was impaired by the hoods on the thermal suits. "No, I can't hear a damned thing."

No sooner than he uttered the words, the Howler literally pounced from out of the foliage directly on top of Cunningham, who attempted to cry out for help, but was cut off in mid-scream. The weight of the huge beast on his chest kept him from raising his weapon. In a split second he bit Cunningham in the face, and proceeded in biting and clawing his upper body in an uncontrollable frenzy. Higdon and Evans were in complete shock and surprise, and realized all they were holding were their ineffective crossbow pistols. The thermal suits were like jumpsuits and both had their service pistols zippered up inside. So Evans pointed and released an arrow which struck the Howler in his side. The Howler screamed in pain. As Evans reloaded, Higdon released his arrow, but having no skills and no practice, he missed completely. As Higdon fumbled with the zipper on his jump suit, Evans released another arrow, striking the Howler in the shoulder. Raising his head to the air, the Howler let out a scream and leapt into the woods, leaving a mutilated Cunningham and a sleeping bag torn to shreds.

The Howler's screams of anguish were heard clearly by Aaron and Rebecca.

"He is in pain. He has been severely wounded," Rebecca stated.

"I can see him. He is alone and running toward the lake," Aaron replied, for he could clearly see the warm blooded creature moving.

"We should attack. We can finish him," she suggested with enthusiasm.

"We will be risking our lives."

"I want him dead! This is our best opportunity. If you won't, I'll attack him and finish him myself!"

"Okay, let's kill him!"

With the Howler disappearing into the woods, Higdon ran to his partner and in a glance, knew he was dead. He could clearly see the AR15 lying next to him, but also saw the revolver with the silver bullets in his ankle holster. He drew the gun loaded with silver bullets, and yelled to Evans, "I'm going after that bastard!" Evans reloaded his crossbow pistol. Together they ran, following the Howler's trail.

The vampires could not see Higdon and Evans, who were still wearing their thermal suits, hiding their warm blooded glow. Rebecca reached the Howler first, landing on his back and biting and clawing, while Aaron landed in front, attacking his head and chest. Unearthly sounds of pain and fury filled the air. Higdon arrived at the scene first, and immediately raised the snubbed nosed revolver and began firing silver bullets. With its 2 inch barrel, the gun had little accuracy outside of 10-15 feet, so the fired shots were wasted. Evans could not believe the sight, and as the huge werewolf tossed and turned, he raised the crossbow and fired. Just as he pulled the trigger, the werewolf turned his back and the arrow hit Rebecca in the center of her back, penetrating her body and piercing her heart. She fell, making a final scream of death. It was only a few seconds in real time, but it seemed as though everything was moving in slow motion. Aaron released his grasp and seeing the two men, took one last look at his Rebecca and took to the sky. With Aaron gone and Rebecca lying on the ground, the wounded beast fled into the darkness.

Higdon finally opened his thermal suit and raised his 9mm service gun. Evans reloaded the crossbow pistol, searching for another target. "We got one," he gasped. They both stood staring at what appeared to be a shriveled up, elderly woman's body. Higdon was speechless.

"They do that," Evans stated.

"Do what?"

"They age quickly once they're dead. I have seen this before."

Both were shaking and filled with adrenaline. "That beast got away," Higdon replied.

"Well, he sure took a beating. I know I hit him with two shots and God knows what damage those vampires did."

"Shit! I fired that revolver before he was in range. I wasted the damned silver bullets!"

"Hey, don't beat yourself up. You may have hit him, but just not in the heart."

"What do we do now?" Higdon asked.

"Well, let's get back to your partner. Is there any chance for communication out here?"

"Not likely. We are way out of radio range, unless we get back to the car. No chance for a cell signal. What of this vampire body?" Higdon asked.

"Leave it. It won't be here when the sun comes up. It will turn to dust. It's just as well, because you don't want to have to explain it."

"Son-of-a-bitch, he killed Jerry. Son-of-a-bitch!" Higdon was in shock.

"We screwed up. No way did we expect that wolf to show up, and I have never seen anything move that fast. Jerry had no chance. He was dead in seconds," Evans stated.

"What are we going to say? How do we explain it?"

"Well, we know we can't mention werewolf, or we'll both be put in a mental hospital." Evans shook his head at the mere thought.

"The only thing we can do is tell the truth. We were staking out a killer, when a huge animal attacked him. That is all that will ever be determined by the evidence. Come on, let's get back and call this in."

* * * *

From high up and far away, Christian and Katherine had watched the sequence of events unravel.

"Obviously, there are those that know of us. We must take great care," Christian began.

"Christian, what was that beast?"

"I am not familiar with it. It appeared wolf-like, but with human dexterity and inhuman speed. I have the feeling it can change form. It may be a type of shape shifter."

"It was more than a match for the two vampires," Katherine stated.

"Apparently they thought they could overtake him once he was wounded. The humans disrupted their attack."

"Were they the residents of this domain?"

"I would assume so," Christian answered. "Now there is only one. We should find him, as he is now alone. Should we not come to a compromise, we will find it easy to end his existence."

"He fled in that direction; let us follow. I would imagine he returned to where they rest."

As they flew across the night sky, the direction in which they saw Aaron flee pointed straight to a mountain, and to the mouth of a cave. Christian could sense it was a perfect resting place, as it was inaccessible by any vehicle, and far from populated areas.

"I know he is there. Stay behind me."

They landed silently, and Christian slowly entered. The cave ran deep and Christian was on guard of any unanticipated attack. He was not truly sure whether there might be more than one vampire, as a lair was a remote possibility. Far into the darkness and into the mountain, he heard sounds of anguish. Those sounds sparked a memory of his own pain at losing his Anne. He began to put aside his sense of confrontation as he came into the presence of Aaron, who was huddled in a corner. Christian just stood, staring at this pitiful sight. Suddenly Aaron realized he was being watched, and immediately knew it was by vampires. Instead of becoming defensive, Aaron simply looked up.

"Who are you?"

"I am Christian, and this is my Katherine. We have been driven from our northern territory and wish to reside in this domain."

As if nothing had been said, Aaron stated, "They have killed my Rebecca. She was my mate of 50 years."

"I understand. You must be feeling great pain."

Aaron looked at Katherine. "Obviously a pain you may never understand."

Christian smiled. "On the contrary. Only a short time ago I lost my mate of 100 years. After the anguish, will come the need for revenge. It will be a revenge filled with reckless abandon. I was driven to walk amongst the population, and feed in public without concern, until I destroyed the human that killed my Anne."

"So this pain will cease?"

"Oh yes, but you will soon be overcome with a rage, and you will also be compelled to seek revenge."

Aaron studied Christian. "I feel threatened. Is that so?"

Christian smiled. "Your instincts are correct, but only for the sake of defense. However, this is no longer true. We mean you no harm."

"I believe that you are much older than I." Aaron sensed a strength and confidence.

"I am, although Katherine is only two years as a vampire. She is a modern woman. She understands this current culture."

Aaron, with his night vision, could not see their tanned appearance. Aside from his Rebecca, he had never encountered another vampire. He studied Christian and Katherine, and instead of aggression, he felt a comfort with being with his own kind. He knew that Christian understood his anguish and felt Christian's compassion. Aaron, after the brief minutes of feeling as though he was truly alone in this world, appreciated the newcomers.

"I don't know what I will do?" Aaron whispered.

"Have you eaten?"

"No. In fact that was what we were hunting when we came upon that beast. I should have stopped her. My instincts were to avoid the Howler after our first encounter years ago."

"The Howler?"

"Yes, he is a werewolf. He has been named the Howler in the local Ozark folklore. He is very old. He is only a beast for the cycle of the full moon. Other than those days, he appears human. He kills publically and indiscriminately. If it were not for him, we would have had an undiscovered existence."

"Interesting. You cannot kill him when he is in human form?"

"He walks in the sunlight. We cannot locate him."

It seemed that just talking with Christian and explaining the general environment made Aaron forget his sorrow, if for only a moment. He told of the Howler and how he wreaked havoc in the wilderness every full moon. He spoke of how easy it was to feed undiscovered. He explained that until recently, their world was secure, and that the trap they had flown into was unanticipated and never before had they encountered a crossbow. He felt there was something strange about the men who killed Rebecca. It was when he told of the two men chasing the Howler, that Christian became interested. When Aaron described the Professor, whom they had killed, Christian felt it was more than just coincidence.

"So, it was after the killing of the old man, that these other three apparently set the trap. Yet, if the trap was for the werewolf, why did they have crossbows? The only time I have ever seen this weapon, was when I was being hunted in Minnesota. My Anne was killed by such a weapon. Is that the weapon of choice to kill a werewolf?"

Aaron thought for a moment. "No. In fact it seemed ineffective. Legend has it that only silver through his heart will kill him. Rebecca and

I were going to try and remove his heart, or his head. Why would they be armed with wooden arrows?"

"They were hunting for us. They were hunting vampires. That is what we witnessed. They had set a trap for vampires and this beast wandered into their trap. They were unprepared. Now one of them is dead, and this Howler also appeared as being wounded."

"He will survive. He always does. Had it not been for his indiscriminate carnage, my Rebecca would still be with me and there would be no knowledge of us," Aaron mourned.

"Tell me of this old man you killed. What happened to the body?"

"I dropped it deep in the woods where it may never be found."

"Can you take me there?" Christian asked, anxiously.

"Yes."

The three walked from the cave and rose into the night sky. They followed Aaron as he descended into the wilderness. There, on the open ground, was the dead Professor, lying on his stomach. Christian turned the body over, and immediately recognized him. It seemed more than a coincidence to find him following them to Branson. Christian paced back and forth, bothered. *'How was it possible that this old man knew our destination?'* Christian thought to himself.

"At least one of the men with crossbows is from Minneapolis. Given they are most likely police, one of them is a detective that I am familiar with. They are surely hunting us."

"Will we relocate?" Katherine asked.

"No, we will kill him."

Talk of killing led Katherine to utter, "I hunger."

"Follow me," Aaron offered. "There is a homeless camp not far from here. Small groups are scattered about, away from the population. Never are they missed."

Taking to the sky a series of small campfires was soon clearly visible. The vampires surveyed each camp, looking for the proper number of humans. Aaron spotted one with three men sitting by their fire, drinking. He motioned for them to land. Setting down lightly, they watched as the men passed a bottle of wine back and forth, and made irrelevant conversation. "We should strike quickly," Aaron whispered. Walking up from behind, there was no chance to escape or struggle. Looking up and seeing the vampires, barely a scream could be uttered before the blood drinking began. As they gorged on their victims, they never noticed that in a nearby tent was a fourth man, who had been sleeping and had awakened.

He peeked out to see this nightmarish sight, and struggled to not make a sound. He could only watch in horror as his companions were drained of life. He covered his mouth, scared that they might hear him breathe. He was frozen in fear, as he knew there was no communication, and nowhere to escape to, so he remained still and silent. It was only after feeding and in the glow of the fire that Aaron looked at Christian, in wonder. "Your complexion . . . is like that of the humans, and as if you have been walking in sunlight?"

"It is a dye. They apply it to your skin. It gives us an appearance that allows us to walk amongst them."

"Do you have this?"

"No, the humans must apply it. We will show you."

The old man in the tent stayed perfectly still in complete shock, as he watched what looked like hideous monsters switch to human form. He could hardly breathe, for fear they may hear him.

"We should take the bodies and dispose of them in the woods. They will never be missed."

The old man watched as each vampire easily picked up the body of each of his friends and disappeared into the night sky. Once they were out of sight, he remained afraid to move, and shaking in fear of their return.

* * * *

Evans and Higdon returned to their clearing and the gruesome sight of Cunningham's body. Higdon just paced about, manically. "We have to clean this up as best we can. We need to get rid of the AR15 and these thermal suits. There is no way we can admit that we were on a vampire hunt. Forensics will determine exactly what happened here, and that is that Jerry was killed by a wild animal. The question is, what the hell were we doing out here?"

"Looking for meth cookers? Looking for a marijuana field? We were helping him set up camp and the animal attacked?" Evans offered several suggestions, groping for anything that made sense.

"And we never fired our service weapons, why?" Higdon asked.

"Because . . . because, we were on our way back to the vehicle when we heard the attack. By the time we got here, it was over."

"That just might fly."

They quickly decided that Higdon would stay with the body and Evans would take the thermal suits, crossbow pistols, and AR15 back to the car, hiding them in the trunk, before calling in the incident. It seemed like hours as Higdon sat with the body of a partner that he was sworn to protect. He actually had not known Cunningham that long, but felt the deep loss of a friend. *'Not the best way to go out.'* As he sat mourning, he vowed to kill this werewolf. He remembered old Jonah's words, that if the beast was wounded, they would look for a man with a similar wound. Higdon knew if he could find him, he would empty his gun filled with silver bullets in his chest. When Mike returned, Higdon simply stated, "We must talk."

It was hours later that both were relieved and the paperwork was finished. Higdon knew that Cunningham's death would be covered up, and the press would somehow put an acceptable spin on his death, as not to taint the city's image. Actually, the incident was not within Branson city limits, therefore it was technically the county's problem. It would be reported that Cunningham was likely killed by an animal while out hunting. He would have a funeral with full honors. There would be no evidence that anything else could have occurred. Once outside, Higdon suggested Elmer's as a place to get a well needed drink and talk privately. After getting settled in a booth in the back and having a few shots and beers delivered to their table, Higdon wanted answers.

"Mike, what the hell have we stumbled into? I have had a brush with the paranormal, but this is insane. What are these creatures?"

"When we were at college, we dreamed of being good cops. With that came hopes of locking up the bad guys and protecting the public from people we could arrest. I lived with that dream for nearly a decade and for the most part, enjoyed living that life. Then, something totally bizarre happened. One of my best friends claimed he killed a vampire. It was all accidental, mind you. It attacked, and he happened to be carrying a crossbow. He swore its mate was chasing after him. I thought he lost his damned mind, until I pumped fifteen 9mm bullets into one, and it smiled at me. I have no idea about this whole werewolf thing, but I do know vampires. You saw them tonight. You watched me kill one. Once that door is opened and you know these things exist, you will never be the same. The night will take on a whole new meaning. When I walk over a sewer cover, I wonder if one is standing below me in a drainage tunnel. When I walk into a warehouse, I wonder if one is hanging from the ceiling. When I view a corpse, I wonder if the massive blood loss is common hypovolemia, or if has it been sucked out. My house has blessed crucifixes over all entrances, and I keep a bottle of holy water at my bedside."

Mike produced a crucifix from under his tee shirt and held it out. "I watched my friend have his throat torn out because he took this off. It changed me. I lost my wife, and most of my department thinks I'm insane because I keep a handheld crossbow within reach at all times after the sun goes down. I am always looking for signs that they are there. More than once one of these Goth kids has had me reaching for a weapon, because of their white make-up and black lipstick. I am not the same man. I will never be the same man."

"What did it do to your belief in God?"

"It made it stronger. There is a reason these monsters are afraid of the cross. I won't preach religion, as we both graduated from a Christian college, but if these things exist, and are afraid of God's blessings, then I know in my heart that angels are also out here."

"What are we going to do?" Higdon wondered.

"I know a lot about these creatures, thanks to experience and a good education by the late Professor Steiner. I also learned tonight that those thermal suits can allow us to be invisible to a certain extent. My vote is that we go hunting, if you can break free."

Higdon grimaced. "I want that werewolf. I want his head on a platter. I don't care how the hell old he is, or what the Ozark folklore states; I'm killing him. I will carry a drop gun and that revolver loaded with silver bullets with his name on them."

"Well, you're kind of screwed, because this is the last night of the full moon. You have to wait a month," Evans replied logically.

"So? I'll wait. I'll wait a month, or two months, or every damned full moon until I put him to rest. What he did to Jerry is something I will never, ever, get out of my mind's eye."

"See? It already changed you. Do you have children?"

"Yes, a little girl."

"How will you react if she ever wants to go camping, or to summer camp? Or even to a high school camping event? That is what changes you. Knowing that these things are out there will make you behave differently. Unfortunately, people will notice. Tonight you witnessed a horror that you can never share, even if you try. Even though my wife saw my hundred stitches on my arm, when I told her of the vampire that did it, she wanted me to see a shrink. She packed up and left after she invited a stranger into our house and I went berserk. Once you know, it stays with you. You can't shake it. You'll never forget it."

"You're telling me not to tell my wife?"

"It's up to you, but I wouldn't if I had it all to do again."

Evans noticed a young man watching them. "We have someone interested in us."

Higdon turned around and noticed Danny, and motioned him over.

"Mike, this is Danny. Danny is a close friend of the department."

"Where's Jerry?" Danny asked.

"Danny, I'm sorry to say that Jerry passed away tonight."

They watched as Danny's eyes welled up in tears. "What . . . what happened?"

"This is confidential. He was on a stake-out for a meth lab and was attacked by a cougar. It killed him."

They watched as Danny's tears flowed freely. "Jerry was my good friend. Is there anything I can do?"

"No, Danny. I can let you know when the funeral will be held, and I guess you can continue helping us and working through me. Jerry told me how valuable you are and how much you have helped the department and the city," Higdon explained. "In fact, you can help me with something immediately."

"Anything. Please, just tell me what to do?"

"If you could, keep your eyes open for a guy who is likely old, but might have some massive wounds. He may have bandages on his shoulder and sides. We need to find this guy."

Danny's eyes widened. "An old guy in bandages?"

"Do you know something?"

"I delivered an order this morning to an old guy. He had what looked to be a shoulder wound with a big bandage. The only reason he seemed strange, is because the old guy had some guns. I mean his arms looked intimidating. I figured maybe he was with one of the shows here in town, like an old acrobat or something."

"Will you work the morning?" Higdon asked.

"I can."

"What time did he order?"

"He ordered two really rare steak sandwiches between nine and ten."

Higdon couldn't believe it. "Really rare steak? Let's hope he orders tomorrow. Either way, you are taking us there. If he does order, all I want is for you is to deliver the food and let us know if he is wearing more bandages."

"Is this guy dangerous?"

"If it's who we think it is, yes. All I want for you to do is give us a nod, and we'll do the rest."

* * * *

Deep in the Ozark's woods the Howler removed the arrows and was literally licking his wounds. In his mindless state there was no reasoning of why the attack occurred or even who his attackers were. All he could determine in his animal state was he sensed he was injured. It was not the first time. His history was one of being hunted and even shot in decades passed. Too injured to hunt, he laid in the safety of the dark woods and slept to regain his strength. As the sun rose and he transformed into a man, the pain of his wounds awoke him. As he examined his body, he could only imagine what had occurred. His healing was twice as fast as that of a mortal man, but the damage was evident, aside from the large wounds made from the arrows, he was covered in deep scabbed lacerations, resulting from the vampire's claws. As he searched for his hidden stash of clothes, he could only imagine what might have happened. He was tired of this curse, yet had no way to remove it. He painfully put on pants, a shirt, and shoes, and he would attempt to walk from the woods looking as normal as possible so as to not draw attention to himself. He did not want someone concerned to offer assistance and try to take him to the emergency room. So with his collar up and head down, he walked a brisk pace to his motel room. Once there, he watched the clock, for he was anxious to order food, as he hadn't eaten and was famished. He was used to being wounded, and had everything he needed to tend to his injuries. Still having a significant wound in his shoulder, he applied a new bandage, and also to his arrow punctures. He had little concern for he knew that within the week all would be completely healed. When the clock hit 8 a.m., he was dialing Elmer's ordering not two, but four very rare steak sandwiches.

It was breakfast time at Elmer's and the owner was surprised to see Danny show up to do morning deliveries. Danny had gotten a good night's sleep, and although he had been helping the police with information, he felt that this was his chance to really be involved and contribute. Although Evans and Higdon only wanted Danny to do a simple identification, Danny had other ideas. He walked over to their table. "The order just came in," Danny announced.

"Remember, we will follow you there. Wait for us to get in position. I will cover the front and Higdon will cover the back. All we need for you to do is ID this guy. If he is obviously bandaged, especially in the shoulders and torso, just give us the nod as you leave. We'll take it from there," Evans instructed.

Danny took his order and proceeded on his way with Higdon and Evans following behind. Once at the motel, Higdon went around the back and Evans sat in the car watching the front door. Danny waited until he was signaled and went to the motel door and knocked. The man peeked out and as with the last time, he allowed Danny in. Going inside, the old man's bandages were clearly visible. Even under his tee shirt, the bulk from the layers of gauze bulged and was obvious. Danny knew this was absolutely the man they were looking for. "$25.00," Danny stated. The old man went to his dresser and just as last time, there were multiple wallets lying about. Danny, being larger and a much younger man, decided he wanted to do more than just give Evans a simple nod. As the old man turned his back, Danny moved up quickly and grabbed him from behind. He actually thought he could wrestle and disable the old guy, and bring him out as a prisoner. Instead he was in for a big surprise.

He wrapped his arms around him from behind, in a reverse bear hug, locking his hands tightly. "You're going with me," he announced. Danny had full confidence that he could easily overpower this old man. Instead, the old man's animal instincts took over. He slipped from Danny's grip and Danny attempted to get him in a head lock, clamping his neck with all his youthful strength. The old man with his face at Danny's side, did what his instincts dictated, and he bit Danny through his shirt, deep into his skin. Danny screamed in pain as he let go, and when he did, the old man pushed Danny through the front picture window. All Evans saw was Danny crashing through the window backwards and falling onto the sidewalk. He immediately drew his pistol and yelled, "Police!"

The old man's only instinct was to escape. Hearing Evans announce police, he ran to the bathroom window, and like a panicked wild animal, dove right through. Higdon drew his revolver loaded with silver bullets as he saw this mass of glass, window frame, and human, come crashing outward in his direction. The old man landed on all fours and as he looked up, Higdon ordered, "Hands behind your head, you are under arrest!"

The old man stared at Higdon for a brief second, and rushed directly at him, growling; it was a sound that was inhuman. Higdon did not hesitate and emptied his gun into the old man's chest, sending more than one silver bullet into his heart. As Evans tended to Danny, who was bleeding and lying in the street, he heard the shots. "Don't move, I'm calling 911," he told Danny, as he rushed to the rear of the motel. There, Higdon stood frozen in place, just staring at the old man who was sprawled on the ground. His gaze was fixed on the old man's face, as it appeared he had the faint trace of a smile.

"What do we do now?" Evans asked.

"Call in for back-up." Evans watched as Higdon produced a .38 from his coat and placed it in the old man's hands. "I had no choice," Higdon stated.

"Jesus, he looks like he is smiling?"

Higdon could only guess. "Maybe he is. Maybe I set him free." He produced his radio. "Officer needs assistance. We have a civilian injured and one fatality. No officer was injured."

When the EMT's arrived, Higdon explained that Danny was an innocent bystander and should be taken to the ER. When the next detective arrived, he examined the motel room and determined that because of the stash of wallets and purses, that the dead man was quite the thief. Higdon explained that it was to be a simple arrest, but the man came at him waving the .38. He would have to surrender his weapon for a day, but it appeared an open and shut case of self-defense.

In the ER, Danny was covered in cuts and bruises and took a number of stitches to the lacerations from crashing through the glass window. Given the multitude of cuts and scratches, the minor bite wound was completely overlooked. It was not a major wound and only enough to break through his skin. No one, including Danny, thought much of it. Danny had no clue that the curse of the Howler had been passed on. He had no idea that he had been bitten by a werewolf.

It was hours later that the scene was cleaned up and Evans and Higdon were seated back in Elmer's.

"Well, that's the end of one Ozark legend," Higdon surmised.

"That old guy threw Danny through that window like he was tossing a rag doll. His strength was way beyond his years."

"Was Danny okay?"

"Yeah, likely a few stitches and he'll be sore tomorrow. Why the hell did he try and grab the guy?"

"Likely he thought he was helping us. The problem is that he never knew he was literally grabbing a tiger by the tail. When that guy came crashing through that bathroom window, he came at me with a look that was pretty scary. So much so, that I did not hesitate to empty my revolver into him. You know how you have that sinking feeling after you shoot someone? Well, this time, I don't have it. In fact, I feel a bit exhilarated. Is that weird?"

"Nah. That's how I feel after killing a vampire. It's more like I have this feeling of accomplishment," Evans replied.

"Well maybe we won't be finding body parts all over the woods, and maybe Jerry didn't die in vain," Higdon lamented.

"Hey, don't be taking the blame for that one. Nobody had a clue that thing would show up, much less how damned fast it could move. We still have one vampire to hunt down."

"How do we do that?"

"I'm not sure at this point. Given what I know from the past, I did kill his mate, therefore, he may be hunting me! I guess I should make myself available."

"Tell me more about these vampires," Higdon requested.

"Well, all that I know came from experience and the Professor's handbook. They are night creatures, so they rest during daylight hours. They can be most anywhere that is hidden from the light. In Minneapolis, we have huge drainage systems where we found them, and one I killed in a deserted warehouse that had the windows painted black. Typically, they are invisible to the average citizen and feed off the less desirable population, such as prostitutes, homeless, gang members, etc. They seem very intelligent at choosing their prey and disguising their kills. They need not totally drain the body of all blood, only what they need to eat and to kill the individual. The crossbow and wooden arrows seem the best and safest way to kill them. Believe me, getting too close is risking your life, as they move far too fast. Here, look at my arm." He rolled up his sleeve and clearly visible were a set of long, deep scars that ran from shoulder to wrist. "I nearly lost this arm to one. I had to drive an arrow through the bastard's heart by hand. The Professor and I were actually down here on vacation when we walked into your crime scene. It looked a bit too familiar to us. There is one particular vampire we are after and we thought he might be here," Evans explained.

"What will you do now?"

"This vampire knows me. It was the same one that killed the Professor. I think I will return to where he last saw me and just wait. He'll find me. However, I won't make the mistake of taking off my cross."

"What will I do now that I am the only one that knows we have vampires here in Branson?"

"You do have certain advantages here."

"What would those be?" Higdon asked.

"First, I have never seen so many churches in such a concentrated area in my whole life, and second, you have no huge drainage system underground. Plus, I have seen very few pieces of deserted or neglected property, and no industrial area to speak of. So vampires are likely restricted to caves and the wilderness. Logically, that is their primary and possibly only vulnerability."

"That is, unless they have gotten a spray tan as you and the Professor suspected. If that is the case, they could be walking around the malls and going to shows."

"Yeah, but only at night," Mike replied.

"God, with all the homeless this economy has created, vampires have a virtual unlimited feeding ground."

"We've got daylight, let's visit the homeless camp," Evans suggested.

After paying the bill, they took a drive to the outskirts of the city to a woodsy area away from the tourist population. As they drove down a rough dirt road, tents and even large boxes became visible, as they were scattered about the area. They could see whole families and gatherings of men grouped together in various settings. Seeing one large group seated on folding lawn chairs in the shade, they pulled their car over. "Let's talk with them," Higdon suggested. Immediately recognized as police, they could see a look of fear on the faces of the group as they were thinking they were about to be evicted from the property. Higdon and Evans approached the group with a smile.

"Hi, folks." Higdon greeted. "We need your help."

"How so?" asked an old man.

"We were wondering if you have had any strange disappearances around here lately," Evans asked.

"Lately? People disappear all the time. Some pack it up and leave in the night and never even say a good-bye."

"Did you ever have some not 'pack it up' and just disappear? Maybe leaving all their stuff?"

"Yeah, we have had a few of those," the old man answered as he scratched his head.

"We're looking for someone that might be preying on your people." Higdon explained. "Has anything unusual ever happened out here?"

The old man looked around as if he was asking permission to tell the story and decided it was okay. "Well there was a guy we called Jake. He left at daybreak. He was camped a bit down the road from here with three other men. They were all old Viet Nam veterans. He left on his own and was scared as hell. He said some demons came to their camp and carried the other three men away. They were all hooked on one substance or another, so his accounting of what happened might not be quite accurate. He said the demons just picked them up and flew away. Damndest tale I ever heard, but he said he was headed for Springfield and wanted to get into a homeless shelter. He told us we should all get the hell away from here. We just think he needed to find Jesus."

"Is their camp still there?"

The old man scratched his head. "Don't know."

Higdon handed him a card. "Here, if anything strange happens out here, call me."

Higdon watched as the old man crumpled up the card and threw it on the ground. "You see any phones out here?" The group all laughed.

Evans stepped in. "I recommend that all of you stay close together. We would not advise anyone to set up any camp away from the main group. Stay together, for there is a definite danger in being alone."

Higdon motioned to Evans to follow him as he walked further on down the path. About 500 yards away was a camp that was deserted with three tents still intact. They could see personal items still left in the open.

Evans looked to Higdon. "Three men missing, three demons. It seems we have three vampires."

Chapter Six

Danny began to feel strange. After leaving the ER and giving the police his report of what had occurred, he went home. He was amazed that he was not feeling the pain from his wounds, which he expected, and it seemed that he would not need the pain killers the doctor had prescribed. All that he really felt was fatigue. Entering his apartment, he proceeded to the bathroom to splash cold water on his face. When he looked in the mirror, the face that looked back at him seemed to have changed. His round boyish face seemed to have a more chiseled appearance. The eyes staring back at him seemed cold. He splashed the water on his face and believed that the drugs that the doctor had given him were causing him to see things differently. He didn't think much of it, because all he wanted to do was sleep. As Danny collapsed on his bed, what he didn't know was that his physiology was changing. As he descended into sleep, he couldn't help but be bothered by sounds; some of which were distant, that he had never been aware of before. It was quiet by human standards, but still he desperately tried to shut out the noise and fell into a near coma.

* * * *

Higdon decided that they had had enough action for one day and that he had been ignoring his wife with his late evenings. He did not share the new knowledge with her, and for the time being he would heed Mike Evans' advice. He could only imagine how Abby would react, faced with tales of vampires and werewolves. Higdon did call the few tanning salons in Branson that did spray tanning, asking them to immediately contact him should anyone suspiciously pale, or acting unusual in any way, enter their businesses. This evening, he and his wife, Abby, would treat Evans to dinner and a show on the riverboat. Higdon felt it was one of the better Branson experiences. There was a nice dinner, time to stroll the three levels of decks, and finally, a great show, all while cruising on the lake.

After picking Evans up at the hotel and introducing his wife, they drove to the dock of the riverboat that Evans already knew all too well. As they walked across the top of the dock, Evans could remember standing under it only a few nights ago. Off in the distance he could see the island from where he had escaped the vampires, and where the Professor had been killed. Abby could sense his serious mood and was a bit puzzled by it.

"Mike, do you not like being on the water? You seem so serious," she asked.

Evans looked to Higdon. "No, I just have some personal memories that I am reminded of."

"We don't have to do this," she offered.

"No, it is fine. Don't pay any attention to me."

Evans couldn't help himself from wondering; *'Now that the sun is down, are there vampires in the vicinity?'*

The riverboat was beautiful and enormous. It was three levels, and had a capacity of 750 people, plus the staff. Although filled with modern technology, it gave all the appearances of an old fashioned paddle wheel. They took their seats on the main floor facing the stage. Mike was impressed as he looked up, as each level had its own dining service. As the salads were served, a live band played various combinations of jazz and ragtime.

"Wayne told me you were divorced. I'm so sorry." Abby felt that Mike's somber mood might be due to the fact that he was alone.

"My divorce was well deserved, as I let my job become my top priority. I let the demands of my job take control of my life. In all fairness, I let the job become more important than my personal life, which was wrong. The problem with our work is that sometimes we cannot share enough and we hold things in. Not because we choose to, other than protecting the ones we love. There are things we experience that are just too distasteful to share. The things we sometimes see, we don't even want our wives to be aware of. The instinct to shield my wife from the evil that I witness on the streets became the communication barrier that caused us to slowly drift apart. My problem is that I would not do it any other way. I could never vent all that I am aware of on anyone. So I guess I'm a bachelor until I retire."

"Do you think Wayne holds things in?"

Evans looked at Higdon, as if asking to be rescued. "I won't go there," he said politely.

Abby looked at her husband. "Do you?"

Most innocently, he asked as if ignorant of the question. "What?"

"Wayne Higdon! Do you hold things inside that you don't share with me?"

Wayne gave Mike the evil eye. "Shit! Now look at what you did! Yes, there are some gruesome things that I don't share with you. I just feel that you might sleep better not knowing of them."

It was now Abby flashing the evil eye at Wayne. "I always want you to share anything that is bothering you."

"Sweetheart, Abby, there is a part of this world that you are much better off not knowing about. Believe me!"

* * * *

Christian and Katherine stayed the day with Aaron in his cave. They awoke when evening set and the sun was low in the sky.

"These are nice quarters," Christian stated.

"It was our primary home for nearly fifty years. We have other shelters throughout this territory, but this was our favorite. This vast area is abundant with caves and shelters. Tell me about from where you come," Aaron asked.

"For a hundred years, I lived mostly in wilderness. I, or we, shunned the population and modern society. Yes, we would, occasionally, travel to the fringe of the city and feed off of those that were mostly undesirables, but we would feed off of large mammals as well. There were also many Native American tribes that choose living in the wilderness, and many more hermit-types than is commonly known, so feeding and existing while being transparent to society was never a problem. Only when my Anne was killed did I boldly walk amongst this modern population, which, at times, still confuses me."

"Did you know your maker?"

"No. He struck and I assume, left me for dead," Christian answered, with a bit of sadness in his voice. "Thus, I had no mentor."

"As with I," Aaron replied. "I was also left for dead. Rebecca was my love in life, so I took her as my mate. We have always existed in this territory. It is filled with humans living in isolation, such as religious cult groups that shun society, and those that are involved with the drug culture; plus, we have those stragglers just wandering the woods and mountains. Food is never a problem. The only real problem we have experienced is that Howler. If it were not for him leaving human remains scattered about, our existence would be unknown. I should have stopped her from attacking him. It was a huge mistake. Do you know of the man that killed my Rebecca?"

"I believe I may know of him. If he was the one accompanying the Professor, we have definitely met. He is with the police and vowed to kill me. I thought I had left him in my past. How they knew we traveled here is a mystery to me. It seems beyond coincidence. I can only guess that they assumed this territory would be appealing to our kind."

"Are there many of our kind? I do know that there are some of us located south, in Louisiana."

"I have little knowledge, for I have led an isolated existence, but I do know that more of our kind exist. I encountered some in Minneapolis. Generally, I felt threatened. I assumed it was a natural instinct."

Katherine remained quiet and just observed as Christian, who appeared almost formal, traded knowledge with Aaron, who looked like a retro modern hippie.

"Will you search for Rebecca's killer?"

"Yes. I will not choose another mate until that is done," Aaron vowed.

"I don't believe he will be here much longer. I believe he will return to Minneapolis. I assume he was accompanying the Professor, and now that he is dead, this man will likely return to his home," Christian assumed.

"If he does, I will follow him there. I want him dead. I must locate where he is staying. Should I fail to kill him here, would you guide me to Minneapolis?" Aaron growled.

"I will. However, this man is educated to our ways and weaknesses. You should be aware that he wears protection, and is equipped with effective weapons. Upon entering the city of Minneapolis, I was astounded. There was no hunting necessary. Besides undesirables, there are many human predators that will view you as their prey. You will never want for food. I boldly walked the streets and no one took the slightest notice of me. There seems to be so many odd types that our appearance raises no concern. Aside from feeding, I actually had to kill in defense of myself. I actually had humans attack *me*! This modern society is in shambles," Christian explained.

"Here, in this territory, we never have to make a public appearance." Aaron related. "This territory is littered with isolated groups that just accept a death or a disappearance as being normal. Most never seem to alert the authorities. There are religious groups, where if a member goes missing, they assume he fled back to the general population. Finding food that is removed from the population is never a problem. There are many types that use the forest to mask their illegal activities, so with them, there is no risk. In this vast wilderness, disposing of the body is never a problem, as there are caves, sink holes, and places where men rarely travel."

"I hate to interrupt, but can we walk amongst the humans and attend a theater again?" Katherine inquired.

"First, we must eat. Where would you suggest?" Christian asked.

"South of here is a compound. These people have removed themselves from society, much like the communes of the sixties. They always have guards posted alone in the wilderness. Should you take one, they will never communicate to authorities. Rebecca and I always rotated our kills, never becoming obvious in any one place. I, myself, will visit the Amish community west of here to feed. The Amish shun society, and have a very closed and isolated community. Then, I will attempt to locate the one that killed my Rebecca."

Katherine and Christian left, and Aaron flew south. Looking down, they could see the warm blooded beings on the ground below them. It was over the Arkansas border that they spotted a group of buildings deep in the woods, miles from the closest town. As they surveyed the area, they could clearly see the guards posted away from the compound. The small fortress belonged to a right wing survivalist group, and the guards were on alert for government agencies that they imagined were spying on them. A little known fact is that the greatest percent of these types of organizations are located in southwest Missouri and northwest Arkansas. For vampires, these right wing types, cults, survivalists, or religious fanatics that have withdrawn from society, make for an easy meal, as they avoid the government and press.

Christian motioned for Katherine to set down. They landed near the guard who was leaning up against a tree, and far from being on the alert. Katherine intentionally rustled some leaves, which got the man's attention. The guard felt it was likely some form of wildlife moving about. He was startled when Katherine walked out from the cover of bushes.

"Lady, are you lost?"

"No, I have found what I am looking for," Katherine answered with a smile.

"Are you looking to join up with us?"

"No, I'm in search of something to eat."

"I can take you to the main building—that is, if you are not with any government agency. You're not . . . are you?"

"No, I am not."

It was at that moment that the guard finally wondered, with her being so far from the highway and town, how the hell did she get out there? So he asked, "Lady, how did you get here? What are you doing alone out in these woods at night?"

Katherine's voice changed to more of a growl. "I told you . . . I am in search of dinner!"

As the poor man watched, her face began to morph into that of a vampire, and her fangs gleamed in the moonlight. "Oh, shit!" he screamed, and turned to run. When he turned, standing directly behind him was Christian, who had already morphed. He grabbed him by the shoulders, biting into his neck. His screams went unheard. They feasted on his blood, draining his body of almost every drop. When they were finished, Christian intentionally left the rifle and two-way radio on the ground to be found, so it might appear as though the man had deserted his post. He picked up the body and they took to the air, back toward Branson. In flight, he merely dropped it into the wilderness, far from the lights and population, likely never to be found by the time the area's predators would finish with it.

"Now, you wish to go to the theater?"

Katherine smiled. "Yes, that would please me.

"Is it possible to board the riverboat?"

Katherine thought on this for a moment, before answering. "I'm sure there would be no problem."

"Oh, I would so love to ride a riverboat once again." Christian stated, remembering days gone by.

"Then, that is what we will do!"

* * * *

Aaron flew west, headed for an Amish community. The Amish maintain a very closed society. Most all infractions are settled within their community and judged by their laws. Aaron knew that when a youth goes missing, the disappearance is usually attributed to youthful rebellion, and assumed he went running away to the city. Rarely do the Amish use outside authorities. So, Aaron was looking for a teenager, possibly wandering away from the community and maybe doing something un-Amish-like. He spotted his potential victim behind a barn alone, drinking beer and smoking. Both these things were against the Amish laws, so he had found his rebel, even though he was dressed in handmade Amish attire with a rope for a belt. Aaron landed and walked slowly toward him, as to not cause alarm.

"Hello friend," the young man called out.

"Hello to you," Aaron answered back.

The young man could see by Aaron's attire that he was not Amish. "What brings you this way?" he asked.

Aaron answered boldly. "I hunger."

The young man smiled. "Well, you are in the right town, because you can knock on almost any door and they will be happy to feed you. It is God's way."

Aaron could not resist admonishing the youth. "Is smoking and drinking alcohol God's way also?"

The youth became embarrassed. "No. But I wish to sample those things of which I am prohibited from."

Maybe it was the fact that Aaron had run off as a young man and joined a commune, but he was compelled to ask. "Are you thinking of leaving this community?"

The youth hung his head down, facing the ground. "Yes, it has crossed my mind."

Aaron smiled, as his features began to change slowly. "It was a mistake separating yourself from your community."

The youth stood there frozen, as Aaron came closer. The young man could see the nightmarish features. He screamed, "You are a devil!"

Swiftly, Aaron grasped his throat. "No, I'm just your common vampire." He tore into the flesh of his neck, holding one hand over the boy's mouth. He drank until he could feel no heartbeat. He left the cigarettes and beer to be found, and took off, carrying the body. As was his habit, deep in woods, he dropped the body. When he returned to the Branson area, he began to envy Christian and Katherine, with their tanned appearance which allowed them to walk amongst the humans. '*I must do this,*' he decided. He began searching for a tanning parlor that advertised with the word "spray," as Christian had told him. Unfortunately, the first one he encountered was in east Branson, and was the exact same one that Christian and Katherine had visited. It was also one that Wayne had called, warning of any pale, unusual customers. To Aaron, it looked perfect, as it was away from the main road and with an empty parking lot, so he set down. Aaron also had one other problem, and that was he never considered needing money.

He set down in the gravel parking lot, and looked in the window. Other than a person sitting at the register, no one was there. So he walked in. Aaron recognized immediately that the attendant was smoking a joint, and was pretty high. "Can I help you, man?" At first glance, the attendant saw nothing unusual.

"Yes, I would like to be painted tan."

"Painted tan? That's funny dude. No problem. Just get naked and get into the booth back there." He pointed to the curtain leading to the dressing area, but Aaron took him literally, and began stripping down in the middle of the store. The attendant watched in shock. It was then that the attendant noticed the colorless body. *'This guy looks like a zombie out of Night of the Living Dead?'*

Aaron walked behind the curtain. "Just get in the booth and make one turn with your arms in the air, and one turn with your arms at your side. Move very slow." With that being said, the attendant pushed the spray button. He walked out and picked up Aaron's clothes, which only consisted of a shirt, jeans, and shoes. As he did, he noticed that Aaron had no wallet, nor did he have any money. *'This damned albino was going to stiff me and not pay. Well I'll fix his ass.'* The attendant scooped up Aaron's clothes, along with his own cell phone, and began running out the door while calling 911. Meanwhile, with the spray still running, Aaron was finished doing his two rotations, yet the spray continued. So he yelled, "Hello? Hello?" More than covered in a double coating of skin dye, he stepped from the booth completely soaked. All that was to be seen of use, was a towel. He only wiped the excess from his arms before he dropped the towel to look into the store. In doing so, he didn't realize that only his arms would become an acceptable shade of tan, and the remainder of his body would become bright orange due to the excess skin dye!

The attendant met the police car in the parking lot. "What's the problem?" the officer asked.

"There's this really white looking dude in there. I think he was going to rob me. He wanted to get really tanned."

"Isn't that why people come here? Why did you think he was going to rob you?" The officer asked, recognizing immediately that the attendant was more than a little cooked.

"No man. Like this guy is like, really white. You know? Like, see through white!"

Looking at the attendant, both the officer and his partner were slightly amused, and knew this guy was very high. "What do you have there?"

"I've got his clothes. This guy has no wallet or money. He was going to skip out, or even rob me, for all I know."

The two officers traded skeptical glances and proceeded toward the front door. Meanwhile, Aaron realized that both the attendant and his clothes were nowhere in sight. Seeing the police car outside, he rushed out the door, stark naked. For a brief instant they all looked at each other in complete disbelief, and then both officers drew their tasers. "Stop! Stop or we will tase you!" one ordered. Moving in a near blur, Aaron took to the sky, as all three men were speechless.

The attendant stood in awe. "Wow man, did you see that? It was just like Superman!"

One officer looked toward the other. "I have only been on the force here for a year, so there is no way am I writing this up."

The other was also in shock. "Well, I'm not either. You think I'm reporting a naked guy flying off like Peter frick'in Pan? They'll be drug testing us and sending us in for a mental evaluation. I didn't see a damned thing. Neither did you." He turned toward the attendant. "And neither did you, loco weed! This never happened. You speak one word of this and I'll be busting you every time you turn around. Throw those clothes away and get back in there and get to work. We'll be keeping an eye on the place."

The other officer asked, "What are we going to report on the response to this 911 call?"

"Simple. False alarm."

The one officer scratched his head. "What the heck did we just witness?"

"I don't have a clue, but I'm not going to talk about it. I just hope I never see anything like that again. We'll park out here for a while."

Aaron was in the sky and naked. So he went to where he had dropped the youth's body and removed the Amish clothes and put them on. Even in the dark he could see his skin had become darker than he imagined. What he could not see was that it was much darker than he had intended.

* * * *

The riverboat dock is surrounded by a park-like setting, adjacent to the wilderness preserve. Katherine and Christian landed in the nearby preserve and walked the park-like setting to the ticket booth. Walking hand and hand, they appeared as any other couple engaging in this romantic evening cruise. Christian was still a bit paranoid, but was aware that no one took notice of them, other than to smile. Katherine took money from Christian and proceeded to the ticket booth, purchasing their tickets. As with the last time, she asked for tickets far and away from the main floor and audience. The tickets she received were on the third level, with a table along the rail, facing the stage. As they walked onto the dock, Christian marveled at the incredible recreation of a boat that he was so familiar with, over a hundred years ago.

As a first mate took their tickets and welcomed them aboard, another mate guided them to the stairwell and to the third level. When they arrived at their level, for a moment, they both felt panic, because photographs were being taken of the attendees for later purchase. When they were approached for the photo, as Christian's instinct had him looking for the closest escape route, he listened as Katherine simply stated, "We wish that no pictures be taken." That said, they were ushered to their table. Christian marveled, as he looked down onto the stage as the band played jazz background music. Katherine glowed, as there they were, at a candle lit table for two, overlooking the stage in this magnificent vessel.

"This is wonderful," Christian stated softly, as his eyes scanned the crowd below. "What type of music is this called?"

"It is called jazz, my dear."

"What will we do when they serve the food? Will they not think us odd for not eating?"

Katherine smiled. "No. Many people forgo eating and just enjoy the music, the cruise, and show. Just mix the food around a bit on your plate."

To Christian, this was all too good to be true. There they were interacting with the warm blooded population and enjoying an evening on a riverboat, about to see a live show. This is something he had not done in a hundred years and only could imagine doing such just days ago. He missed his Anne, but as he looked at Katherine, he was happy that she was introducing him to a whole new wonderful dimension of his world. He never knew he could have such freedom. The only thing he could not seem to understand is why everyone was so casually dressed. In his day, attending such an event was only done in formal attire. Christian relaxed, and leaned on the railing, gazing down at the stage.

On the first floor, Mike Evans was scanning the dining areas and looking up at the balcony level as he made pleasant conversation with Wayne and Abby. Staring up at the third level, he could not believe his eyes. It appeared as though the man whose head was at the railing looking down, was Christian the vampire. His face drained of color as he maneuvered his chair, trying to see if the woman accompanying this man resembled Katherine. All he could think was, *'Could this possibly be?'* If it was Christian, he was sporting a tan and actually looked healthy. It was not the pale, sunken eyed creature that he had faced in Minneapolis. *'This is impossible! This guy can't be him. He is tan and is smiling? No frick'in way is that a damned vampire.'*

Abby saw the expression on Mike's face. "Is something wrong?"

"Not really. I just think that someone I might know is sitting up on the balcony."

Now Abby and Wayne also began staring up in Christian's direction. At that exact moment, Christian looked their way, took notice of three people staring at him, and had vague recollection of Mike Evans. He began to remember their final confrontation on the roof, standing over Ted Scott's dead body.

"Mike, whoever it is seems to upset you. You sure don't look happy to see him," Abby commented. "Is this a problem?"

Mike was unsure of what to do next. *'How can I get a closer look?'* he wondered. He decided to make up a story for Abby's benefit. "He is a guy . . . I . . . I arrested some time ago. I am just surprised he is on the street already." Mike knew if he said the word 'vampire' she would think him completely crazy.

At the same time, Christian turned to Katherine. "We may have a problem." He looked around and saw the exit door to the outer deck directly behind them. "We may have to leave."

Katherine was confused. "Why? What is it, Christian?"

"There is a man on the main level. He vowed to kill me in Minneapolis for taking the life of his friend. I believe he may be coming for me."

Katherine looked about. "He could not have a weapon, as they would not allow it on this boat. These chairs we sit on are metal. I don't think he could arm himself and present a threat. Let's wait and see if he approaches. Somehow I don't believe he will cause any action to create panic or alarm aboard this ship." Katherine also eyed the exit door. "Should he intend to do us harm, we will leave quickly. Let's just see what he does."

Mike rose from his chair. "I think I need to use the men's room."

Wayne looked concerned. "Mike, I'll go with you."

As they walked, Higdon asked, "Mike, what's wrong?"

"I think my vampire is sitting up on that balcony."

Wayne was skeptical. "Come on, a vampire on a show boat? That doesn't make sense."

"Well, I know who I saw. Either it's a lookalike, or I swear it is him. If I can see the woman he is with, I will know for sure, as I know what she looks like."

"If it is him, what the hell are you going to do?"

"I don't really know. I have no weapon, or I'd try and kill him. Believe me, the first thing I looked at was a chair leg, but the chairs here are all metal and other than that flag staff on the stage, I don't see any wood anywhere that I can use as a stake. At the very least, I will confront him and let him know I intend to keep my promise."

"What if he decides to kill you?" Higdon asked.

Mike pulled the gold crucifix he was wearing under his shirt into full view. "I have this. Only when my friend Ted took this off, did he get torn to pieces. He can't touch me."

"So you're going up there?"

"Yeah, I am."

"If it is him, what do you think will happen?"

"I . . . I'm not sure?"

"Well, I'm going to cover you," Higdon stated firmly.

"With what? Even if you had your service weapon, believe me, it would be worthless."

Mike took a deep breath and began walking the winding staircase to the third level, with Higdon following close behind. Christian already knew they might be on the way, since he had observed them as they left their table and did not return. So he watched intensely at the entrance to his dining level. When Evans and Higdon reached the third level, Evans gave Higdon a look that clearly projected the fact that he was opening a can of worms. He opened the door slowly and stepped into the balcony dining area. There along the rail he could clearly see Christian, and from the back, it appeared Katherine was with him. As he stepped forward with Higdon behind, Christian arose and stood at the table. "What wrong?" Katherine asked.

"This is a matter I will try to handle in a civilized manner. Should it become a problem, prepare to leave quickly."

Mike was not exactly sure of what to do next. More important, was that he could not predict how Christian might react. He stood staring, with his fists clenched at his side, as beads of perspiration ran down his face. It was almost surreal. There before his very eyes was the vampire that had killed his close friend, standing relaxed in full public view. Christian was just as confused. He could see that Mike had no weapons with which to attack, and Higdon also stood empty handed. It seemed like they stared at each other for minutes, before Mike decided to slowly approach the table.

"Wait here," he told Higdon. Mike slowly walked toward Christian.

Christian had no fear, for unarmed he knew he could overpower Evans in a second. He reached for an unoccupied chair and moved it to his table. As Evans got near, he simply uttered, "Please, sit."

As Mike sat down, he looked at Katherine, and could see the difference in her appearance. Her eyes were cold and unfeeling, with no trace of recognition. Not knowing what to say, only sarcasm came to mind. "So? What's a vampire like you doing in a nice place like this?"

Christian smiled. "I see you maintain a sense of humor."

"It's one that I can lose quickly when facing a murderer," Mike replied.

"We would simply like to enjoy our evening."

"I had a very close friend who has no evenings to enjoy because of you." Mike responded, most seriously.

"I was not at fault. He demanded the confrontation. I had no choice. I would not have killed him, given any alternative. It was he that killed my mate, and as you can see, my revenge was satisfied." Christian glanced toward Katherine.

When Mike looked her way, she studied him. "You look vaguely familiar. Have we met before?" she asked.

"No, not formally."

Mike was fighting his instinct to take control as his training dictated, as negotiating was not his strong suit. Having read Professor Steiner's manuscript, he was careful not to make any lengthy eye contact. He knew that if Christian was going to turn violent, it would have happened instantly. So he sat and decided to talk and gather what he could learn. Just studying them both, he could see how a vampire in human form could appear alluring, mesmerizing, and hypnotic. They were not the evil looking image that one might expect; instead, Christian appeared handsome, well bred, and outwardly confident. Katherine looked well groomed, dressed very tastefully, with a glow of a woman in love.

"I see you have discovered the spray tan."

"Yes, Katherine educated me to this modern process."

"The attendant is missing. Did you kill her?" Mike asked directly.

"No, we paid for the service." Christian, true to his vampire instinct, could lie without showing any tell that might be read by Mike. "Your friend, who is watching over us, does he intend to do us harm?" Christian asked calmly and directly.

"No, not at this moment. He has little knowledge of vampires. I am wearing protection, as I am sure you are aware."

"Yes, I am. Please keep it covered. Should I be forced to defend myself, it would cause quite a scene, which I am sure you wish to avoid."

"Now that you know I'm here, will you attempt to kill me?" Mike asked directly.

"I have no desire to kill you, but there is one here that does. You see, when you came upon that werewolf, you killed a female vampire. Her name was Rebecca. She was the mate of a vampire named Aaron. It is he that wishes to take your life. My only interest is to defend myself and Katherine, if need be."

"Do you expect me to be aware of who and what you are, and simply do nothing?"

"Yes! Why not? Only a short time ago, you had no knowledge that we even existed. We have no need to be publically known. In most cases we only take what we need to survive from your undesirable population. Had Ted Scott not murdered my mate, you would be walking around in ignorant bliss," Christian rationalized.

"He was only defending himself. Ted never meant to do anyone harm. In fact, your mate's death was totally accidental. She simply fell onto his crossbow," Mike explained.

"I smell no fear in you."

"You are correct. I do not fear you. I do, however, fear what you are capable of and the fact that all these people surrounding us and enjoying their evening are ignorant of your kind and walking around unprotected. I guess *they* are in ignorant bliss. Is this Aaron the one that killed the Professor?"

"Yes."

"I know what he looks like, and I will look forward to our meeting. I am at the Chateau Hotel—tell him bring it. I, too, have the need for revenge, as he killed the Professor—my good friend.

"Are you fearless or just stupid?"

"I am protected," Mike stated smugly.

In a flash so fast that Mike did not see Christian move, he looked down and Christian's hand was touching his chest.

"I recommend that once you leave this table, you keep your protection in plain view. As you have seen, I could have had your heart in my hand, had I desired," Christian stated most seriously. "Aaron may not wish to confront you as you might assume. He is capable of striking without warning. I can only advise you and warn you that he is blinded by revenge."

Mike's face turned a bit pale, and Katherine decided to join the conversation. "Had you not known of us, why would you care if undesirables disappear?"

"Were the three homeless men considered undesirables?" Mike replied.

"You were not there. They were three drunken thieves planning their next crime. It amounts to three people you won't have to arrest. At least in our world, there is no plea bargain," she responded indignantly, having been a lawyer when human. "At least when we deal with these types, they are off the street for good. I find it absurd that you are concerned with us, as you have a society filled with warm blooded monsters."

Christian felt that their eventual confrontation might possibly be avoided. "Why not allow us to exist in secrecy. We wish you no harm. Do have any idea how many illegal drug operations lie deep in these woods, or how many lawless groups planning violence exist in this wilderness? These are people you would never miss. There is no reason to believe we will ever become known. It is only what they call the Howler, a werewolf that leaves carcasses scattered about. He is the mindless threat to be eliminated."

Mike smiled. "We just might be looking into that."

"I was told he was very old, generations old."

Mike was not about to give Christian any information. "We know little of this being. As far as I know it is all Ozark folklore."

Christian smiled knowingly. "So it was not you that we saw chasing that beast after he tore one of your friends apart, when you killed Rebecca? You did admit to killing Rebecca, didn't you?"

"I did."

"You know, we could really help each other concerning that beast."

From a distance, Higdon watched, as it appeared Mike was conversing as he might with normal people. When he saw Christian's hand on Mike's chest, he prepared to move in, but noticed Mike did not even flinch, and did not seem threatened. He found it frightening that this normal looking couple could be vampires. He found himself looking about, studying other couples, wondering if more vampires were present. Over the railing, he could see Abby looking in their direction, as dinner began to be served. He couldn't help himself, and wanted a closer look. Slowly showing open hands, he walked to the table. "Excuse me. Mike, dinner is being served."

Mike stood to leave, but decided to introduce Wayne to the vampires. "This is Christian and his . . . his mate, Katherine. Hopefully, we will not meet again, but if we do, we may have to kill them."

Christian smiled. "Wayne, may you and Abby both enjoy your evening. Tell Abigail, who is waiting at the table below, that she is stunning."

Both Mike and Wayne looked surprised. Mike stuttered. "I . . . I never mentioned her name?"

Christian smiled, as if amused. "We vampires have excellent hearing and also find it easy to read lips."

His words brought a chill to Wayne, as he realized that Abby could possibly become a target in this cycle of revenge. "She has no part in this," Wayne replied.

Christian pointed to Katherine. "Neither did Katherine . . . at one time. But true revenge is absent of rules or boundaries. I hope this game might end now."

Mike and Wayne walked away slowly, not looking back. They did not share a word until they reached the first level, and before entering the main dining room, Wayne turned to Mike. "We'll talk later."

When they reached the table, Abby was curious. "How did it go? Is everything okay?"

Wayne explained that they simply had a discussion and everything went well. As he soothed Abby's worries, he noticed that around her neck was a heart necklace he had given her. He knew at that moment that a blessed cross will be her next gift, as well as one for his daughter, as soon as possible. As Wayne looked up at the balcony, Christian glanced his way and flashed a smile, giving a slight wave of his hand, which sent a spike of fear down Wayne's spine. Wayne knew that with his human appearance, Christian could easily make inquiries and locate his family. As they sat eating dinner,

Wayne believed they only had two choices. One was to let the vampires exist and hope they stay invisible to the city, or two, find them when they are vulnerable and kill them, or die trying. He found himself not eating, and just pushing the food around on his plate. He looked over at Mike, who was doing the exact same thing.

At the after dinner break, Mike and Wayne went out walking the deck, while Abby stood in line for the powder room. Mike was in a somber mood.

"I really dragged you into a mess. I am so sorry."

"Look, we were picking up body parts before you arrived here. The way I see it, besides Jerry, I likely also would have been killed through pure ignorance. So take the weight off your shoulders. I guess we have a decision to make as to whether we let him go his way, or whether we hunt him down and kill him."

"What actually worries me more is that other vampire. If he didn't see me actually shoot his mate, he may be looking for both of us. He is the one we need to find and deal with first, before he finds us. If you can do this without causing Abby alarm, I would get a number of crosses for your house, have them blessed, and put in plain view. Also, you will have to explain to never invite any stranger into the house after the sun sets. I hope you can do this without Abby thinking you're nuts. This was the road that took me into a divorce. My wife thought I was losing my mind."

"Well at least I can leave werewolves out of the conversation. Tomorrow we can put Jerry to rest knowing he didn't die for nothing. All I know is that you better give me some lessons using those crossbow pistols, for if it's my vote, tomorrow night we go hunting."

"If you're sure you want to do this, I can stay as long as I have to, as I have weeks of vacation stored up," Mike replied.

"Well, if that's the plan, let's go back and enjoy the show. I may need you to back me up when and if I decide to open up to Abby about all this."

* * * *

Having clothes, Aaron decided to try his new appearance. He thought a safe place to start might be the downtown boardwalk. He figured it was the perfect place. It was near the wilderness, providing easy escape, should that become necessary. He landed near the bridge that crosses into Hollister, and walked along the lake until he reached the boardwalk. Once on the boardwalk, he walked along as if he was just another tourist. Having not walked amongst the public in decades, he was self-conscious and a bit paranoid, so he was very aware when the first person he encountered did a double take when he passed. He did not go much further when a couple spotted him, and the woman pointed in his direction. This caused him to become nervous. He could see crowds of people ahead shopping, and he could hear a live band playing on the outside stage. He began to look forward to hearing a live band, but the next couple not only pointed, it appeared they looked away laughing. Aaron was perplexed, but it seemed instead of being able to mix with the humans unnoticed, everyone he encountered looked in his direction. He decided to turn around and return to the wilderness. What he did not know, was that aside from the odd Amish clothes, the spray tan had been over applied, and his skin was not tan—it was bright orange. Since he had only wiped his arms with the towel, so only his arms appeared a normal color and that was all he could see. So he was totally confused.

He returned to the island and stood on the bank as the riverboat docked. As he watched, he replayed Rebecca's death in his mind. He remembered his attack on the werewolf, and getting a glimpse of two faces, one of which was armed with a crossbow. It was this man that he needed to kill. As he stood on the bank watching the warm blooded people crossing over the dock onto dry land, he observed an unusual sight. He spotted a couple walking along with humans that were not warm blooded. He instantly knew Christian and Katherine had ridden the boat. It was then that he suddenly realized that Christian and Katherine had witnessed the event, and could possibly identify the man he needed to find. He hoped Christian would point him to the man he wanted to tear to pieces. For now, he would return to his cave and mourn.

Katherine and Christian returned to the cave to take their rest. They found Aaron sitting in a corner in sad silence.

"Did you enjoy your evening?" he asked, as if he could care less.

"Yes we did. There was a tense moment when in the midst of the cruise, we were confronted by Rebecca's killers. At first, I thought a public display of violence was eminent, but instead we just talked."

Aaron jumped to his feet. "Who are they? Where are they? I will tear them to sheds!"

"There is only one. He stays at the Chateau. He is prepared, so be aware that he will have protection and weapons, should you confront him. He also wants revenge, as you killed his friend."

"Who was his friend?"

"It was the old man that we viewed, that was killed on the island."

"Are you saying, it was the man that escaped us that killed my Rebecca?"

"Yes, that very man."

"I know what he looks like. I will find him."

"I believe you may not have to look so very hard, as he will also be looking for you. I believe the old man was his mentor."

"I did what you recommended, and it seems that it does not work. I had my skin dyed tan, but when I attempted to walk amongst the public, every person I encountered took notice of me. I felt they could sense that I was not one of them."

In the lightless cave, Christian, with only night vision, could not see Aaron's overly tan but orange appearance. "I do not understand. Maybe it was just you being paranoid."

"No, they were staring and even pointing. Some even seemed to laugh and find humor."

"When the sun rises and this becomes dimly lit, I will tell you of your new appearance."

"On the next night, I am going to find this man and tear his heart out!"

Christian could only think of his promise to Mike Evans—that they would remain invisible. He wondered if he should stop Aaron from possibly entering a hotel and causing a public display? He enjoyed being regarded as a myth, and certainly did not want anything to happen that might cause the authorities to start vampire hunting, but he knew Aaron was out of control!

Chapter Seven

Danny awoke and felt completely rested. Since he had slept for almost a complete day, he had missed work. He looked at the clock, and it was 11 A.M. It didn't faze him that he had been asleep for eighteen hours. He literally awoke without a care. He picked up his cell phone and saw he had a dozen messages. He began playing them.

"Danny, let me know how you are."

"Danny, the memorial service for Jerry will be tomorrow morning at ten. Call me."

"Danny, we heard what happened; let us know when you can come back to work."

"Danny, are you okay?"

"Danny, call me!"

. . . and on and on. One by one, he deleted them. The Danny that was caring and dependable was gone. He tore off all the bandages, and realized that every cut and bruise was healed. He took a shower and dressed, and for some reason, the bright colors and youthful attire did not look appealing. Instead, he felt comfortable wearing black. He felt different. As he looked at himself in the mirror, there was a dark entity staring back. For no reason he could define, he just wanted to be outside and walk, or even jog or run—but he needed the open air. He left his apartment located in the old downtown area without his car keys, and left the door unlocked without a care. He felt strange, as his sense of smell was heightened to the extent that he could smell the neighbor's cat; except, he never knew that his neighbor ever had a cat. He sniffed and suddenly realized that he could 'read' the air. Each distinct odor seemed separated and identifiable. As he walked outside, he also became aware that his peripheral vision had expanded and not only could he see a wider range of objects, his vision was distinct and specific far to his right and left, even if he was facing forward.

Danny casually walked to the boardwalk and as he did, he watched as the funeral procession for Jerry Cunningham slowly moved down Main Street. Although Jerry was his close friend, Danny no longer felt the least bit of connection. He looked down at his hands that appeared slightly larger and stronger. He began to jog, except the pace he moved at, though he felt it slow and relaxed, was equal to a normal person running. He wanted to jump, and saw a four foot fence at the end of the boardwalk blocking a construction site. At a pace that was even and steady, he jumped the fence without breaking stride. He could see the woods ahead and was drawn to continue running. As he ran through the woods, he realized he was aware of everything that should be invisible to a normal man. As he traveled, he looked around like he was seeing the world for the very first time. He spotted a tiny bat buried in a tree trunk. He could identify a snake slithering in the dry leaves. The splash of a fish seemed loud. He could hear hummingbirds and even a dragonfly, as he ran by. He disturbed a fox, which took off running. Danny ran after him, keeping up, and knew he could even catch him, had he wanted. He stopped and knew he had covered miles in distance, yet felt no fatigue. Strangely, he never questioned his metamorphosis and accepted it as if was a 'gift.' It was pure instinct to learn about his new 'self.' As he walked through the woods returning toward his apartment, he realized he no longer plodded through the brush like man; instead, he moved with cat-like skill, not disturbing the foliage.

Reaching the boardwalk, he paused and realized he could hear people talking half a block away. As he walked, a woman with a Yorkshire terrier passed, and the little dog backed away and growled. "Gosh? He never does that?" the woman exclaimed. Danny just smiled. As he saw his reflection in the store windows, he seemed to look leaner. He liked the muscle definition of his arms, and began flexing as he walked. He knew he was stronger than he had ever been. As he passed a trendy restaurant, he realized he was starving. He took no notice that he ordered a rare hamburger and downed it in two bites. What Danny didn't know, was that his taste for meat would grow and his preference for raw meat would begin to dominate his mind. He would soon say goodbye to the old Danny and say hello to the new . . . Howler.

* * * *

The funeral being over, Higdon and Evans went to Elmer's to have a drink and contemplate their dilemma. Evans only had one train of thought when it came to the vampires, and that was to kill them all. Higdon had mixed feelings. He argued that in their professional life, they spent their days hunting down predators of various sorts, only to have the liberal justice system put these same criminals back on the street. He felt sick that pedophiles, murders, and drug dealers could make use of the "plea bargaining" that prosecutors were only too anxious to negotiate. The statement that Katherine had made kept replaying in his mind. *"At least when we finish with them they are no longer on the street."* Higdon argued that if this was true, and Christian and Katherine stayed invisible to the public, only removing *"undesirables,"* they may be more a blessing than a curse.

"You know a lot more about this than I do, but when that vampire was in Minneapolis, who did he kill?"

Evans had to think a bit. "Well, mostly types that were gang related or criminal types. He did kill a rookie cop, but likely only because he was confronted, as the rookie made the mistake of drawing a gun on him. Actually, when I think about it, he easily could have killed me and instead, let me go."

"See? I mean, what the hell? If he stays in this territory and only wastes drug growers, dealers and criminal types, who really cares?

"The problem is that vampires lie. They may tell you anything they think you want to hear."

"Well, the fact that he didn't kill you is a fact. Actually, the fact that he didn't kill us both the other night is also a fact."

"So you are saying just leave him alone and ignore him?"

"I think we should try to meet with him again and make the ground rules clear. If he keeps away from children, tourists and citizens, we stay out of caves and leave him and Katherine alone."

"How do we find him?" Evans asked.

"I think if we were to go out alone in the wilderness, he will find us."

"I still have a vampire to deal with. If he is seeking revenge, I should get that over with. I will go back to that island with my crossbow pistols and wait. I'm not going to have him following me back to Minnesota."

"Mike, there is no way I will let you face him alone. If you are going out there, let me back you up. I can wear that thermal suit and he won't even know I'm there. I can at least get a shot off."

"Hey, I appreciate it, but if that's the case, you better start practicing with that thing. First, your range is short, maybe five yards. However, at five yards with a vampire, puts you in the danger zone. Besides practicing, the best advice I can give you is to keep an arrow in your hand, because if you miss, the vampire will be right on you. There will be no chance to reload, so the arrow in your hand becomes your only defense in hand to hand combat. Having an arrow in my hand saved my life, even though the vampire almost amputated my left arm. There are no second chances at close range. You may want to carry two loaded crossbows. You have to be able to hit a four inch circle, dead center. Until you can do that, don't think about it. Just sticking them with arrows only pisses them off."

"Five yards don't sound like all that much," Higdon replied. "That should be easy."

Evans smiled knowingly. "The distance is really not the factor. It is coming face to face with a monster that wants to tear you apart and then hitting a four inch target, is slightly different. Seriously, assuming we can get rid of this vengeful vampire, could you really live here knowing that the other two are out there somewhere?"

Higdon thought for a moment. "Let me ask you . . . do you really think they are the only two out there in the first place? They just uncovered over twenty bodies on a New York beach in shallow graves. They discovered the remains of over forty people in New Mexico. I would bet that the method of death, regardless of what is determined, involves massive blood loss. Do you honestly think we can kill them all? Do you think that if we kill Christian and Katherine, that some other not-so-agreeable vampires will not move in? It's like the devil I know, opposed to waiting to see what the next devil might be like . . . and you know there will be another one coming! God, I wish I never was exposed to this shit. I was ignorant and happy."

"So you're saying, yes, you can look the other way and live with that."

"I'll put it like this. In Branson, we have over 35 registered sex offenders. As a person sworn to protect the public, I have to sit and wait until they commit some heinous act before I can do a thing. Now, we all know the pedophiles will, because they are incurable. If I could make a deal to make them 'go away' before they re-offend and hurt some child, would I? Would I look the other way? You bet. I could easily live with it. If this vampire sucks the blood out of some meth cookers, I see it as a double bonus. First, the bad guys are made to go away for good. Second, imagine all the meth that is taken from distribution, even for a short time. If we could get his word, I would try my best to forget I ever have seen a vampire."

"Well, if I go out on that island and sit waiting, maybe they'll all show up. Who knows?"

"Okay, what's our next move?" Higdon asked.

"You should get some practice in, if you're really going to back me up. Me? I'm going to take a nap. After all, it's going to be a long night. Remember, five yards and try to hit something the size of a grapefruit. If you can do that a dozen times in a row, then close your eyes, because you may flinch when you actually see what comes at you. In Minneapolis, I flinched and missed, and was shaking too much to reload. Fortunately, I used the arrow to stab it in the heart. You don't ever want to get that close."

Higdon watched as the owner came their way and took the opportunity to ask, "Have you heard from Danny?"

Old Elmer just scratched his head. "No, in fact we're a bit worried. Everyone has been calling his cell, but all they get is his voice mail."

"Well, he had a rough fall. He was lucky he didn't get cut up worse than he did. He's likely taking the medication the doctor gave him and is sleeping through it. If you don't hear from him soon, I'll go check on him. Does he have family near here?"

"No, as far as I know. I believe his parents retired to Florida somewhere," Elmer replied as he retreated to the kitchen.

Mike left for the hotel, leaving Wayne alone in the booth thinking about his situation. He had to call his wife Abby and explain once more why he would not be home at a decent hour. He figured if he could just make up a story that would hold for a few days, all this might be over. He knew it had to be, because there was no way he would allow any of this to affect his family. He dialed his wife.

"Abby, I don't know when I'll be home . . . no, no, this is serious. We have a serial killer traveling through here. Mike and I are going on a stake out . . . no, I promise. This will all be over in few days. You know I love you."

Wayne felt a bit guilty, but didn't lie. He was after a serial killer, except not human, and he hoped it would be over in a few days. No way did he want his wife to know creatures like this even exist. Wayne Higdon was not beyond having a vigilante philosophy. When he was with Springfield Police, he knew of and even collaborated with a vigilante group of sorts.

Vigilantism was almost a tradition in these Ozarks, going back to tales of the Baldnobbers, who were rumored to protect the innocent and right the wrongs of the justice system. Higdon had knowledge of a number of vigilante groups, including one that was made up of ex-police, most of them tired of the revolving door called the judicial system. So? He would allow a vampire to reduce the ranks of outlaws of various types. If Christian would keep his word, and the result was that his family and the everyday citizens of Branson were safe, he could easily live with that. All he had to do was help Mike Evans kill this Aaron vampire, and not let any of this become public knowledge. He left to do his target shooting and to pick up a grapefruit.

* * * *

Danny walked along the boardwalk, analyzing his new strength and agility. For the first time in his life, he felt strong. As he walked, he moved his arms about and appeared he was doing some martial arts exercises or isometrics to those around him. He started to realize his arms not only had a new strength, they also had lightning speed. For years, he felt this loyalty to Branson, as he was born and raised there, which left him helping the police as an informant. Now, he felt a new loyalty and sense of personal domain. As he walked, a few people recognized him and waved or said hello, but went completely ignored. As he passed a stylish pub popular with locals and tourists, Danny sensed a foul odor. It was a chemical odor that he found offensive. He stopped to discover the source. Near the front door stood a young man standing in one place, yet in constant motion. Danny instantly knew the foul odor was meth, and this was a dealer waiting for potential customers. Danny's new instincts took over. In his new mind, this was a violation of his domain. However, he would not think of informing the police—instead he walked over to the man. They traded glances and Danny did not appear as undercover or 'smelled' like a cop, so they guy nodded him to come over.

"Let's do business," Danny said seriously, but quietly.

"Hey, around the corner," the man replied, looking about in all directions, making sure they were not being watched.

They walked to the side of the building and the man reached into his pocket and stated, "Twenty."

Danny grabbed him by the collar and the man quickly realized that the grip was so forceful, that any resistance would be unwise. "What do you want?" he asked nervously.

"Empty your pockets." Danny said it in a way that meant business.

"Man, you don't want to do this. I mean, this would be a huge mistake!"

"I will not say it again. Do it! Empty your damn pockets!"

The man emptied his pockets on the ground, including vials of crack and meth, and a few balloons containing heroin. Danny stomped on the pile, smashing it into a mess filled with shards of glass, as the man grimaced.

"That was a terrible mistake."

Without any emotion, Danny stated, "Now, give me all your money."

"Man, this cash belongs to Bobby Raye. Believe me, he will not be happy."

"Bobby Raye? Is that supposed to scare me? He sounds like a B-list country singer." Danny laughed. "Give me the damn money!"

Between the roll in his pocket and his wallet, the man turned over nearly three thousand dollars. Danny smiled. "If I see you here, we can skip the whole physical routine. Just walk around the corner, empty the drugs on the ground and hand over the cash. Give this Bobby Raye my regards. Tell him Branson is now off limits."

"Dude, if I were you, I would get out of town, because Bobby Raye is not one to mess with," the dealer warned.

As he released the man, Danny looked him directly in the eyes. "If this Bobby Raye, or his friends, come looking for me . . . for one, I'm easy to find. But more important to you, is that I will know it was you that described me and were responsible for sending them. I may not be happy with you the next time we meet." The man saw something in Danny's eyes that frightened him beyond what might be a normal threat.

Danny walked away smiling as he counted the money. He made an immediate decision to no longer be a police informant and instead, he would rid Branson of any bad elements himself, or make them pay for doing business. Danny decided he would work this night and was looking forward to doing a few specific deliveries!

* * * *

It was the time of the year in the Ozarks when the nights turned just cool enough to settle on the warm moist ground and leave a thick mist in the valleys. As Mike and Wayne pointed their boat toward the island, it became the perfect setting for the horror they had planned to experience. Wayne had the thermal suit so his warm blooded image would not be visible to any vampire overhead. Their plan was simple. Mike would sit in the open, waiting for Aaron to see him and attack. Mike would not make the same mistake his friend, Ted Scott, had done. He would not remove his blessed cross. He hoped he would face Aaron and take him down on the first shot. Should he miss, it was the sign for Wayne to take his shot, and Mike would take his second shot. Should the blessed cross not repel Aaron, Mike had a stake tucked into his belt, in case of hand to hand combat. Wayne also carried a stake, in case he would have to enter the fight. They rode silently until they reached the shore.

"Hopefully, we won't have to worry about this vampire after tonight. We have three shots and two stakes; if that don't do it, I don't know what will."

"I do!" Wayne replied.

"What else could we have gotten?" Mike wondered.

Wayne reached under his thermal suit. Producing a huge child's squirt gun, he grinned.

"What the hell is that?" Mike asked.

"It is called a super shooter. It's a squirt gun."

Mike looked perplexed. " . . . and?"

"It shoots about fifteen feet, and it is filled with holy water!"

"You're kidding me?"

"No. If my timing is right, I will make it a bit easier to take that first shot. I really don't have confidence in my crossbow skills yet. I guess being a novice at this had me thinking outside the box."

"Jesus Christ, you are brilliant. How did I or the Professor never think of that? We just have to make sure we get him. Should he get away, he won't be dumb enough to face off with us again, so after tonight, it will be sneak attacks on his part if he lives through this. We must make absolutely sure he dies tonight."

* * * *

Christian and Katherine awoke from their rest to find Aaron pacing about. They could tell his mourning was over, and that revenge was the only thing on his mind. Christian could sense Aaron was in a reckless state.

"What do you have planned on this night?" Christian asked, already anticipating a violent-type response.

"I am going to his hotel and I'm going to tear his heart out!" Aaron stated in anger. "After I tear his heart out, I will drink from it and throw his body off the roof!"

Christian frowned. "In doing so, our presence will become public knowledge. This is not the wise thing to do."

"I don't care about being wise. I want my revenge. I want to kill that man. Depending on my mood, I just may bring him here and bleed him for a week before I kill him."

Katherine joined the conversation. "That would be a very bad idea also. First, they carry cell phones which also function as tracking devices. It would bring them right to our cave. Then, the hotel has surveillance cameras. Whatever you do, when they review that recording, they will realize your image is not visible. It will certainly be proof that we exist. After that, they will hunt for us," she explained.

"I don't care! I want him dead and I will chase his ass down Main Street if need be. Christian, you certainly should understand how I feel."

"That is exactly what puts me to worry. I understand you have no care as to whether we are exposed, or even if you are destroyed yourself. That is why I will not allow you to do this in that reckless manner."

"Allow me? Allow me? Who do you think you are? You, who have tasted the ultimate revenge, would prevent me from mine? You are in my domain! Although you are older and likely stronger than I, you will have to destroy me to keep me from what I crave." Aaron faced Christian defiantly.

"I would not relish a conflict with my own kind," Christian replied.

"Then stand out of the way and allow me what is due." Aaron turned and walked from the cave, disappearing into the night sky.

Christian looked to Katherine. "I feel conflicted. I understand his need, but I am reluctant to allow him to become a public spectacle. Should that occur, we will have to flee this territory."

"Flee this territory? With the modern media, should vampires become public knowledge, there could be no place to hide. It will be like Bigfoot, where everyone is looking for us . . ." Katherine replied dryly.

"Bigfoot? What is this Bigfoot?" Taking it literally, Christian looked down, examining his feet.

Katherine laughed. "No; it is just a name the media has given a creature that is said to have been seen, of mythical proportions. He is large and leaves large footprints—thus, Bigfoot."

Christian was baffled by the humor. "He leaves big footprints, so they label him Bigfoot? It sounds like something the Indians might do."

"The modern media is much less civilized than Native Americans." Katherine's comment just left Christian confused.

"Let us go and observe his rampage. Aaron is likely traveling to the hotel. If I had my wish, I would provide him the opportunity to satisfy his lust for revenge and have this over with."

Into the dark night sky they flew. Taking the direction toward the hotel, Christian could see a warm blooded being alone on the island. This just seemed far too easy of a meal. Flying closer, he could see it was Mike Evans, and he was armed with crossbow pistols. Christian also knew that somehow they were able to cloak their warm blooded image, so he anticipated more than one man possibly being there. It appeared an obvious trap. He wondered, *'Is it for me?'* He motioned for Katherine to land about fifty yards from where Mike was sitting. As they came closer, he could see that clearly Mike was waiting for a confrontation. Christian decided to approach and initiate conversation from a safe distance.

"Are you waiting for me?" he asked.

"Is that you Christian?"

"Yes. Can we talk?"

"Yes," Mike responded.

"Will you put your weapons down? There is no need, as we will not bring you harm."

Christian watched as Mike set both crossbows on the ground and held his open hands in the air. Christian sensed Mike was not alone. "Will you have your friend come into view and put his weapons away, as we will not harm him."

Mike motioned to Wayne, who reluctantly stepped out from the brush, setting his weapons on the ground in clear view. Once Christian saw this, he moved forward with Katherine close behind. He trusted that there was not a third man still hidden.

"If you are not waiting for me, I assume you wait for Aaron." Christian's eyes examined Higdon, and he could see the jump suit, but could not understand how it blocked his warm blooded image.

"Yes. I want to get this over with. I realize that he will be following me until either he kills me, or I kill him. Seeing as there is no other solution, I am prepared to meet him."

"Aaron came this way. How he did not see you, is a mystery, other than he was intent on going to where you are residing."

"He is headed to the hotel?" Wayne gasped.

"Unfortunately, yes. I believe that was his intention."

"Oh my God!" Higdon uttered in disbelief. "That hotel is a hub of activity. This could be something that Branson can't put on the back page!"

"My friend here wanted to talk with you," Mike pointed to Wayne. "You see, I will leave here soon. Either on a bus, or in a casket, but this is his home. He believes you both can come to an agreement."

Christian turned to Wayne asking, "Is this true?"

Wayne stepped forward. "Yes. You stated last night that you would strictly eliminate undesirables. Is this true?"

"Yes. We can only judge by their location or immediate behaviors, but that will be our intent. We have no need for the public or officials to become aware of our presence."

Wayne was compelled to explain. "I am a policeman. Being most honest, my job is frustrating. Much like Katherine stated, our legal system truly is failing. Not only can criminals plea bargain and obtain light sentences or be released on probation, our jails are over populated and they are releasing criminals back on the street to commit more crimes. I have no problem with the bad guys disappearing."

Christian smiled. "This sounds like we might collaborate."

"Only with your word that no children—good, bad or otherwise—will ever be harmed. This, plus police, tourists, and innocent citizens should also never be harmed." Wayne stated.

Katherine laughed. "It is not like we can do background checks, but we are intelligent in our choices and discreet in disposal. We would never harm a child, and never have need of entering the population to feed."

"Can I have your word?" Wayne asked.

"I will give you my word. We agree. Now I ask, will we not live with the threat of being hunted at times when we are vulnerable? Can we also agree that we will not be hunted?"

Wayne agreed. "No one will ever know of you, much less hunt for you. In fact, anyone that appears hunting for you is fair game. I, myself, will tell no one of your presence. You will remain a myth and subject of folklore, as far as I'm concerned."

Christian smiled. "Then we have an agreement. May I also ask, what manner is this fabric that it cloaks your warm blooded image to us?"

Wayne opened his jump suit, showing the inner fabric. "This is a thermal suit. Actually, it is made to contain heat, in the case that someone is cold. I, too, have a question. Should I ever have the need, how can I contact you or send a message?"

Mike interrupted. "Are you really going to put your trust in this thing?"

Christian looked to Mike, annoyed. "I could have torn your heart out twice, yet I did not, even though I knew you were a definite threat. What more proof do you need?"

Wayne felt the need to explain. "Christian, you are the lesser of many evils. If I could, I would give you the sex offender registry, and you would have enough food to sustain you for years. We have over a thousand on that list alone in the Springfield and Branson area. The drug pushers and manufacturers could also sustain you for a year. If you keep your word, I can easily live with that. Now, how can I contact you?"

Christian looked Wayne directly in the eyes. "It is all about the blood."

Wayne looked confused. "Please, explain?"

"I need to taste your blood. After which, we will always have a mental link. Should you need me, or come under stress, I will know."

"You've got to be kidding? You want to bite me?"

"No, not necessarily. I merely need to taste your blood. If you simply cut your finger and offer me a drop, it will suffice."

Wayne took a pocketknife out of his pants and exposed the blade. While Mike observed in disbelief, Wayne cut his index finger. As the drops flowed he held out his hand and Christian put his palm under the flowing drops. As they watched, Christian tasted it, with an expression as if he had tasted a fine wine. He offered his hand to Katherine, who also tasted Wayne's blood.

Wayne felt no fear. "Will you now be able to read my mind?"

Christian laughed. "No; I will only be able to heed your call and feel your extreme emotion. We now have an unbreakable bond."

All standing in silence, the crack of the police radio was startling. "Detective Higdon? We have a 911 call at the Chateau Hotel. The caller describes violence and chaos. We have cars on the way."

"Oh shit!" Wayne uttered.

Christian calmly stated, "It is Aaron."

* * * *

What Aaron had done was of near comedic proportions. The Chateau Hotel was a complex in itself. Set away from the main entertainment area, it commanded its own peninsula, surrounded by Table Rock Lake. In the night, from a distance, it appeared like a palace, as it stood high above the surrounding water and wilderness. In a city where nearly all buildings were a single story, this twenty story structure stood like a tower, visible for miles. The driveway leading to the valet parking was a half mile long alone. It was magical, as uniformed doormen graciously greeted visitors and opened a door leading to a huge entryway, and a four story atrium. Just this lobby alone covered a space half the size of a football field. Glass elevators whisked the guests up and into their rooms. For most people familiar with such opulence, they might expect the name "Trump" to be stamped on the cornerstone. So it was unusual when the doormen observed an Amish young man walking about, as if confused. They watched as he eventually came in their direction. As he came closer, his overly sprayed orange tan tested their self-control, as it was laughable. Though he appeared a lost soul, the doormen greeted Aaron and opened the door while containing their smiles.

The doormen were used to unusual sights. This was Branson, with a hundred different shows and over a thousand entertainers. In reality, Aaron looked no more strange than one of the entertainers from the cast of "Cirque De Magic," who all wore mime make-up. For all they knew, an Elvis look-a-like might walk up next. So, one doorman asked the other, "What do you think?"

The other smiled, "Well, he could be from an Amish show?"

Aaron had no clue as to his strange appearance. He walked into the atrium and marveled at the sight of the open, foliated atmosphere. He looked about at the many customer service desks, and chose the one with a sign stating 'check-in.' As he walked toward the desk, he noticed a family with various aged children, and a few were pointing toward him. His sensitive hearing could hear the one child say, "Look, mom! He looks like an Umpa-Lumpa!" Then an older one stated "Man, he's more orange than Snookie!" Aaron gave them a serious stare, and proceeded toward the check-in wondering, 'What's an Umpa-Lumpa? What is a Snookie?' He had no idea, but he was beginning to bristle, because it was apparent that they found his appearance humorous. He was indignant, as no one had ever found him humorous—after all, he was a vampire, and in general, he would only put fear into people.

Now, he could see the woman at the check-in counter beginning to grin. Anger began to rise from within. Before she could even ask to help him, Aaron demanded, "I need to know the room number of a man called Mike Evans. He came here with an old man from Minnesota."

The clerk attempted to handle him tactfully. "I'm sorry sir, but for security purposes, we never give out room numbers. I can call his room and see if he is in." The clerk picked up the phone and Aaron watched in a bit of confusion, for no one had ever dismissed his demand in decades.

"I'm sorry sir, he is not in. I can give you his phone number and you can leave him a voice mail."

Aaron had no idea what voice mail was, and he was beginning to get agitated. "I want his room number! Are you deaf, or just a complete idiot?"

As tactful as she could be, she attempted to explain. "Sir, for the security of each guest, we never give out the room number. If you are a friend, just leave a message. If you don't wish to use our voice mail, I'll be happy to write the message down for you."

Severely frustrated, Aaron gave a sarcastic smirk. "Okay, take this down. Ready? Write this exactly as I dictate. I am going to find you and tear your heart out . . ." As he spoke, his voice changed to a more of a growl, and the desk keeper's face began to become pale. "You will suffer beyond your worst nightmare. You will beg for your death." As Aaron looked around, he noticed more people snickering and pointing at him. He had no understanding of the reason. All he could surmise was that he was a vampire, and should be feared. His strange orange color was such a focus of attention, that no one but the desk clerk saw his eyes begin to glow a bright amber.

As he looked about, she said, "Sir, I will make sure he gets this message." Incredibly, she maintained a calm appearance as she reached over and pushed a button, which silently summoned security. Unfortunately, the security personal at this high class hotel is not armed. Never would anyone think weapons would ever be necessary. The biggest problem the hotel ever faced was escorting an occasional drunk from the bar to their room or to a cab. So it was a disaster in the making when the security guard walked up and stated, "Sir, I need to escort you from the premises." Aaron continued looking about the atrium and ignored the guard completely. As he was trained, the guard made the mistake of grabbing Aaron by the arm. It was then that Aaron realized he did not want to walk amongst these people. In his mind, they were all inferior and worthless. *'Laugh at me? I'll give you morons something to laugh at!'*

The atrium, being so large with trees and foliage spread throughout, made all but those who stood close unaware of what was about to happen. Aaron felt the grasp on his arm and turned and grabbed it, snapping the arm like a twig. As the guard screamed in pain, Aaron's eyes were now becoming red as he transformed into a hideous killing mode. As the girl at the desk screamed and pushed the security button again, Aaron picked the guard up like a mannequin and threw him into the fountain, sailing through the air some ten yards away. Branson, being known for its constant entertainment, made some hotel guests watch from a distance thinking it was all some kind of show.

Aaron was enraged. "Now, is this funny?" He grabbed the desk station that was attached to the floor and tore it out, holding it over his head before throwing it directly at some bystanders. Coming from the back, the two arriving security men only saw Aaron from behind and they both grabbed him. One tried to put him in a headlock, but let go as soon as he glimpsed the monstrous face; but it was not soon enough, and Aaron immediately bit a chunk of his arm off and spit it out. As the man watched his blood squirt into the air, he yelled "Call 911!" Incredibly, people in the farthest part of the atrium could catch glimpses of the action and moved forward to get a better view of the show. Seeing this, Aaron grabbed the second guard, holding him high in the air before throwing him directly at the people moving his way. Seeing a man literally flying out of control in their direction initiated immediate hysteria. People began screaming and running in all directions. Aaron was now completely out of control and seeing the Concierge station, he proceeded to tear it from the floor and throw it, as if it was cardboard, at one of the glass elevators, sending glass flying in all directions. Seeing and hearing the noise and chaos, the doormen ran, scattering for safety.

The exclusive beauty of the Chateau, being on its own peninsula and away from the city, now became a severe negative, as it would take time for the police to get there. This gave Aaron plenty of time to create havoc.

"No one's laughing now!" Aaron screamed as he continued his rampage, destroying everything in sight. He trudged about the atrium, as everyone disappeared, except those lying injured, screaming or moaning.

"How funny is this?" He tore out whole trees and kicked out every glass door and window in sight. A vampire on the rampage can create a massive amount of damage in the five minutes it took for the first police car to arrive. The atrium looked like a tornado had struck. Seeing the flashing lights, Aaron sneered as he merely rose into the air and crashed through a panel in the glass ceiling and into the night sky. As the glass rained down from overhead, the police entered with guns drawn.

One policeman could only gasp, "What the hell happened here?" The second one looked about. "Where's the perp?"

The man lying near with a broken arm pointed upward toward the ceiling with his good arm. The cop closest was puzzled. "You mean he went upstairs?"

"No!" the man moaned. "He flew up through the ceiling!"

Most seriously, the cop looked at him and asked, "Have you been drinking?"

Both cops looked up, and clearly one of the glass panels in the ceiling was missing, and glass covered the floor beneath it. They began scratching their heads in wonder. One immediately began calling for medical assistance over his radio. They could see another security guard lying unconscious across the room. Blood from the other security guard was splattered everywhere, and one cop immediately began applying a tourniquet to halt the bleeding. Police poured in, with most standing in shock at the scene they observed.

As the policeman applied the tourniquet, he asked. "What did he look like?"

"He was Amish and orange," he mumbled weakly.

The cop looked at him confused. "Orange? Like he was dressed in orange?"

"No, he *was* orange. Everyone was staring at him and he went nuts."

The cop was perplexed. "Was he Amish or Asian?"

"No! He was just a guy who had orange skin. Then he turned into a damned monster."

"He turned into a monster and created all this damage himself . . . alone?"

"Yeah. There was no real resistance, as he just tossed Bob over there like a rag doll. He tore the desks right out of the floor."

The cop could see the holes in the marble floor where service desks were once positioned. He knew they weighed hundreds of pounds. "You're saying one man ripped those from the floor by himself?"

"Not only that; you'll find what is left of one over there by what used to be an elevator."

The cop was totally confused. Finished with applying the tourniquet and with paramedics now on the scene, he looked to his partner. "This one is for the detectives. No way do I want to be writing this shit up. We got here, the perp had fled, and we secured the scene. Look at this place! It looks like hurricane Katrina came through here. This guy is saying one guy did all this. And the best part is, he escaped by flying out the ceiling! Let's step off and sit on the sidelines."

Mike and Wayne arrived to a dozen squad cars and EMT vehicles. Two men were already being removed on gurneys. "Oh shit!" was all Wayne could utter. As they walked in and surveyed the damage, Wayne asked the first officer he encountered, "Any casualties?" He found it unbelievable when the answer was, "No."

They walked amongst the rubble, seeing a desk station embedded in the remains of the glass elevator, as they stepped over trees that had been torn out and were lying about.

"How the hell will Branson explain this?" Wayne mumbled.

"This is just the beginning. This vampire is completely out of control. Let's talk to the desk clerk."

As they walked over to her, they could see she was wrapped in a blanket and obviously traumatized. "Miss? Can you tell us what happened?"

"I can try. This young man came in. He was about six foot tall and slender, dressed in Amish clothes. He looked like he didn't belong here. Possibly homeless. The strange part is, he was orange. I believe he was sprayed with way too much of that dye that tans your skin. It was so unusual and obvious, that everyone was staring at him. It was like he didn't have a clue that he looked so obnoxious. He asked for a Mike Evans, and just went berserk when I would not give him the room number. He left a message that I had to write down. It's somewhere in the rubble. He turned into a monster! He broke Wally's arm. He bit a piece of Tom's arm off. He threw Bob all the way across the room. It was like he was as strong as Superman! The way he looked at me, I thought he was going to kill me," she sobbed.

Tenderly Wayne asked. "Do you remember what the message was?"

"Yes. It was for a Mike Evans, and he said he was going to tear his heart out and something about making him suffer horribly. It was terrible."

Mike just looked at Wayne seriously. "We have got to go back out there. We have to kill this guy. The sooner, the better!"

Chapter Eight

Aaron flew into the dark night sky still filled with rage. Having complete disregard for his very being, his blind anger was also fueled by hunger. He looked down at one of the many campgrounds on the outskirts of the city. There, amongst the trees, was a lone camping recreational vehicle parked with a young couple sitting outside enjoying the night on their lawn chairs. Aaron landed silently. Keeping his 'human' appearance, he walked up, startling them. When he appeared, they assumed he was a young Amish man. As he entered the glow from the lights of their trailer, the young woman nearly laughed out loud at his orange skin. It was obvious that this should have not been his normal complexion. They assumed he was just passing through on his way to another campsite. They both nodded an acknowledgement of 'hello.' Instead of continuing to walk passed, Aaron stopped and stared at them both. He was famished, but also curious, as he did not know why his appearance brought humor everywhere he went. As he stood there staring at them, they tried to ignore him and hoped he would continue on his way. They had no fear for the Amish are well known to be a gentle people.

"Why do you smile at my presence?" he asked.

They really did not wish to engage him in conversation. At this point, they were not threatened, but only wanted their privacy and not to entertain unexpected 'guests.' "Oh, I was just smiling as friendly gesture." The woman answered, hoping he would just go away.

Instead, Aaron became agitated. "You lie!"

With that response, the man stood up and was much bigger than Aaron. "Look man, we don't want any trouble. Just go on your way and let us be."

Aaron smiled. "You wish! I want to know why people are laughing at me? Tell me!"

The man smiled. "Look, all you have to do is look in the mirror. You are as orange as a construction workers vest. We don't see people with orange faces walking around that often." He began laughing, along with his wife. With a slight hint of demand he stated, "Look, we just want to sit and enjoy our vacation if that's okay with you, so we'll see you. Just move along." He assumed that would suffice, and Aaron would continue walking. Instead, he barely saw a blur and Aaron had him by the throat.

"Who is laughing now?" Aaron asked rhetorically.

Although he felt the force of Aaron's grip, the man responded, "You have two seconds to let me go . . ."

As his wife watched frozen in fear, Aaron laughed. "Ha! You have two seconds to live." Instantly, he transformed into a hideous being and bit the man savagely in the throat. His wife began screaming and fumbling for her purse and her cell phone. Aaron dropped the man, who was still alive, and grabbed the wife. Muffling her mouth and biting her neck, he drank and drained her blood as her husband watched in horror, struggling for his own life. When her heart had stopped, Aaron opened the door of the RV and threw her inside. He then turned to the man clinging to life. "Maybe next time you see an orange face you won't think it so funny!" He growled. "Oh wait! I forgot . . . there won't be a next time!" Aaron slashed at him and gave his neck a twist, breaking it. The man was dead instantly. Aaron then moved his body into the RV and threw the folding chairs inside, slamming the door. Aside from the blood splatters, from a distance it would appear as just another RV parked, and the carnage would likely not be discovered until days later.

Aaron's hunger was satisfied, but his anger was not. He took to the sky, and nearing the hotel, he could see the light show made up of police and emergency vehicles. He was satisfied that he had given them a display of his power. Below him, the riverboat was on an evening cruise. With the show and dinner cruise in full gear, he landed on the deserted upper deck of the riverboat. For now, he would ride and observe while planning his next move. He was obsessed with finding his mate's murderer.

* * * *

Christian and Katherine left the island and went south after Mike and Wayne raced to the hotel. They stopped on a mountain to discuss their future.

"What should we do?" Katherine asked, admiring the distant view.

"I'm not sure. Depending on the degree of disturbance Aaron created, this whole territory may become unsafe."

"But I like this territory."

"We may have no choice. Should he continue, it could become dangerous, as they will begin hunting him and exploring all the caves."

"Make him stop!" Katherine demanded.

"I wish I could, but I understand his deep feelings for revenge. He will either get his revenge, or die trying."

"Well, than the sooner he dies the better!" she hissed.

"I am inclined to allow him his due."

"At the expense of losing this domain?"

"Why? Why do you not wish to merely relocate again?"

"I like this domain. It has everything we wish for. Did you not enjoy the theater and the riverboat? This territory is perfect. I'll be damned if I'll give it up!" Katherine's eyes were both full of anger, and pleading with him.

"Please, I am conflicted on this issue. Let's change to another subject." Katherine nodded, complying.

"I have never asked . . . exactly how old are you?"

"One hundred and twenty-six years." Christian answered, as if deep in thought.

"How did you exist outside the population?" Katherine wondered.

"It was easy. I was born at a time of vast wilderness. Cities were small. Isolated travelers were many. I found it easy to survive with no need to travel into populated areas. As you will find, many people walk the wilderness. Further north, individuals go ice fishing alone, staying out all night. Indians still wander the woods in certain areas. There are more hermits than are known, plus there are always criminal types fleeing the cities and hiding. All become fair game. I saw the horseless carriages become a common method of travel, and even the airplanes take to the air. I observed various handheld communication devices, but know very little of them. I have no need. Do you miss your modern life?"

"No. Ours is a perfect existence. I feel free. I don't feel hot in the summer or cold in the winter. My financial burdens are gone. I now look back at what I used to eat, with disgust. I actually existed on ingesting dead things! Now, I can fly! Do you know how many humans dream of such power? No, I don't look back. This detective Higdon, whose blood we tasted, I understand his concerns. There are so many undesirables that could easily be removed from society and if we did this, it would actually be helping them. We would become super heroes."

Christian was puzzled. "What is a super hero?"

"Typically, they are of a vigilante mentality. The warm bloods believe in many of various fictional people with mythical powers, but they share one common denominator. The super heroes get rid of the criminal-types, as a vigilante might do. I find it strange that this same society that celebrates these heroes who execute personal justice, have ruined their society with laws that actually protect criminals. Let me ask, what would they have done to someone that abused a child in 1885?"

"In most cases he would have been hung instantly. It could be after a brief trial, but other times immediately by a public mob. This would have been an unacceptable crime."

"Today, people that harm children are considered ill and are many times set free after a short time spent in jail."

Christian looked perplexed. "They consider them ill? Do they feel they can be cured of their illness?"

"No! Exactly the opposite! They understand that they can never be cured."

"Why then on earth would they set them free?"

"That is the nonsense I don't miss. They have distorted the laws and the judicial system. That was what I did as a career. I worked very hard at finding loopholes in contracts so men could legally cheat each other. In criminal law, they more or less conclude that any penalty, regardless of how meaningless, is adequate. All they care about is that the individual has been processed through the system."

"This makes no sense."

"Exactly!"

"This modern world confuses me. When I had warm blood, the rules and laws were very simple. For any serious crime, the penalties were harsh. If an individual killed a criminal who had stolen from him, it was considered justifiable. If one harmed a child in any way, it would have been judged as unthinkable and they would likely be dispatched on the spot. This problem with substance abuse baffles me, as I do not understand it. What is this about? In my day, there was alcohol, but aside from rumors of opium dens, people did not solicit these things. When I was in Minneapolis, a man I fed on was selling things that appeared to be illegal, and solicited me. He called it, 'shit, nose candy, snow,' and other things. What is this substance?"

"Likely, it was cocaine. It is a white powder that you breathe into your nose and it intoxicates one."

"Does a good whiskey not do the same thing?"

"It is different. The affects are immediate and beyond those of alcohol. Plus, one can still remain functional to a point where their intoxication is not obvious."

As Katherine tried to explain illegal drugs and other problems of the modern world, Christian was baffled. It seemed so much of what she described flew in the face of basic logic. As she listed the various illegal substances, he was overwhelmed that these drugs were readily available on the street. In his mind, he wondered, *'What has happened to law enforcement?'* As he listened to her description of widespread money lending, he was completely baffled that people could live their lives in debt. He could not fathom it. *'They borrow for food and entertainment?'* When she described spousal abuse and halfway houses, he began to wonder how the society deteriorated so much in a short century. In his day, a man took great pride, regardless of his means, in the fact that he was free of debt. The image Katherine described was a society of people imprisoned by their own conspicuous consumption and insatiable appetite for material things and intoxications. He understood a society where ethics and morals no longer applied, and where widespread cheating was acceptable if presented in deceit. He began to fully understand the gift he had given her. As Katherine continued, he truly wondered whether he even cared to understand a society that evolved into pure nonsense. In his logic, a man driving a car that is owned by a bank should have no pride other than being that of a chauffeur. He could absorb no more.

"Enough! You were trapped in a world that lacks dignity, ethics, and morals. And they call us evil? I will not feel grief in feeding off this modern society. Too me, it sounds as though death might be a gift."

Katherine smiled. "Poor Christian. I have made you depressed. I only meant to help you understand why this Higdon would allow us to remove undesirables and turn his head away. It would give him great satisfaction knowing these criminals are removed forever. There is no plea bargaining or probation in our world."

Christian looked confused. "What is this plea bargain?"

"I will explain at another time. It will merely depress you. Let's eat! I'm starving."

"Fine. Let us take flight and look for an undesirable. But frankly, I feel death would be a relief to any man in this distorted culture."

They took to the night sky and within minutes, spotted a single warm blooded being moving slowly along the dark rural highway. They landed in his path, expecting him to attempt to flee. He was rolling an old antique wagon wheel along the highway and singing some little known country song. He looked at them in amazement.

"You two just fell out of the damned sky! I'll be damned!"

Katherine looked to Christian. "It is obvious that he is quite drunk."

Christian laughed. "Drunk? He has taken inebriation to a new plateau. What are you doing with that wagon wheel?" Christian asked, as he recognized it as being from his era.

The man was using the huge wheel to prop himself up, as his balance was completely gone. "I stole it! I stole it from that motel up the road. You gonna fly me to jail?"

"We are not the police. Are you not afraid?"

"I live in Branson! I see shit all the time. If you're not the cops, get the hell out of my way!" The old man turned his attention back to the wheel.

"He is unfit," Christian stated. "If we fed on him, we would literally be flying into trees."

"Let me just taste him," Katherine begged. "Call it a 'before dinner drink.' Please?"

"Go ahead, but bite him on the wrist."

As the man stood staring at them, trying to decide who or what they were, Katherine grabbed his arm and Christian held him. "Hey, let me go! Git your hands off me!" he yelled.

Katherine grabbed his arm and sunk her teeth into his wrist. "AAAHHHH!" he screamed. "What the hell are you doing? She bit me! Damn it! She bit me!"

Katherine giggled. "My, it is truly a wonder that this man is still alive. His blood is at least a third alcohol. If he is not the town drunk, he should be!" Meanwhile, the man was upset and kept screaming.

"Damn it! She bit me! What the hell did she bite me for? I'm telling the cops!"

Christian let the man go and turned to Katherine. "Let us depart. This is not someone to feed off of." In leaving, Katherine thought she would have some harmless fun. She grabbed the man by the collar and lifted him a few feet in the air. He was silent and stared in awe, as if he could not decide whether this was reality or a dream.

"When you call the police, you can also tell them that you were flying!" She rocked him back and forth, giving him a weightless sensation. Gently, she set him down, as he was dumbfounded. "You can tell the police that you met Superman and Superwoman! Watch as we fly away!" They slowly arose high into the air and vanished from view, leaving him standing completely confused.

It was only minutes later that after getting a 911 call that a wagon wheel was stolen, that the police spotted old Kenny, a well known town drunk. The young officer laughed. "Christ! It's Kenny again. What the hell is it with him stealing that wagon wheel all the time?" They pulled over and the young policeman began scolding him. "Kenny, Kenny, Kenny! What the hell are we going to do with you?"

Kenny just looked at them, and in his condition, did not recognize them personally and wondered how they even knew his name. "How do you know my name?" he asked in wonder.

"Kenny, this is about the tenth time we have been through this. Now, start walking that wagon wheel back from where you found it! I really don't want to lock you up." The policeman knew the owner would forgive Kenny and not press charges, as this prank had become routine.

Kenny stared at them in confusion. "You're not locking me up?"

The young cop smiled. "No, but you are walking the wheel back from where you found it. Right now!" Besides letting him walk back, which might sober him up a bit, they took no chances of having him inside their car and vomiting, which was their previous experience.

Kenny turned back, rolling the wheel in the direction from which it came, and stopped and blurted out some slurred words. "Hey, I saw Superman tonight."

Both cops now began laughing. "Did you meet the Easter Bunny too?"

Kenny now frowned. "Hey I met him, and Superwoman too! She bit me!" He held out his arm to show the fang marks on his wrist, but the cops paid no attention.

"Well, when we see her, we will arrest her for biting a citizen who was stealing a wagon wheel. She will be in big trouble."

Kenny thought for a second. "Okay, then. You tell her she should not be biting people!"

Both cops just laughed. "Kenny, get your ass moving. We're following you back."

Christian and Katherine flew deeper into the wilderness. Far from the populated area, they spotted a trailer nestled amongst the trees. They could smell the foul stench of chemicals filling the air. Katherine smiled. "These are definitely undesirables!"

When they landed, Christian asked, "What manner of undesirable is this? How do you know?"

"They are here, far from the population, with the reason that they are also far from law enforcement. That foul smell is the chemicals they use to manufacture illegal drugs. They are surely criminals. There will be no retribution for removing them from society."

"How do we get to them?" Christian asked most innocently.

Katherine smiled as she adjusted her dress to show slightly more cleavage. "So, you don't think they will invite me in?"

"Why, I ask, do they live in such boxes? Are they Gypsies?" he wondered.

Katherine laughed. "I swear, sometimes your perception just cracks me up. No, these are trailers or mobile homes. They are merely a convenient and inexpensive way of living."

"Is this a safe method of dwelling?"

"In fact, it is not. During tornado season, they are frequently and easily destroyed by winds. Now that I think about it, it will be a great feeding time, as the people who live in these 'boxes' sometimes completely disappear rather routinely, and no one thinks anything of it."

"Are these people who are making these chemicals with such a foul odor, types that we may really want to feed on? Are they the types that this Higdon would like us to remove from his society?"

"Yes. It is these type people who make and sell this poison that rarely, if ever, use it themselves. When or if they are ever caught, it is this type of crime that courts love to negotiate to lesser charges. People such as this spread this poison to hundreds, maybe thousands, of people—including children—yet they routinely walk free from true justice. Should we make these people go away and destroy this place, it would make this Higdon very happy."

"Then let us feed!"

Katherine smiled as she walked from the woods toward the trailer. Outside, she could see two huge Pit Bulls chained near the door, which was their alarm system . . . but this type of alarm system does not work with vampires, as the two giant dogs cowered and hid under the trailer. The only light was that coming from inside, filtering through the windows. Katherine knocked softly. With a radio blasting, no one heard the knock, so she pounded louder. Inside were two men cooking meth. One motioned to the other to answer that door while he went for his weapon, as when they turned the music down, not hearing the dogs barking was an alarm in itself. As one pointed a gun at the door, the other opened it just a sliver. Katherine had mussed up her hair as to look disheveled. One look at the beautiful woman appearing lost and confused gave him confidence to open the door widely.

The cooker smiled broadly, as if a gift had been delivered. "What are you doing out here little lady?" As he asked, his scanned the area, and he could see she was alone.

"My boyfriend dumped me out here and I have been walking for hours," she stated sadly.

"Lady, you have been walking for hours in the wrong direction. Had you went the other way, you would have been in town by now." As if in second thought, he asked, "Where are my dogs?" He was looking around the outside puzzled.

"There are two cute dogs sleeping under this trailer," she answered innocently.

"Sleeping?"

Katherine quickly interrupted. "May I come in and use the bathroom?"

She certainly appeared no threat, so he gladly invited her in while giving his partner a wink, as if they were about to get lucky, whether she agreed or not. Once Katherine was invited in, she brushed passed the man at the door, grabbing him by the shirt and pushing him out from the door where Christian was waiting but before he could finish the sentence "What the f—?" Christian was sinking his teeth into his neck and gorging himself. Meanwhile, Katherine turned to the other man wearing her vampire's face. "SSSHHHHH!" she hissed.

The man stepped back in fright, but he still aimed his gun at her.

"So, you thought you would assault me, didn't you?" she growled.

He shook his head. "No, I wasn't going to do nothing!"

"You thought you were going to rape me!" she growled.

The frightened man knew he had nothing to lose, but also knew that if he fired the gun and it was useless against this monster, he was surely dead.

He felt he would fain innocence. "Look, I had no intention of harming you. Maybe Tom did, but I didn't. Please, let me go."

"Oh, you will go, but it will be to another world."

As she moved forward in a blur of speed, he fired one shot before she was tearing his throat apart. As she tasted his warm blood, she knew her assumption was correct, as his blood was pure and absent of the drugs he was concocting. She dropped the body and looked around at all the volatile chemicals. She walked out the door. "Here, let me take his body. Christian, we should let those dogs go free."

As she carried the body that Christian had drained back into the trailer, Christian unhooked the dogs that ran whimpering into the wilderness. Meanwhile, Katherine dumped the body inside next to where she had left hers, and looked at the Bunsen burners sitting on a counter that was filled with accelerants. "These idiots should not be allowed to play with fire." She smiled as she tipped the Bunsen burner over, and the flames began spreading across the counter in a blanket of flames. Without looking back, she exited the trailer. "We better step back," she suggested.

They flew a short distance and watched from the trees. The flames began to grow and suddenly, the trailed erupted into an inferno, followed by a series of explosions. "Kind of like the Fourth of July, isn't it? Hard to believe, but not only did we eliminate two criminals, we likely saved a number of people from their poison."

"Why did it explode?" Christian questioned.

"These poisons use accelerants as their base. Workers such as those are literally sitting on a bomb. I simply lit the fuse," Katherine stated in satisfaction.

"So we are actually helping their society?"

"Yes, it is a strange thing. If a vigilante had done the same thing but killed those men with a gun, he would be hailed a hero. Because of the method in which we kill, we are considered monsters? Different methods, same result . . . strange . . ." Katherine mumbled.

"Can we travel and see this town that is so famous for entertainment?" Christian asked anxiously.

"Yes, let's travel the boardwalk."

They took to air and landed under the bridge, walking up to the edge of the boardwalk. Katherine felt confident, but Christian was still slightly paranoid of walking amongst humans. As they strolled, hand and hand, they began entering a population of shoppers and party goers flowing in all directions. Christian was amazed as they passed the stores with their elaborate displays of clothes, jewelry, and things he was just bewildered by. He marveled at the mannequins wearing modern fashions. The simple shops that he had known were long gone. They could hear live music coming from a distance, and as they approached, Christian was again stunned by the wonderful sounds. He watched Katherine, who seemed comfortable and relaxed, but he couldn't help but feel out of place. He looked out at the lake and as the lights glistened on the water, he asked, "May we ride the riverboat once more and this time, without a possible interruption?"

"Well? What do you think so far?"

"It is all wonderful. All this and we still have our solitude and a safe distance. There is no doubt that this is now our domain."

They returned the same way in which they came, and were soon in the air approaching the riverboat. They observed a warm blooded being on the island and knew that it was likely Mike Evans. As they came closer, they also observed Aaron riding along on the upper deck of the returning riverboat. Both knew that a confrontation would be soon coming.

* * * *

Danny had decided that he would work this night, doing his normal food deliveries. This was no longer the carefree, friendly Danny of the past. Instead, it was a dark and brooding Danny who felt on the edge of hostility. He welcomed the night, for some reason beyond his understanding. Typically, as he prepared for work, his mind became that of an investigator, collecting information for the police. He even carried a notebook to take down specific facts . . . but not tonight. He looked at the roll of money he had taken from the drug dealer, and smiled, as his agenda included more than just deliveries. He realized that he would no longer rely on tips.

As Danny, being known as a passive lighthearted young man, entered Elmer's, a local, known for verbally bullying people, sat at the bar and decided to hurl a few insults.

"Here he is! The old delivery boy! In this economy, you must really be begging for tips! Maybe you should do a little dance for the customers, delivery boy!"

Danny's normal reaction was to walk on by without a word, but this time he stopped and turned towards the bar. Danny didn't understand why, but his blood began to boil. He looked the man directly in eyes.

"Why don't you teach me? You look like you've been dancing for people your whole fucking life!"

Danny had never confronted anyone before, and even the bartender was shocked.

The man at the bar was forced to respond to save face. "You want to dance with me? We can take it outside." He felt confident that Danny, as always, would just walk away. Instead, Danny actually grinned and stepped forward.

"Fine. You feel like going home all beat to shit, let's go! You better get used to drinking your beer through a straw!" Danny turned toward the door and motioned. "Come on! I'm sick of you shooting that big fucking mouth off all the time."

The bartender quickly intervened. "Now, no trouble! Danny, Elmer needs you in the back." Danny glared at the big mouth who knew he would not mess with Danny anymore. The bartender was shocked, but felt that the trauma Danny had experienced, plus losing his friend Jerry Cunningham, had affected him.

Instead of his friendly hello, Danny didn't say a thing. He grabbed a pile of tickets for outgoing orders and began sorting through them. This was unusual, and old Elmer took notice. "Are you looking for something special?" Danny didn't answer, and Elmer began to wonder if Danny was himself. As Elmer watched, Danny sorted out a number of orders in a separate stack. When he finished, he looked at Elmer and stated, "Here, set these up for me. Give the rest to Jack."

"Well, good evening to you too! Are you okay, Danny?" Elmer was a bit concerned.

"I'm fine, boss. I'm fine. Get me the orders and I'm on my way."

Elmer heard what Danny said, but his expression and manner in which he spoke was foreign. There was no joking, and Danny seemed much too serious. Elmer also came to the conclusion that Danny was suffering the aftereffects of his injuries and loss of a friend. Quickly, he put the orders in the thermal bags and Danny was on his way. There was a method to Danny's choice of orders, as he had recognized a number of the addresses as doing illegal activities. His plan was simple; without Cunningham and with his new, more aggressive personality, Danny intended to put simply them out of business. His first stop was at the exclusive Palace Pointe gated golf community. This was one complex that local police could not touch, because of it being a gated private property. Besides having expensive houses, it had an area of condominiums that could be leased, and it was the perfect place for a house of prostitution, as police could only enter if called on 911. Customers set up their appointments by phone, and were given a code to enter through the automatic gate. These places flourished, for in Branson, there was no shortage of older men looking for young available women. Danny knew where a number of these set-ups were, and was about to do what the police could not.

With his Elmer's sign on his car and with the security guards familiar with him, Danny breezed through the gate and toward his destination. As he drove, he laughed at the thought of security, because most all the guards were elderly, working in their retirement years and unarmed. This so-called exclusive community, with no police able to patrol, had no protection at all, in reality. Danny parked his car and carried the order to the door. It was a corner ground floor unit with a great view of a fairway on one side and mountains on the other. It had four bedrooms, which most always were filled and busy. When Danny knocked, looking through a peep-hole, he was instantly recognized. The huge, muscular doorman let him in. It was like entering a party. There were a few customers sitting on the sofa watching TV, and a few of the women dressed seductively, walking about.

"Hey, Danny, how you been? How much we owe you?" The doorman/ bouncer asked.

Danny smiled a wry grin. "How much do you have?"

"What do you mean?"

"I'm robbing you, you muscle headed idiot."

The doorman was confused. "No, really . . . how much for the food?"

Danny smiled. "Look, let me speak a little slower and clearer so you understand. I . . . am . . . robbing . . . you! Now, this is what is going to happen. You can either gather up all the money and hand it to me, or I'm going to throw you through that patio door before I even bother to open it. After that, I will trash this place and the customers will freak out. Then the girls will likely run and never come back, and you're out of business. Oh yeah, someone will call the police, and eventually they will get here and you will have to explain this mess."

The bouncer stood listening, and did not believe what he was hearing. "Danny, I don't want to hurt you, so I hope this is some kind of a joke. Ha, ha . . . not funny. Now, how much?"

"Lifting weights must have made you deaf." In a flash Danny reached for his neck and simply put his grip inside the big man's collar bone. Only a slight amount of pressure causes great pain. As Danny applied pressure, the man dropped to his knees in agony. Danny looked him in the eye. "Did you know it only takes 17 pounds of pressure to break this bone? A person doesn't have to be that strong to do that. It can easily be done by a weakling like me. Now I know the cash drawer is in the kitchen; where is it?"

The two men on the sofa saw what was happening and sensed something was wrong. They quickly left through the patio door. The girls seeing what was happening, retreated to the bedroom. Danny released his grip and knew what was coming next. No sooner than the man was on his feet, he threw a punch that was hard enough to break a brick. Danny easily dodged it, and immediately the bouncer threw a second one, which Danny also dodged. He shook his head in disappointment. "I was hoping it wouldn't go this way."

With a speed that was unnatural, Danny simply hit the man in the throat, instantly leaving him choking. Danny followed that with a kick to the groin, causing the bouncer to double over. Danny then went to the kitchen and opening the first drawer, pulled out a 9mm semi-automatic. He tucked it into his pants. Keeping one eye on the man still doubled over and choking, he went through drawer after drawer, becoming agitated. "Where is the cash?" he yelled down the hall. "Hey, will the head whore come out here?"

A girl in her mid-twenties came out from a bedroom and seeing her bouncer doubled over and choking, she knew this was serious. "You know this is one of Bobby Raye's houses. He is not going to be happy. You don't want to do this," she warned.

Danny laughed. "That name slays me. Bobby Raye sounds like a hillbilly singer."

The fact was that Bobby Raye controlled all vice in southwest Missouri, and the center of his operation was north, in Springfield, only 30 minutes away. He was known for protecting his operations.

"I'm serious! He will fuck you up!" she warned.

"Look, I will ask you once. After that, your pretty face goes through that glass door. Where is the cash?"

Her jaw tightened, and she pointed to a drawer in an end table located in the living room.

Danny smiled. "Now, was that so hard?" He walked over and opened the drawer, which contained a little gray metal cash box. Opening it, he found a stack of hundreds. It appeared there was thousands of dollars.

Below the drawer was a door, and inside was a variety of drugs, primarily cocaine. He pocketed it all. Out of the corner of his eye he could see the bouncer straighten up and come running at him full force. Danny side stepped and used the force and direction of the bouncer to push him over the sofa, and completely through the floor to ceiling window. In a thunderous crash, he landed on the patio, dazed and bleeding.

He looked toward the hooker and calmly stated, "I would call 911. He is going to need them. Oh yeah, tell them I robbed your whorehouse while you're at it. Ha!"

Danny began leaving, and as an afterthought, he turned and yelled. "Oh, your food is on the table."

Danny knew that they could not report anything to the police, except possibly making up some kind of accident excuse. This secure, gated community that protected them from police, also made them vulnerable to being cleaned out. Driving out through the security gate, he waved to the old security guard who was hunched over and half asleep. Danny was on his way to his next destination. Right down the road and up the mountain, in a trendy area of houses, he pulled into the driveway. Taking his food order, he knocked on the door. The man saw Danny and smiled. "Come on in!"

Danny knew this was a huge dealer of pot. Danny walked in and set the food order down on the dining room table. Danny was aware that he lived alone, and by the food order, could tell he had no guests. "What do I owe ya?" he asked.

"Oh, I'll take all your cash and all the pot you have here," Danny stated, seriously.

The man laughed. "Dude, that's not funny. Really now, what do I owe you?"

Danny grabbed the man by the throat.

"Look, I don't want to hurt you. I want all your cash and your stash. When I leave, you are going to either stop dealing, or move to another town." Danny stated in a growling voice.

"Hey man, this is not my stash. If I don't have the cash to pay for it, I'm a dead man!" he pleaded.

"Then it seems your decision is an easy one. You're going to have to get out of town," Danny answered simply.

The man looked at Danny, and seeing the 9mm tucked in his jeans, he decided it was best to do what Danny asked. He reached into his pocket and produced a wad of bills, handing it to Danny. He opened a drawer, which revealed at least a pound of marijuana.

Danny smiled and asked him, "This is it?"

"Yeah, that's all I have. I swear."

Danny looked at him seriously and threatening. "So you're saying that if I search and find any more cash or weed, I can blow one of your knee caps off?"

The man knew Danny wasn't kidding. "Okay, I just might have some more." He pulled up the couch cushion and lifted a panel, producing a huge stack of bills and a brick of marijuana. As he handed it to Danny he stated softly, "I'm a dead man now, but so are you."

"Tell your supplier who I am and that he's next."

"Are you serious? Do you know who he is?"

Danny laughed. "Don't tell me. Let me guess. Some guy named Bobby Raye. Yeah, I know, he's big and bad, and will fuck me up. I guess we will see."

The dumbfounded man felt Danny was completely suicidal, as Bobby Raye was sure to send his enforcers looking for him. Danny had no concern at all. In his car counting his cash, he had almost a year's wages sitting in a pile, tax free. He stopped at a dumpster and tossed all the drugs and the gun where he thought they belonged . . . in the garbage. There was also another reason he tossed the weapon, and that was because he was afraid that his last stop might put him in a position to have to use it. The last food order was a large one that was going to people that Danny was well acquainted with. They were bikers, and by the food order, he knew he would be facing at least four of them. They were known for dealing meth in the area. Danny knew this was to be a true test of his new strength and his fury.

The house was just outside the city limits, and as Danny pulled up, he could see four motorcycles in the driveway. It was strange, as Danny felt no fear; in fact, it was like he was looking forward to releasing some of the hostility exploding from inside. He picked up the food order and walked to the door, knocking with authority.

A grizzly face looked out from a window, and he could hear a man yell, "It's the food guy." The door swung open and a biker motioned Danny in. Danny scanned the room, for he knew this time when he made his demands, it was likely that violence would instantly erupt. Instead of asking for the total, the biker threw a fifty dollar bill on table and mumbled "Keep the change, kid." Danny looked around and could see no weapons in clear view, so he made a statement that would likely do nothing more than incite violence.

"I'm putting you out of business."

The four bikers stood looking at each other in confusion, before the obvious leader spoke. "Look kid, we have no reason to hurt you, so if you're looking to get beat up, go to some bar and start some trouble somewhere else."

The largest one, who was covered in tattoos, grabbed Danny by the collar. "Come on, let's go."

Danny couldn't see his own eyes, but they changed color from an innocent blue to glowing a dark amber. He clamped on the man's wrist, spun around, and with a simple strike, broke his arm at the elbow. A second man threw a punch and only felt air, as Danny dodged it and struck the man upwardly and solidly in the nose, breaking it, which caused his eyes to instantly tear up, and blurred his vision. Danny grabbed the third man and threw him into the fourth, sending them both backward. Danny picked up a kitchen chair and slammed it over the third man's head, knocking him unconscious. While the other men moaned, Danny addressed the last biker.

"Look, do I need to continue? Where are the cash and the drugs?" Danny had his eyes on all four, hoping that a gun would not come into the picture.

"I ain't giving you shit!"

Danny just smiled. He sprang forward, striking the man in the center of the chest, which stunted his breathing. He then grabbed his head and slammed it against the wall a few times. As the other men rose to help their friend, they could see the blood visible on the wall and knew their leader was severely injured. "You bastard!" the one biker yelled, trying to see clearly while his nose was gushing blood. He lunged at Danny. Danny kicked him in the groin and began slamming his head against the table before letting him fall to the floor. Danny looked to the only conscious member, who had the shattered arm.

"You want to point me to what I want, or do I break the other arm?"

Seeing his friends unconscious, he reasoned that none of them would ever know he gave up the goods anyway. "Under the sink, man."

Danny opened the cabinet under the sink, and there were a few bundles of hundreds and a trash bag filled with vials of meth, along with balloons of what was likely heroin. He tossed it on the table. One biker on the floor began to stir, and Danny kicked him in the head without a thought.

"Weapons?"

With his good arm, he pointed without a word to the closet. In the closet behind some clothes were an AK47 and a box of handguns. Danny tossed the cash and drugs into the box with the handguns, grabbed the AK47, and headed for the door. "Should I call 911 for you?"

The biker glared at Danny. "You know you are fucked. Hell is going to rain down on you."

"Enjoy the food!"

Danny headed for a strip mall and drove around the back. Once again, he dumped the weapons and drugs literally in the garbage. He piled all the cash into the box, which now was filled with hundreds. From years of deliveries, he knew where all the places of vice were located. He knew this was his last night working for Elmer's. He decided this was to be his new lucrative occupation. He also knew he would have to relocate, as all these crooks would easily trace him from Elmer's to his apartment, so he would have to move quickly. Everything had gone exactly to plan. There were only two things that Danny didn't anticipate. One, he had amassed more money than he ever imagined. The second thing was that he was totally unaware that one of the bikers was an undercover cop!

* * * *

Christian and Katherine watched from a distance as the riverboat made its final turn toward the dock. They could see the warm blooded glow of who they assumed was Mike Evans, sitting in clear view on the shore of the distant island. As they watched, Aaron stood at the rail of the top level of the riverboat, while the show concluded inside. When the boat became parallel with the island, it was clear that Aaron saw the warm blooded being on the shore. He began pacing, and both Christian and Katherine knew exactly what was to happen next.

Katherine turned to Christian. "Will we get involved?"

Christian was deep in thought. "I am still conflicted as to who dies tonight."

Chapter Nine

Mike Evans and Wayne Higdon left the hotel and assumed Aaron would soon be searching the area, looking to kill Evans. They decided to set the perfect trap. Taking all of their gear, they made their way to the island, thinking that if Mike sat on the shore, his warm blooded imprint would easily be seen from the air. The plan was simple. Higdon, wearing the thermal suit that would make his presence invisible from the air to a vampire, would hide in the woods located near the shore. Wayne even had his night goggles, so that he could see any movement in the dark. Although he would have a crossbow, his main weapon would be a basic high-pressure squirt gun filled with Holy water. This simple weapon would allow Higdon to drench Aaron from 15 feet away, should Evans miss. Neither had a clue what dousing Aaron in Holy water might do. Would he be rendered powerless, thus becoming a sitting target, or would he fly off in pain? They hoped they would soon find out.

Higdon picked his position carefully and would sit motionless beside a tree covered by bushes from the shore side. In effect, he was invisible. Evans sat out near the water. On the sandy shore, he was very visible from the air.

"How long will we sit here?" Higdon asked.

"I'm staying as long as it takes. If we get near dawn, it will be over, for it will be likely that he never saw us."

"I'm going to let you get that first shot before I squirt him with this thing. When I hit him with this Holy water, he just might fly off," Higdon guessed.

"Wayne, let me take both shots, if you can. I will take one, and as he charges, I will take my second. If he does not drop, just start squirting. If he remains stationary, then take your best shot. I will be reloading."

Their plan was set and both could see the riverboat approaching, making its final turn toward the dock. Little did they know that Aaron was riding on the upper deck. When the boat became parallel to the island, Aaron could not believe what he saw. There, sitting on the shore, was a solitary man. He knew it was Mike Evans, the focus of his revenge. With his keen night vision, he could only see one warm blooded being, but he was fully aware that they had the ability to cloak their presence. Although his blood began to boil with anger, his instincts were telling him to beware. Aaron decided to take to the air and land deeper within the island, approaching his target from the wilderness. As the riverboat neared the dock, Aaron was in the air and soon landing in the woods. He could see through the foliage and trees that Evans was sitting there, crossbow in hand. He could also see a second weapon near him on the ground. It was easy to surmise that Evans was going to attempt to take two shots. With vision that would allow him to see Evans trigger finger twitching in the darkness, Aaron smiled, for the odds of Evans getting a shot off that he could not anticipate and dodge were slim.

Aaron's vampire instincts were telling him this was far too easy. Since Evans had left his friend and fled the last time they had met, this showdown was suicide, in Aaron's logic, so he looked for the 'catch.' He stood motionless in the dark and within the shadows he was invisible. His eyes scanned in every direction. It was when Higdon simply scratched his nose that Aaron saw the movement. He was confused, as he could not see a warm blooded imprint because of the thermal suit Higdon was wearing, but he knew someone was there. Crouching next to a tree and with no warm blooded glow, Higdon appeared like a rock to Aaron, so he would inch closer. Silently and slowly he moved toward the mysterious movement. Within seconds, Aaron was standing behind Higdon and could smell his human scent, as well as his fear. His immediate instinct was to kill him quickly and proceed toward Evans, but that may compromise his revenge, for Evans just might flee to the water. So he decided on another plan. Aaron took his hand and in a quick move, slammed Higdon's head against the tree. It was a single strike and other than Higdon's body collapsing on the ground, making a slight noise as it landed on the dry leaves in the brush, there was no other sound. Evans heard the stir.

"Wayne? Is everything okay?" Evans called. His cry was met with no answer. "Wayne, are you there?" The eerie silence brought no response and Evans knew something was terribly wrong.

Evans jumped to his feet, taking aim, and began scanning in all directions. He shouted, "Wayne?"

Slowly, Aaron walked from the woods into clear view, standing some 30 feet away. "Your friend is sleeping."

Evans did his best to appear brave. "Well, I heard you were looking for me."

Aaron, despite his instinct screaming at him to attack, wanted this to last and savor every moment of this killing. "Yes. I called at your hotel, but they told me you were not there. So here you are, facing your demon, so to speak. I must admit, you are either very brave, or completely suicidal."

"I was told that you would follow me, regardless of where I went, so rather than prolong the inevitable, I chose to get this over with. Did you kill Wayne?"

"No, not yet. As I stated, he is sleeping," Aaron sneered. "I sense you are wearing protection."

Mike knew Aaron was referring to his blessed crucifix. "I once had a close friend who faced a vampire, and he made the mistake of taking his off. It was fatal."

Aaron smiled. "I can endure the pain, and as you seem so familiar with my kind, you must know that it will not fully protect you from me tearing your heart out."

Evans bravado seemed to kick in. "I will only tell you that I have killed your kind before. You all talk as if you are invincible, but I know your weakness!"

Evans comment made it clear to Aaron that caution might be called for. He slowly stepped forward, keeping his eye on Evans hand. Evans called out. "Wayne?"

Aaron smiled. "You are alone, my friend. Your friend will not be waking up anytime soon. It is just you and I, so let's get this over with."

Evans slowly raised his right hand, taking his best aim at Aaron's heart. "Bring it," Evans stated, most seriously.

A vampire's vision is so keen that Aaron could see each bead of sweat on Evans forehead; so watching Evans trigger finger tense up was clearly visible. Aaron knew Mike was about to pull the trigger. Mike needed to disrupt Aaron's concentration. "I'm going to send you to wherever I sent your mate."

At those words, Aaron froze in his tracks with a flash of Rebecca coming instantly to his mind. Just that instant gave Mike his opportunity to fire on a stationary target, and he did. In a fraction of a second the arrow was released and hit the target, but Mike's aim was off and the arrow sunk into Aaron's shoulder. Mike reached for his second weapon, assuming Aaron would soon be upon him. As he raised the second crossbow holding his last chance at life, he looked up and Aaron had not moved. Instead, he stood sneering.

"One down, one to go," Aaron growled. Evans watched as Aaron's face was morphing into a hideous monster. "Prepare to die, Mister Evans."

As Aaron rushed forward, Evans fired. He missed Aaron's heart by only inches. Evans reached for his last hope, and that was the arrow in his belt which he would attempt to drive into Aaron's heart. He now knew what his good friend Ted had felt, because certain death was rushing at him. As Aaron leaped into the air and Mike flinched, anticipating being put upon, he opened his eyes and instead heard the sounds of growling and screaming. He could see what appeared to be Aaron, locked in battle with someone or something, as a blur of fury was difficult to make out in the darkness. As Evans stood in amazement, the movement stopped, and he could see Christian holding Aaron down. In was two monsters interlocked.

"I want my revenge!" Aaron screamed.

Christian just looked at him sadly. "I cannot allow you your revenge. I can only offer you peace." With that said, in a flash, Christian tore out Aaron's heart. He threw it at Evans feet. "Do what you must," Christian ordered.

Evans took the wooden arrow in his hand and drove it though the heart and Aaron screamed a guttural, final gasp. His body withered as Christian arose, morphing back into his human appearance. "This is the third time I allowed you to live," he stated quietly. "You better tend to your friend."

Mike ran to Wayne, who was still completely unconscious. After checking his pulse, Mike began shaking him. Removing the hood, Mike could see Wayne bleeding from a gash on the side of his head. As Mike moved him out and to the shore, Wayne began to become conscious, but confused. "What happened?" he asked. Seeing the blood dripping down his onto his shirt, he wondered, "Did the vampire bite me?"

Relieved that Wayne was okay and alive, Mike answered, "No; it looks like he slammed your head into the tree."

"When? I never saw him?" Wayne was puzzled.

"He was a lot smarter than we imagined. He came up from behind. You never saw him coming. I guess he would have killed me, had it not been for our vampire friend."

"What?" Higdon uttered in confusion.

"Christian. He likely saved my life. He took him down. He tore his heart out and threw it to me to destroy."

Higdon looked about. "Where is he?"

Mike turned, and Christian was gone. "I . . . I guess I owe him my life." Mike walked to where Aaron's body lay. Only a shriveled up corpse with two arrows stuck in it and huge cavity in the center of its chest was on the shore. He pulled the arrows out and walked to Higdon, "Let's get you to the hospital."

"What of the body?" Higdon questioned.

"Believe me, it won't be here once the sun comes up."

Mike helped Wayne into the boat and loaded their gear, and they were off to the ER. Once there, they simply gave the excuse the Higdon had suffered a fall. He was quickly given a few stitches and diagnosed with a mild concussion. When the doctor finished, Higdon asked him in casual conversation, "So how was your night?"

"Unusual," the doctor quickly answered.

"How so?"

"Well, usually we get a few heart problems—old people, you know. That, and a few car accident victims. Tonight, beside your head trauma from a fall, I have had two broken arms, and a number of people with various lacerations. I've been doing a lot of stitching up. Just unusual."

The detective in Higdon had to ask, "Any common denominators? Was there a brawl somewhere?"

The doctor thought for a moment. "Yeah. Most of them were a lot of big, tough guys. You know, some biker types, and a huge muscular guy that said he 'tripped' and fell through a window. I'm guessing some scuffles went on somewhere. All I heard about was some mess that took place at the hotel. From what I overheard, some meth-head walked in and went berserk in the lobby." Wayne knew immediately that Branson had put its 'spin' on what would be in the news.

Leaving the ER, Wayne and Mike headed to Elmer's for a well needed drink. Being near closing time, Elmer's was empty, so they sat at the bar.

Knowing Wayne and seeing his head bandaged, Elmer, always curious, asked, "What happened?"

Wayne smiled at Mike. "Actually Elmer, I took a fall and went head first into a damned tree." He made it sound as truthful as can be.

Old Elmer grimaced. "That had to hurt. Can I ask you a favor?"

"Shoot," Wayne replied.

"Can you keep an eye out or check on Danny?"

"What's with Danny?"

"Well, he took some food orders for delivery and never came back. I'm a bit worried. It's not like him."

Logically, Wayne questioned, "Any customers complain about not getting their order?"

"No, not a one."

"So, Danny did his deliveries and just went home . . . are you worried about the money for the orders?"

"Nah. Danny is always good. We're talking sixty to eighty bucks. I'm more worried about Danny not coming back, as he didn't seem like himself." Elmer went on about how Danny seemed withdrawn and quiet. When he mentioned Danny selecting specific orders, Wayne's detective instincts took over. Higdon wondered and asked, "Did he select them by neighborhood or by the size of the order? What do you mean by 'select?" Elmer went on to explain that Danny seemed to pick out a few orders, and obviously delivered them, but that he never returned. In reality, Elmer was worried about Danny. Higdon assured Elmer that he would check on Danny, and gave him the 'get lost' signal, as he wanted to talk privately with Mike.

Mike looked at Higdon seriously. "You know you have made a pact with the devil."

"I know."

"You think you can live with that?"

"I guess I have to. There is no doubt that he could have let that vampire kill you, and God knows I would have been next. Instead, here we are drinking a cold beer. If you strip away all that we have been fed by the media about vampires just killing everything in sight, and view it as we know to be true, what do we have? Even in the worst case, I would rather deal with him, than a pedophile. Maybe he will really eliminate some of the bad elements. I really wish I could send him on a quest to shrink the sex offender registry, or make the drug dealers disappear. What is the worst case? We have to hunt him down and kill him. What would that take? It would mean a short hunt of the caves, a squirt from the super shooter, and a stake to the heart. Somehow, I trust him. He has nothing to gain. He could have merely left, and we would never find him. He and I must talk."

"All I know is that he saved my bacon. Damn, as much as I practiced, I missed with two shots! I have to agree with you. He really did have three chances to kill me and didn't. The thought of him drinking blood makes me a little queasy, but in perspective, not as queasy as the serial killer we caught up north that was chopping people up and eating parts of them. After this week is over, you know I'm coming back as soon as I can to see how all this turns out."

As they talked, a rough looking biker came in with his arm in a cast. Higdon immediately thought about the doctor mentioning a few broken arms. It appeared to Wayne that the cast was brand new.

"Fall off the bike?" Wayne asked while Evans snickered.

The biker looked at Wayne most seriously and stated, "The color of the day is blue."

With that statement, both Wayne and Mike knew he was an undercover cop. "What's up?" Wayne asked.

The biker looked straight ahead and kept his head down so that he did not appear conversational from a distance. "You're Higdon?" Wayne nodded positive.

The undercover cop continued. "I came here because a delivery guy, supposedly from this place, delivered a food order. He was the clean-cut type. He had no tats, piercings, or anything. One of the guys said his name was Danny."

"Sounds like him. He's a real good kid. He is a good friend to us, if you understand," Higdon replied, without calling Danny an informant.

"Well, this good kid is now either some kind of crook or a vigilante, and if Hell's Ravens find him, he will be scattered around Branson in multiple garbage bags."

"What? What the hell did he do?"

"This 'kid' came into a Raven's safe house. He boldly told us that he was robbing us. Because there were four of us and all being veterans of street wars, we thought he was joking. I honestly thought any one of us could flatten him. When we balked and laughed at him, he began beating the piss out of us. I was the first to grab him, and my intention was to throw him out before he got hurt. Instead, he broke my fucking arm. This bastard moved so fast, I don't think anyone got a hand on him or even touched him. One of the guys is in the hospital with a major concussion. This kid walked out with thousands in cash, a stash of heroin, crack, and meth, plus an AK47 and about six to eight handguns. We distribute for Bobby Raye. This will not be taken lightly. Find this kid, because on the street, he is a dead man. Higdon, find this kid. Get the shit back and maybe this can go away. If not, Bobby is likely to send some real muscle up here, and you know that he gives two shits about Branson's image. He will bloody the streets."

Higdon thought for a moment. "Okay . . . if I can find Danny. That is his real name, by the way. If I can get all this stuff back for you, we can keep this quiet and keep Bobby Raye out of it?"

"Let me put it to you this way; Hell's Ravens do not want to tell Bobby Raye that some 'kid' came into our house and beat the crap out of four of us and walked out without a scratch or a bullet being fired. Our lives are on the line here. Bobby would believe that we set it up and made up this bullshit, and robbed his dope. I mean, who would believe some punk beats the shit out of four Ravens and cleans us out? If I heard this story, I wouldn't!"

Higdon's cell phone rang. "Higdon here. Yeah, where? Yeah, I know who it belongs to. Throw it into holding. I'll handle it." Wayne looked at the biker. "Well, it appears we've got your weapons and drugs. No trace of any money."

"Where? How?"

"It seems a citizen saw someone throw some stuff away in a dumpster. He thought it looked suspicious and called the police. One of our guys brought it in. I can get it checked out and back to you in the morning. Where do I leave it?"

"No way can I tell the Ravens the cops returned it. Leave it at this kid's apartment. Let me and one of the guys bust the door down and 'take' it back. There was no money?"

"No. This kid lives in the apartment building only a few blocks away. He's at 101 Elm Street. We'll go over there right now. If he has the money, I'll put in the bag with the drugs. Everything will be back in order but the healing."

The undercover cop asked, "What if he doesn't have the money?"

"If we find him, he'll have it. If we don't find him, I don't know what to tell you? We will leave whatever we find so that you can save some face and get it back."

"You know we will trash his place either way."

Higdon smiled. "Expected."

"Can you keep the heat away around noon? I can't give up my cover and these Branson cops will kick my ass."

"I can make that block out of bounds for an hour," Higdon promised.

The undercover cop left, and Higdon and Evans finished their drinks. "Come on, let's go see Danny."

They drove the few blocks and Higdon could already see that Danny's car was nowhere in sight. They entered the building to find the door unlocked. As they looked around, both could recognize that Danny was gone, and was likely never coming back. Evans just scratched his head. "This kid beats up four bikers, takes their cash, weapons, and drugs, then throws the drugs and weapons away and splits? Where to?"

"I'm told his parents are in Florida. Who knows? All I know is that I need some sleep. I need to pick up that shit at the station and plant it here, so that our biker brother can find it . . . and I really want to know what the hell happened when I was unconscious. I have no idea what this kid was thinking or where he went, and frankly, I don't care. All I want is some sleep!"

* * * *

Sitting in his car in the dark, Danny was plotting what to do next. He knew that the people he had robbed only really had one alternative, and that was to hunt him down. So the first thing his did was vacate his apartment, for he knew they could easily trace him from working at Elmer's. Having not earned much, aside from his clothes, he was a minimalist, but not by choice. His income did not afford him much. So there he sat, with all he valued easily stacked in the back seat of his car. *'What is happening to me?'* he wondered as he contemplated his next move. He was fully aware of the changes, both physical and mental, but he had no understanding as to why? Everything about his being was enhanced. His strength seemed unlimited, as well as his speed. He had yet to test their limits. The things that guided his life seemed to become part of his instinctive behavior. Just as he was dedicated to being an informant and helping stop crime, he was instead driven to act.

He glanced at the box in the back seat, which held uncounted thousands, and he smiled. He knew he could get more anytime he wanted, as he knew where nearly all of the illegal activities were. Regardless of being robbed, they could never report it to police. He stared at himself in the rear view mirror. *'Who is this new Danny?'* He had never been aggressive and forceful. The old Danny was passive and quiet. *'Who am I?'* he wondered. The changes in his physiology were of almost mythical proportions, so there was only one person who had knowledge of such things, and that was old Jonah. Danny had known Jonah since he was a boy and they had a relationship that was warm and friendly, almost grandfatherly, although Danny had always considered him 'a little bit out there.' Except, Danny now found himself 'a little bit out there,' and this made Jonah the man to see. He started the car and pointed it in Jonah's direction.

Being in the wee hours, it was unusual for someone to knock on Jonah's door. "Who the hell is it?" Jonah bellowed.

"It's Danny."

Jonah swung the door open and was smiling ear to ear. "Danny!"

"Jonah I need your advice and help."

The old man was beaming, as he always liked Danny. "Just tell me what you need, and you've got it."

"Can we sit?" Danny asked.

Jonah led Danny to his living room and two comfortable overstuffed chairs. "How can I help, young man?"

"Jonah, something happened to me."

Danny began to explain the last few days and how he was helping the police and made the mistake of trying to capture their suspect. He explained how he was thrown through the plate glass window, by what appeared to be an old man. He told of the detectives killing the old man. As Jonah listened, Danny told of sleeping almost coma-like, and awakening to a whole new set of instincts. He described his changes in strength and speed, and a driven aggressive behavior. As Danny spoke, he noticed Jonah's brows furrow and exhibit a look of concern. When he finished, Jonah began asking questions.

"Has your eyesight improved?"

"In fact, yes. I seem to see everything more clearly and my peripheral vision is much broader. Most amazing, is I think I have night vision . . ."

"Has your diet changed?" Jonah asked.

"Yeah . . . yes. I ate a near-raw hamburger today. I have never eaten anything rare in my life."

Jonah could only say, "My God, Danny, Danny, Danny . . . my God."

Danny was now worried. "What is it, Jonah?"

"Were those detectives you were helping named Higdon and Evans?" Danny nodded. "They killed that old man, didn't they?" Danny nodded again. "But this old man was strong enough to throw you through a window?" Again, Danny nodded positive.

"Danny, Danny, Danny . . . did this old man bite you?"

"Yes!" Danny exclaimed. "Yes, he did." Danny lifted his shirt to show a healed scar.

"Danny, I believe you are a werewolf." Jonah said it softly and sadly.

"A werewolf? Nah! No way."

"Danny, I know what you are telling me. Higdon and Evans were hunting the Howler. That old man was the Howler. They shot him dead with silver bullets. Did they ask you to grab him?" Danny shook his head. "Grabbing him was a mistake. When he bit you, he passed on the curse. Danny, you are now the Howler."

Danny arose and began pacing the room. "Great! That's just great! I'm a damned werewolf? What the hell do I do now? I don't want to hurt anyone. How do I get rid of this curse?"

Jonah lamented. "Danny, there is no way to remove it, but you can control it somewhat. During the cycle of the full moon, I would leave. I would take some clothes and go deep in the woods, far away from the population. Go far enough away that you will not make human contact. This way, you will live off the wildlife and will not bring harm to anyone. For three days, during the full moon, when night falls, you will transform into a beast. While you are a beast, you will be mindless and subject only to your primal instincts." Jonah sat silent, but as if realizing it for the first time, he stated seriously, "Danny, you are immortal. You can be wounded, but only killed by a silver bullet to the heart."

"Jonah, how do I live this life? What the hell am I going to do?"

Jonah sat back. "Sit, Danny. I may not be able to tell you what to do, but I can surely tell you some things not to do. I can only pass on stories handed down from those who hunted werewolves many years ago. My first advice would be to find a place to live away from people that might observe your comings and goings and take notice of your behavior. Don't live in one place too long. Maybe stay a year or so, and no longer. Stay away from domestic animals. Dogs, especially, will sense what you are and be immediately threatened. Eat in private. Your preference for rare or raw meat will make people take notice and remember you." Danny knew this to be true from firsthand experience. "If you are wounded, try not to make the wound obvious, if possible. When you are in the wild, you will be the strongest predator in the woods, but you might get into a skirmish, as animals do. When you go to the wilderness, bring clothes, and bandages." Without warning, Jonah picked up his empty cup and threw it at Danny as hard as he could. Without flinching, Danny caught it. "Try not to show your abilities in public. All these things were on my grandpa's list of how to spot a werewolf. Most of all, try to make your disappearance during the full moon a secret. Let no one be aware of that routine. Most people do not believe werewolves even exist, so it is likely that you will never face a silver bullet."

"Do you have one?" Danny asked.

"Yep. I have a whole box."

"Can I have one?"

"Why would you want one?"

Danny looked deep into Jonah's eyes and spoke slowly. "In case I want to end it all. In case I can't live this life. A gun I can get easy, so just give me a single bullet."

Jonah arose and picked a bullet out of the box and threw it to Danny. "Danny, Danny. Actually, if you can find a way to make a living that accommodates your schedule and you isolate yourself during the full moon's cycle, you can have a charmed life."

Danny shook his head. "Some charmed life. I spend eternity alone, always moving, always lying, always paranoid."

"You need not live alone. You can date. Just be careful not to reveal your abilities."

"Jonah, I am doomed to a lonely life." Danny hung his head.

"Now mind you, I'm not suggesting anything, but if my Alice were alive, I would have welcomed being with her forever. Not a day goes by where I don't miss that woman."

"Are you saying I can take a wife?"

"Yes . . . er . . . no, more of a mate for all eternity." Jonah snickered at the thought. "Hell, if you choose the wrong woman, it will be hell!"

"What would I do? Just bite her?"

"You do that, and you'll be together for all time."

"Can I come and talk to you after tonight?" Danny asked politely.

"Danny, you are always welcome here, except during the full moon. During that time you will be an animal. You will kill to eat without regard. My Grandpa told a story of a man that turned into a werewolf and tore his whole family apart. During those days, you will not be able to reason. Danny, during those three days, never, ever, come anywhere near here. I only have a short time left on this world and I want every minute. I will shoot you dead. In fact, having my .38 loaded with silver bullets, might make me the only person that can shoot you dead. I love you as a son, but during the full moon I will not know you. Understand?"

Danny was only beginning to truly understand.

*   *   *   *

Christian and Katherine flew to their mountain and sat on a ledge outside a cave that would become their home. Staring out at the dark lake that had become a mirror of the sky above, they inhaled the pure beauty of the night. They had not spoken a word from the time that Christian had helped end Aaron's life. They sat in silence, as Katherine knew Christian's action weighed heavy on his mind. Finally, Katherine felt it was time to break the silence. She moved close to him and placed her hand on his.

"Christian, what did you do?"

"You saw what I did. Reluctantly, I helped end Aaron's life."

"Why does it bother you so?" Katherine, as relatively new vampire, knew that killing without conscience was a blessing that all vampires possessed, so this was a reaction that appeared as an emotion that she didn't quite understand.

"I robbed Aaron of all his eternity. Once, when I faced that old man and could not cross the threshold to kill him, I told him I would find him and end his life. He answered me with something so profound that it has remained in the forefront of my mind. He said, 'So you end my life? I only have but a few years left. If we find you and kill you, you will lose all eternity.' He was so very correct; so taking Aaron's eternity burdens my mind."

"Was there another choice?" Katherine asked.

"I would like to believe not. I know firsthand that Aaron's anger and fury would not be satisfied, even if he killed this man. I knew he would not have regard for his being until he found a mate. He would have continued killing with complete disregard. He would have become a significant threat to our existence. I would like to think he is at peace."

Katherine smiled and squeezed Christian's hand. "You are very old and thus, very wise. There is no doubt your instincts have served you well. I would not second guess your action. Yes, Aaron is at peace. There was no doubt he was in great pain and anguish. Every night was torture to him. He no longer viewed what he had; he only mourned his loss. I don't think he ever could have recovered from his loss. His cup would have always been evaluated as half empty. How did you recover?"

Christian looked upon her fondly. "I was fortunate. I met you. Had I not, I would have continued killing indiscriminately, likely until someone did to me as was done to Aaron. You fulfilled me. In the end, had not Ted Scott demanded a confrontation, I would never have killed him. After finding you, I was content to walk away."

"Why was I so special?" Katherine asked, of course, wanting to hear every word.

"You are a thing of beauty. You are cultured, intelligent, and consider the night as a gift and not a curse. The one characteristic I admire, is that you kill for sustenance, never for cruelty or sadistic enjoyment. Anne had a cruel and careless tendency that I always had to control. When I look at you, I see beauty."

If vampires could blush, Katherine would have been blushing. "What of this Higdon?"

"I am not sure."

"Do you think we can trust him?"

"We already have," Christian stated firmly.

"How can we be sure we abide by his wishes?"

"Discretion. Discretion has never failed me."

"Have you ever put your trust in a warm blood before?"

"No. However, it seems they have a whole new world in which to cope. Because of you, I have been exposed to modern culture and I do not like what I see. It seems they have become as tribes. I see a world where despicable types are free to sell various mind-destroying potions on the street freely. I see groups of racially varied men preying on the weak in uncontrolled gangs. Prostitution is rampant. Then, there are these homosexuals who band together as a tribe and culture of their own. Higdon talked of pedophiles that have proliferated and prey on children. He even spoke of them not having justice any longer and setting them free. I see homeless everywhere and a society that overlooks their plight. In perspective, are we not worth his trust? Should he be a good and moral man, his job has become an impossible one. How does he maintain law and order with no absolute solution, other than death? I believe that is what we represent. We are his absolute solution to the extreme portion of his problems."

"Should we just continue unguided, hoping that our choices are correct?"

"To a certain extent, yes. However, I believe we should communicate and review our boundaries."

"So, we will meet with him again?"

"Yes. He does not seem to fear us. I always sensed a fear in this Evans, but Higdon is different. Either he viewed us as an asset, or was blissfully ignorant. There is also the possibility that he is just very brave. I am not repelled by him, for some strange reason. I do sense he views us as the lesser of many evils, but he possesses no hatred of our kind. If in satisfying our hunger, we can also assist Higdon in mending society, I see no harm."

"What of this Howler?"

"My instinct still dictates to take care. I know little of werewolves. At least we know to be aware of him during the cycle of the full moon." Christian did not know that Higdon had thought he had eliminated the werewolf. "I suspect that this Howler suffers a curse of some kind. Whether he can be reasoned with or not, remains to be seen. Aaron described him as being mindless, ruthless, and with incredible strength that is beyond ours. This, of course, also remains to be seen. This is a subject to ask Higdon. I wonder if the warm bloods are aware of this Howler? If they are, do they have a solution to eliminate him? We must find out, but until then, we will take great care."

"Should we feel fear?"

"Fear is something we never feel. We may have traces of emotions—some instilled, others from distant memories—but fear is not among them. We are vampires. We never feel fear, we instill it in others. I will never seek confrontation for the sake of confrontation itself, but must I face this Howler, it will be with full fury, as this is now our domain."

"Our domain . . . I like the sound of that."

* * * *

It was twilight, and Danny drove slightly west to Reeds Spring. The highway was empty and deserted, as it matched the whole town. Once it was a tourist and visitor's stop on the way to Branson, but a few years ago it was literally condemned to death. A new bypass was built that took traffic around the town, which slowly left an empty Main Street. Businesses eventually left or went bust. Now, it appeared a ghost town, with little to no traffic and boarded-up store fronts. With reduced tax revenue, city services were cut to a minimum, and the pot holes began to appear in the road. At this time of day, with the mist taking on the glow of daybreak, this appeared the perfect location for a werewolf.

Danny knew where he was headed. On the deserted road outside of town, amidst overgrown acreage, was a rundown house. Beside the road was a 'trailer for rent' sign. Danny drove on a weed covered path that was once a driveway, and knocked on the door. He was greeted by a voice that was obviously upset. "Who the hell is knocking at this time of the morning, damn it!"

"Sir? I want to rent that trailer," Danny yelled.

Needing the money, the old man quickly opened the door. "Well, it's pretty far back, if you want a look."

"How much?" Danny asked.

"Well, it's all furnished and comes with utilities. I'd like to get $400 a month."

"Sounds great. How about I give you two months in advance?" Danny offered.

The old man smiled ear to ear, as no one had even looked at it in a year. While Danny went to his car and got the money, the old man wrote a receipt. When Danny returned, the old man asked, "Who do I make the receipt out to? What's your name, boy?"

Knowing the old man was likely unfamiliar with anything current, Danny answered, "Make it out to Charlie, Charlie Sheen."

"Okay Charlie. Let me get the keys."

As he did, Danny looked back at the trailer some five acres beyond the house, near wilderness. '*Perfect,*' he thought.

The old man handed him the keys and issued a strong warning. "Now, Charlie, no parties. And if I even smell you cooking drugs, I will shoot you in the ass myself!"

Danny smiled. "Sir, I like peace and quiet and living alone, and I don't touch drugs."

Danny drove back to the trailer, and it was all he needed. It looked fairly new on the inside, as it was hardly used and sealed up. He emptied his personal belongings and sat, staring at the sunrise. He was aware of one problem, and that was the street people he had robbed would be looking for him. His car and license plates were traceable. However, being a Missourian, he was aware of all the laws. In Missouri, any vehicle categorized as a 'farm' vehicle did not need license plates, and in fact, the driver of such vehicle only had to be over sixteen and didn't even need a driver's license. Danny knew both Honda and Suzuki made vehicles about the size of a jeep that qualified and were 'street' legal. So his next stop was just down the highway to the farm vehicle lot. There, he would trade his car, destroy his license plates, and it would be the final act in order to 'disappear.' All he had to do is remember that his new name was 'Charlie.'

By mid-morning he was driving his used Honda. It resembled a combination Jeep and pick-up, as it had a flat bed for hauling hay. It was actually kind of trendy looking. Driving it, there were no license plates to identify him, and he could only be stopped if he broke the law, as this was an official 'farm' vehicle. Having left his apartment, deserted his job, and gotten rid of his car, he was '*in the wind*,' as they say. Feeling the stubble on his face and looking in the rear view mirror, he realized he had also taken on a whole new look, and he liked it. The old 'clean cut' Danny was gone.

As he left Reeds Spring and entered Branson West, something was calling him. For some strange reason, he felt the urge to enter the Branson West Animal Adventure. It was a tourist attraction that had mostly animals that were germane to the state. However, in order to attract tourists, they had some larger animals, like tigers and lions, as they were also licensed as a sanctuary. Danny pulled over and stepped out. They had just opened, and he paid his $12 and walked down the path lined with arrows, guiding a visitor's direction. As he walked, he felt a strange sympathy for all these proud animals. He began to notice something strange. As he passed each cage, the large cats immediately moved as far from Danny as they could get. He understood their body language, as they were retreating and submitting in fear. There was no doubt they all feared him. He remembered Jonah's words to avoid domestic animals, but now he knew it also applied to most all animals with the exception of dogs . . . and wolves.

Going further down the path and past the large attention-getting cats, the animals became smaller. The raccoons retreated in fright. Ahead, he could see a young woman inside a cage. It appeared she was sketching an animal, or possibly taking notes. When he moved closer, he saw that the focus of her attention was a wolf. He watched from a distance as, like him, she was wearing all black. Rather than the image of an 'artist' with an easel, she was, instead, sitting relaxed with the pad balanced on her thigh, with her legs crossed and unconsciously kicking her lower leg back and forth, as if in concentration. When he moved closer to the cage door, the wolf took immediate notice. It was the first animal that did not retreat.

Danny walked a bit closer to the gate, and as he did, the woman looked up, as he caught her attention.

"May I step into the enclosure?" he asked.

She smiled. "Your funeral. If she doesn't take to you, you'll know pretty quick and just step out."

She was a bit surprised, as the wolf looked to Danny with interest, and showed no aggressive or defensive body language. The girl studied him. It seemed coincidence that he was also dressed in black—her favorite color.

"She's beautiful. Does she have a name?" Danny asked.

The young woman pointed to the wolf's legs. "See the dark marking on her feet? We call her Boots, but I affectionately call her Booteet."

Just hearing the name, the wolf approached slowly, as Danny opened the gate and stepped in. The woman had no idea of what to expect. Typically, the wolf avoided most people and even the handlers. She expected Booteet to bolt for the enclosure. Instead, the huge female wolf moved toward the gate and rolled on her back, in complete submission. The young woman stared in awe.

"I have never seen her do anything like that! You must be emitting a strong 'alpha' signal."

As she moved closer, Danny realized how naturally beautiful she was. He was captured by her thick, brown shoulder length hair glistening in the sunlight. "Hi," he said, timidly. "Do you mind?" He began scratching the female wolf on her stomach. Meanwhile, the young woman stood, completely amazed.

"She is gentle, but not that gentle. How did you do that?"

"Animals always seem to either love me or hate me," Danny explained.

She extended her hand. "Hi, I'm Laura."

Danny hesitated. "Hi, I'm . . . Charlie. Charlie Sheen."

She laughed. "Come on now. I'd sooner believe Mel Gibson!"

Danny smiled. "I get that all the time, but that's my name! He actually stole my name, because his is really Carlos Estavez. However, I don't do drugs, nor do I hang out with hookers."

Laura laughed. "You're for real?"

"Yeah, just call me Charlie. Is this wolf always this tame?"

"Actually, no. She allows me to feed her, and now and then pet her, but until now, I thought she was wild and that I had an exclusive relationship."

"What is your favorite animal, Laura?"

"The wolf. I think she knows that, which is why she tolerates me. Don't say it, I know. Most people like the lions and tigers, but she is my baby. Wolves are smart and resourceful, family oriented, loyal, and fearless. Look at how beautiful she is. Yeah, it's weird. Much like my favorite bird."

Danny asked. "That is?"

"The Raven. The Raven is not only beautiful, it's one of the smartest birds on the planet and contrary to popular belief, is actually a symbol of good fortune."

As she talked, Danny could feel her love and admiration of what she spoke of, and began to feel drawn to her. He looked deep into her light brown eyes. "You're an artist?"

"I try."

"Can I see?"

She showed the sketch she had been working on. Danny studied it. "You captured her regal personality. I would know by viewing this sketch that Booteet, here, is your subject."

As he studied her sketch, she studied him. Blonde and tall, there was nothing ominous about him, but she felt a darkness below the surface. He looked directly into her eyes. "Laura, can I call you sometime?"

Returning the look, Laura saw something deep within Danny's innocent blue eyes. Something that was drawing her in.

She lifted his hand and pulled a marker from her pocket. As he watched, she wrote her phone number on his hand. "Here, now you won't lose it," she laughed.

Danny immediately took his cell phone from his pocket and dialed the number. Laura walked to the bench where she had been drawing and picked up her phone. "Hello?" she answered, in a cartoon character voice.

"What the hell kind of voice is that? Betty Boop?" Danny laughed.

"I like to do that. Deal with it," she retorted.

"Laura, you think we could share a **bite** sometime?"

Chapter Ten

Wayne Higdon was up early and raided the property room at the police station. He quickly gathered all of the weapons and drugs taken from the Hell's Ravens that Danny had stolen, and also borrowed an additional five thousand in cash from confiscated drug money. He hoped it would do, as he had no idea how much Danny had actually stolen from them. Higdon wanted to help his undercover friend, and also wanted to avoid having the area's king of vice, Bobby Raye, from focusing on Branson. He drove to Danny's empty apartment and planted everything as if Danny had hidden the stuff. He put the weapons in the closet, the drugs under the sink, and the money under the mattress. He then left for breakfast and joined Mike Evans at Elmer's.

"Wayne, I think I will leave tomorrow on the morning bus. I think my work is done here and can no longer be of much help."

"Will you do me a favor, Mike? Go with me tonight. I'm going to test my communication ability with this vampire and get a better feel for what I am dealing with."

Mike smiled. "Buddy, you are dealing with the devil."

Higdon thought for a moment. "You're right . . . but if I can get the devil to rid me of some demons, why the hell not?"

"What is it you are going to test?" Mike wondered.

"Can I really call him? Can I channel him to a specific target?"

"Hmm . . . do you really think you can use him as a weapon? I don't think so. You see, he can't go into private residences unless invited, so all he can pick off are those who are out in the open."

"The bad guys can't stay indoors forever . . ." Higdon responded.

"So you're envisioning a vampire hit man?"

Higdon paused in thought. "Yeah . . . something like that."

Mike shook his head. "I'm not sure if you're dreaming or having a nightmare. I will be back in a few weeks to see how this all pans out, and yes, I'll go with you tonight."

"By the way, did you hear the news or see the headlines?"

"Nah; when you live it like we do, it gets old. How they distort and spin everything makes me sick."

"Well, Branson reported that some meth-head tore up the hotel. They gave a vague description and stated he is sought after," Wayne reported.

Mike just laughed. "No mention that he escaped by flying up forty feet and crashing through a sky light?"

"Hey, this is Branson!"

*　*　*　*

Branson has many motorcycle clubs that visit, such as the 'Gold Wings,' a group of seniors that drive elaborate three wheelers with side cars, so the sound of a large group of motorcycles didn't raise an eyebrow until these bikers came into view. The sight of a dozen Hell's Ravens, and people scattered or went indoors. The procession pulled into the old area of downtown and parked clustered in front of Danny's old apartment building. Anyone observing could see by their expressions that they were not visiting Branson for the entertainment. A few onlookers watched as they stomped their way into the building, and anyone nearby could hear the crash as they literally broke down the door. Once inside, they began destroying everything in sight. They quickly found their weapons and drugs along with their cash. However, after counting the cash, it was seven thousand short. The leader was angry as he made his determination. "We can make up the seven grand ourselves to keep Bobby off our asses, but that kid is dead. I will personally give five large to the Raven that brings him in . . . or . . . any parts of him that I can recognize."

If there were such things as 'good' bad guys, Hell's Ravens were it. For the most part, they stayed out of sight of the tourists and never gathered around any tourist areas. They did distribute drugs and were part of Bobby Raye's distribution network, but they abided by the Branson image. They rarely did anything to bring negative press to their conservative tourist town. They also kept other bad elements out of Branson who might not function with the same discretion. So it was unusual that after trashing Danny's apartment that they piled into Elmer's. As they grabbed a number of booths, their presence was greeted by a hush. As they filed in, Wayne could see that it was likely that by planting the goods at Danny's, he had satisfied them, as they all seemed in a good mood.

Mike had to hide his smile, as one of the hulking bikers carried in with him a tiny Shih Tzu.

"Don't laugh," Wayne warned.

"Come on, you have to admit . . . it's a little funny," Mike snickered.

"I always lived by what my dad once told me. 'Big dog, fear the dog. Small dog, fear the owner.' This appears the ultimate example of that rule."

The undercover cop who was playing the role of a biker gave Wayne a nod, letting him know that all was okay, as no words could be exchanged between them. The Ravens were all aware that Higdon and Evans were cops, and were on their best behavior—not that they would cause trouble, since Elmer's was a local pub and on 'neutral' ground. Higdon was not surprised when the leader motioned for Elmer to come over to his table.

"What can I do for you, gentlemen?" Elmer asked.

"You have a delivery man named Danny?"

Elmer scratched his head. "Well, I once did, but he literally disappeared. We have not seen or heard from him in days. We suspect he may have gone to visit his parents somewhere in Florida."

"Well, if you should hear from him, let him know that we would like to see him."

The Ravens wanting to see Danny didn't sound good, so Elmer asked, "Is he in trouble?"

The leader smiled. "Nah! We just owe him a little something and want to pay him back." The other Ravens all laughed.

"If I run into him, I'll tell him." Elmer walked away, befuddled.

Overhearing the conversation, Wayne was worried for Danny and commented to Mike, "When the Ravens owe you something, it usually means it has something to do with great pain and a trip to the ER, if one is lucky! I hope I can find Danny first and warn him."

"What's your day like?" Mike asked.

"I'm taking the day off and taking Abby shopping. You?"

"I'm heading back to what's left of the hotel and I'm going to soak in the pool. Will you come to pick me up this evening?"

"Yeah. Don't bring any weapons."

Mike shook his head. "Shit! You really do trust that monster."

* * * *

On a mountain top west of Branson in Kimberling City, sat a little known restaurant called "Ma's." That is where Danny took Laura for an early lunch. They sat facing each other and she studied his movements. There was something strange and different about this 'Charlie Sheen,' but she couldn't put her finger on it. She stared at him with her penetrating eyes.

"Tell me the truth. Is your name really Charlie Sheen?"

His eyes met hers. "To the rest of the world I am Charlie Sheen, but to you, I am Danny."

Her curiosity peaked. "Are you a fugitive of some kind?"

Danny smiled. "No, not as you might imagine. I have no problems with the law. However, I do have some problems with some lawless types."

Laura was puzzled. "So . . . criminals are looking for you?"

"Yeah, you might say that."

"Why?"

"I guess I'm now a professional vigilante. That's how I make my living."

"Who pays you?" Laura asked.

"They do!" Danny laughed.

Laura was definitely confused. "Explain."

Danny explained that there were a number of vices that ran rampant in Branson. She was amazed as he related that he would merely clean them out and temporarily shut them down. In doing so, because these people are involved in criminal activities, they can never call the authorities and can only come looking for him. So Danny was now Charlie Sheen, driving an unlicensed, untraceable vehicle, and living in a remote trailer. Laura began to view him as almost a super hero. She could only wonder where this level of courage could come from—or was it simply reckless abandon or a death wish?

Men are typically looked upon as predictable in their sexual preferences. The vast majority believe that every man longs for the Playboy centerfold. Nothing could be less true. Men vary in their preferences like flavors of ice cream. Some men like tall women, some prefer short. Some men like blondes and others brunettes. Some men prefer ultra-feminine, while others like women who are athletic and competitive. However, the real key to a man's interest has nothing to do with any of these variables, nor any others one might imagine. The one common denominator that even some men are not aware of themselves is that the key to a man's very soul is in the woman's eyes, and Laura's warm, brown eyes captured Danny. Danny had always been a free spirit and was never prone to any permanent relationship, so it was a whole new feeling looking into her eyes when he realized this was to be his '*mate*' for all eternity. He needed to know if this were even possible? So he began probing. As they conversed, he found she was an only child and her parents were living in Kansas. She had few friends and spent most her time with the animals. Laura was a very independent woman. He decided that she could easily become his mate without many social complications.

"You're just staring at me," she stated, as his gaze had been fixed on her.

"I find you beautiful," he said softly. She blushed.

"Come on, look at me. I am in work clothes and I have no make-up on. Beautiful, I am not. Have you had your eyes checked?" she kidded, being a bit embarrassed.

Danny studied her jewelry. "What's with the skull ring?" In his thinking, it was an indicator of a "dark" side, whether she knew it or not.

"I just happen to like it," she answered innocently.

"Where did you learn to draw like that?"

"University of Missouri, Kansas City."

"Well, I'll tell you something. I'm no art expert, but from what I saw, being able to project feeling like you did . . . that kind of talent is not taught in school."

"Thank you. Maybe drawing Booteet brings out a certain feeling in my work."

"I don't see a watch?"

"I hate watches! What's with the interrogation . . . Charlie?"

"I want to know everything about you. Will you have dinner with me tonight?"

"I'd love to," she answered, as her attraction to Danny was near equal to his, as there was something dark and mysterious below the surface that she was drawn to.

After lunch, he followed her back to the compound where she returned to the female wolf's area. Laura was amazed as her Booteet, upon seeing Danny, came running over and once again, rolled over on her back in complete submission, begging attention. Danny scratched her stomach and praised her, as she rolled back and forth, enjoying the moment. Laura just stood off to side and watched. Then, a strange thing happened. When Danny stepped away to leave, the wolf sprang to its feet. Booteet looked at Laura and growled, moving slowly away. Laura called out to her, and was completely ignored in return. Now, she was totally confused.

"Booteet has never reacted to me like that before?"

After making their arrangements to meet for dinner, Danny left. Laura then went to see what the problem was with the female wolf who had always befriended her. The wolf shied away and hid within the enclosure. Laura was completely puzzled as to why the change in the animal's behavior toward her? Of course, what Laura was unaware of, was the female wolf was drawn to Danny and now sensed Laura as competition!

* * * *

The sun set and the lights of Branson glistened. As usual, the town came alive with tourists and traffic that moved at a snail's pace down the main drag, Route 76. Far in the distance on a mountainside, Katherine and Christian surveyed their domain. They scanned the mountain tops, the deep valleys of woods, and the lake that reflected the dark sky like a huge mirror. Off in the distance, the glow of the city illuminated the wilderness for miles.

Katherine sighed. "Beautiful, isn't it?"

"Yes, this is a special place."

"Theater?" she asked.

"Possibly," Christian replied. "But not before we eat."

They took to the sky and scanned the ground, searching for any warm blooded movement in the darkness. They could easily see the small warm blooded beings scurrying in the night, but nothing of the size they desired. The human body contains 6 quarts of blood, and a vampire only needs 3 for a good meal. Katherine and Christian never had a problem sharing, so one human victim was enough. It was always a feast when more than one victim came into view. That was the case when they observed two motorcycles driving toward Branson on a dark highway. With his keen vision, Christian could see the biker vests and knew that these were not innocent citizens. '*Undesirables,*' he immediately thought.

"Shall we go for a ride?" he asked.

"I always love this!" Katherine replied.

They swooped down and hovered above the motorcycles. The drivers were totally unaware that vampires were just above their heads. It was Katherine that landed on the back seat of the biker trailing behind. With the roar of the engines, his scream went unheard. Katherine grabbed him around the waist, as if she was taking a normal ride. The driver could not see his unexpected rider, but the fact of being grabbed scared him into a panic. The motorcycle swerved; Katherine merely lifted him from the motorcycle as it tumbled off the road. His first instinct was to defend himself, and as she set him to the ground he turned and swung, wildly punching at air.

"Get the fuck away from me!" he screamed.

Katherine smiled. "You know what you are?"

"Yeah, lady, but I have no idea what the hell you are!"

"You are an undesirable!" Katherine's face began to morph into one of a beast, and her teeth dripped saliva. All the brave biker could utter was, "Oh shit!"

In a flash, Katherine was upon him and biting his throat. His final glimpse was the sight of his companion's tail lights fading away. Katherine gorged until she heard his heart stop.

This was not the first time Christian had done this, so he knew that if he lifted the biker quickly, the motorcycle would veer out of control and crash, which is exactly what he did. As the biker screamed, kicked, and became hysterical, Christian bit a gaping wound in his throat. He fed until he was satisfied and the heartbeat went silent. He then threw the body with force onto the wreckage. Aside from a few unusual wounds, it would appear as a double motorcycle accident.

As Katherine joined Christian, he smiled. "This is hard to fathom that we are actually helping this society."

"It speaks for the sad state of their culture."

"If this is all that Higdon requires, I do not predict that we would have conflict."

"Have you ever lived with a warm blood knowing you exist?"

"Only after my pursuit of Anne's killer did anyone know I existed. For 120 years I was transparent to the world of humans. Now, it seems strange to deal with one. In fact, I did not know I was capable of such trust."

Katherine gave a slight smile. "You know, we can kill him at any time."

"But we will not. For one, he needs us, and two, his friend—this Evans—would attempt to avenge him. For now, I am satisfied with this arrangement."

"Can we walk among the people?" Katherine pleaded.

"If it makes you happy, let us go."

They took to the air and floated over the dark mysterious valleys as they made their way toward town. Christian, still being a bit uncomfortable walking and mixing with humans, understood that this was a treat for Katherine. He knew that he could eventually achieve her comfort level, but for now he preferred the openness of the boardwalk. They landed in the edge of the woods along the furthest border of one of the outdoor parking lots. They walked hand and hand, and quickly observed a warm blooded being moving between cars. They watched, as he broke a window and was stealing items from the car. They both had the same thought. '*Undesirable!*' They shared a mischievous glance, and already knew what the other was thinking. Since they already had fed, and they knew this '*undesirable*' could not report anything to the authorities, they would have some fun and toy with him.

"Let me begin first," Katherine whispered.

She moved between cars and intentionally made some noise so that the man could be aware that she was there. "Please help me!" she pleaded.

He looked around and seeing nothing but her, he questioned, "Help you with what, lady?" As he asked, she saw his eyes look her up and down, and in this dark deserted parking lot, she knew what he was thinking.

"There is someone following me," she stated in a frightened voice.

He looked around again, and still seeing nothing, he asked, "Who? Where?"

The man did not hear Christian come from behind, nor see him morph into the face of a beast. So Katherine just smiled and replied, "Look behind you." When he turned, Katherine also turned into her '*vampire*' face. The man spun around and was speechless. He began backing away until he backed into Katherine. Without turning around he managed to utter, "What the fuck is that?" When he turned to face her, seeing her form, he literally became hysterical, screaming and jumping over the hood of the car, trying to escape. Christian grabbed him by the back of his shirt. The man just screamed.

"Let me go! I didn't do anything to you! Please, please!"

Christian growled. "Silence! Fortunately for you, we have already eaten, or I would make short work of your life. You see, I only kill what I eat. You are committing criminal activities in my domain. I would not continue with this illegal behavior."

The man was shaking uncontrollably and could hardly speak. "I won't. I promise. Please let me go." He began to cry.

"You are pitiful! Never let me find you here again." Christian released him and as he passed Katherine, she hissed, deep and loud.

As the man ran away not looking back, they returned to their human form. Katherine laughed. "I believe he wet himself."

Christian wondered. "Would this Higdon have wanted me to kill him?"

"I don't believe he wishes us to feed off of petty thieves."

"Then let us walk."

Hand and hand they proceeded to the boardwalk and joined the crowd moving along the lakefront. With their tanned and healthy look, they drew not a glance, except for those admiring their appearance. Christian, for the first time, was beginning to feel comfortable. He began asking questions to satisfy his curiosities. Observing a large flat screen television in a store window, he asked, "From where do these images originate?" Katherine went on to explain the various ways that images could be displayed. Christian felt pure enjoyment without a care of his surroundings. He knew Katherine was correct in choosing this as their domain.

They walked hand and hand along the boardwalk, which was now lined with more chic shops and displays. They slowly approached a sidewalk café. Christian stopped in his tracks and stared at a couple, seated at a table for two. His mood turned serious and Katherine sensed a problem.

"What bothers you?" she asked.

"Can you feel it?"

"Feel what?" She was confused by the change in his demeanor.

"Concentrate," he stated sternly.

She turned her senses to her surroundings, and felt exactly what Christian was sensing. "I feel it. It is definitely negative. I feel repelled."

"Look to the café. That young man sitting with a woman is not human. He is warm blooded, but could present a threat. I have only come across this type of being once in my existence. Let us observe and learn."

Their attention happened to be on Danny and Laura, who were enjoying a coffee and watching the passersby. Danny had taken Laura out for the evening, and although the Branson boardwalk was not his preferred choice, he looked to please her. To anyone else, they appeared the ideal young couple . . . but to Christian and Katherine, who were keeping their distance, they were a mystery.

"What do you think he is?" Katherine asked.

"All I can determine is that he is not human and he is not a vampire."

"Will that woman he is with become a victim?"

"I don't feel that. I feel she is with him of her own choosing, though she may not understand what he truly is."

As Christian and Katherine lingered, pretending to window shop, Danny and Laura sipped their coffee and held hands as lovers might do. Then, Christian picked up another onlooker who was staring at Danny. This man motioned to his large burly companions, and pointed in Danny's direction. He happened to be the drug dealer that Danny had robbed the previous day. As Christian and Katherine observed, the three men walked toward Danny and Christian could sense the hostility in the air. "Watch," Christian whispered.

Only a small wrought iron fence rail separated the café area from the crowd walking the boardwalk. All three men stepped over the fence and approached Danny's table. Danny immediately recognized his previous victim and said to Laura, "Just get up and leave. I'll meet you at the car. Please, no questions." Laura was confused, but did exactly what Danny stated, sensing something in his voice that was most serious. As she quickly left, she brushed against the three unsavory looking men. They stood surrounding Danny who was sitting calmly, still sipping his coffee. The man who he had robbed became agitated, as Danny acted like they were not even there. Then, the dealer spoke.

"I admit, you are one cool dude, but now is the time for payback. You can start by forking over the money."

Danny just smiled. "It seems you brought along a few friends to accompany you to the hospital. Have you called 911 yet?"

"You are funny, but the only one going to the hospital is you!" he threatened.

No sooner than he said the words, Danny arose. In a flash, he grabbed a chair and hit the man full force, knocking him across tables and sending him flying. He then faced the two remaining men, one of which was already reaching toward him. Danny grabbed his head, slamming it to the table. Without even looking, he launched a powerful side kick, causing the other man to tumble over the wrought iron fence backwards. Danny then boldly reached for his wallet and dropped a fifty dollar bill on the table. Then, he simply stepped over the wrought iron fence and disappeared into the crowd. The only thing about this whole sequence was that it happened at almost an inhuman speed, and one that only a vampire could clearly see.

"That was quite a display," Christian stated. "I sense he has great power, as there was no emotion attached to that action. That reaction was merely a casual reflex. Had he wanted to kill those men, regardless of their size, he easily could have done so. We must learn more of this creature. Whatever you do, remember that feeling. Always keep safe distance. I have no knowledge of what manner of being that was, but I do sense that it is not to be trifled with."

"Well, since this is only the second one you have come across in over a hundred years, hopefully he is a rare being," she reasoned.

"But this rare being may have residence in our domain. We would be wise to remain diligent of his presence."

They continued their stroll, enjoying the lights and music, and viewing the elaborate window displays. Upon seeing a beautiful dress, Christian commented, "This would look wonderful on you."

"What would you have me do, reach in and take it?" Katherine laughed.

Christian reached into his vest. "Did you forget we have plenty of money?"

Katherine smiled. "You think I should?"

"If it makes you happy, then why not?"

It was the first time Christian had ever been in a 'ladies' store, and he enjoyed it. Being tall, dark, and handsome, he drew looks from all of the ladies he encountered. When Katherine came out in her new dress, she was smiling, as she felt it looked elegant. Suddenly her smile evaporated when the sales girl stated, "Here, see how beautiful you look!" as she pointed to a full length mirror. Christian immediate began looking around, and became aware that he was also standing near a full length mirror. He looked to Katherine and she understood that they must leave immediately. If one human became aware that they had no reflection, complete hysteria might develop.

"No, it's just not me." Katherine backed into the dressing room and as she did, Christian quickly left the store, waiting outside. When Katherine joined him, he stated the obvious. "I guess we must always remember who and what we are."

Katherine grabbed his hand. "Well, it was a nice thought, but really, we have no closet in that cave anyway!"

They both laughed at the thought, as they enjoyed their stroll.

Back at the sidewalk café, Officer Ennis was trying his best to put some logic to the report he was going to have to write. He had one known drug dealer with a broken collar bone and a concussion. Then, he had two well known tough guys, both over six foot and 250 pounds, busted up. One with his head split open and the other with broken ribs and a possible punctured lung. All anyone had seen were these three approach a young man described as rather clean cut and ordinary, who was said to have done all this damage. It just made no sense. He approached the owner of the café.

"Sir, are you sure there were not more men involved here? I know you don't want the reputation for having bar brawls breaking out, but I am familiar with those three that are on their way to the ER, and it is just hard to believe that one guy did this to them. Are you sure this is all that happened?" Officer Ennis was completely perplexed.

The owner scratched his head. "Honestly, they never came into the place. The young couple shared some barbecued chicken and was having Cappuccino, and those three stepped over the railing. The next thing I knew, I heard a crash and came out and saw the three guys lying on the ground and the couple was gone. The young man had left a fifty dollar bill for eighteen dollars worth of chicken and coffee. The onlookers all scattered, but I heard that this young man defended himself very well. I assume because they came over the railing that they must have attacked him, but I'm not really positive. The witnesses left very quickly . . . all but that young man standing over there. He watched it."

The owner pointed to a kid who was leaning against a lamppost. Officer Ennis cringed. The young man was covered in tattoos and had piercings throughout his face and neon streaked hair. Ennis walked over and asked, "Did you witness anything here?"

The young man looked at him and grinned. "Yeah, I saw this guy open a can of whoop ass on those muscle heads."

"How did it go down?" Ennis asked.

"This couple was having some caffeine. Like, you know, they were just chilling. Out of nowhere these three dudes jump the rail and it looked like they was hassling him."

"Hassling him, how?"

"Man, it looked like they were getting all up in his face, you know?"

"Then what happened?"

"I think he asked his girlfriend to leave, because she split. Then it was like he went all Bruce Lee on them. I mean he kicked their ass in two seconds. I mean, Spiderman has nothing on this dude. It was amazing!"

"So he was just defending himself?"

"Yeah, like, I would guess so. I have seen those busted up dudes before and they are bad news wherever they go. I just thought it was so cool. For a second I thought they were filming a movie or something. It was that awesome. I think I even cheered."

"You cheered?" Officer Ennis questioned.

"Yeah! I said, 'Dude! Give it to them bastards.'"

Officer Ennis walked away and didn't waste time even getting a name, as he judged by his eyes that this kid was high on something. Officer Ennis had been on the Branson force for three years and as far as he was concerned, he would just add this whole incident to his list of weird Branson happenings.

* * * *

Danny and Laura were driving to his trailer when she asked, "What exactly happened back there?"

"Oh, just some guys that I had a misunderstanding with. I took care of it."

"Well, you look no worse for the wear?"

"I simply explained to them my situation, and we came to an agreement."

"So that loud crash that I heard as I left was them agreeing with you?" she laughed.

"Nah, a waiter just dropped a tray of food."

Laura had no idea why, but it was love at first sight with Danny. He was good looking, but the attraction went far beyond appearance. There was something magnetic about him. She realized he was mysterious and that she had no idea of what his secrets were, but she wanted to be with him. They drove west to Reeds Spring, where he took her to his trailer. She was impressed, as she found it to be neat and clean. "Do you have family here in Missouri?" she asked.

"No; my parents retired to Florida some years ago. I guess I have some family in Illinois, but I have never really known them. I'm alone here."

"You grew up here?"

"Yeah. Born and bred."

"You must know a lot of people around here."

"I once did when I was in high school, but most left for bigger cities and I took to making night delivers during college. I saw so much crap happening around here that I became an informant for the Branson P.D., but my contact died recently. He had a partner who seemed like an okay guy, but instead I decided to do what the police can't. I mean, they have to do surveillance and have witnesses and read them their rights and all that bullshit. Since I know where all these places are, I just fleece their ass and what can they do? Call the police? It is the perfect way to make a good living, plus, it's all tax free."

"What if they have guns?"

"So far, I haven't faced that yet."

Laura just shook her head in wonder. "Danny, you are either the bravest man I have ever met, or definitely the most insane."

"Well, this isn't Chicago where bullets would be flying. In Chicago, those guys tonight would have likely shot me in a second. This is Branson! Everything is kept on the down low. These A-holes that exist by breaking the laws don't really realize they have no protection from the law either. Actually, if the general public did the same thing, crime would take a huge dip. Think about it. These drug houses and whorehouses can't be calling 911?"

"How did you decide to even do this?" Laura wondered.

"I used to deliver food to all these places that did various illegal activities. I would report them to my friend, Jerry Cunningham. As a cop, he had to observe what they were doing. Sometimes he would try and entrap them or attempt to catch them in the act. Most times, even if an arrest was eventually made, they were back in business the next day. Once Jerry died, I went through some changes. I'm not the same person. If I told you the whole story, you would think I was crazy. In fact, I'm not even sure what my story is, or how it ends."

"Tell me!" Laura demanded. She desperately wanted to go beyond the surface.

For some reason, Danny felt he could confide in Laura, so he began to tell his story. He told of how he meant to help the police and decided to become a hero in a failed attempt to capture what appeared simply as an old man. He explained how this old man had incredible strength and threw him through a window, but not before biting him. He told of how after leaving the hospital he had incredible fatigue, and how he slept for almost two days. After waking up, he realized he was changed in many ways. He had speed, strength, improved vision and hearing, but most of all, he had a new attitude toward activism. For some strange reason, he felt like he could attack the criminal element himself, without police involvement. All the cash was just a bonus. For some reason, Danny felt he could let Laura know his most guarded secret.

"Laura, can I trust you? Will you not think me completely insane?"

"What Danny? You can tell me." Her dark eyes reflected complete understanding and deep interest. She brushed her thick hair back and reclined, in anticipation of what he was about to divulge.

"Laura, I believe the old man that bit me was a werewolf. I believe he passed the curse on to me." Instead of laughing as he expected, she remained listening intensely. "I awoke and I could see things I could never have seen before. I have speed beyond what is capable for a normal human and my strength has become tremendous. I have senses I never had before."

"Like?" She wanted examples.

"Like go to the back of this trailer and look out the back window. If you open the curtain a sliver, you will see a fox sniffing around. I can sense him and can hear him."

Laura slowly and quietly went to the rear of the trailer and peeked out the window. There, in the darkness, was a fox in clear view, searching for or stalking something. She was amazed. She slowly walked back and sat down. "What do you think will happen to you?"

"Well, from what I have been told by the only man familiar with these things, is that when the full moon rises I will turn into a wolf. Not just a wolf, but a mindless animal capable of harming whatever crosses my path. His advice to me was to retreat to the wilderness and stay away from the population during the whole cycle of the full moon."

Laura sat there silently.

"I know, say it . . . 'Take me home.' I don't blame you."

"Danny, wolves are never mindless. They may defend their territory, but they always maintain some bit of logic. There is no such thing as a 'mindless' wolf. Who was this old man who told you of this?"

"His name is Jonah, Jonah Blevins. He is near 100 years old and is familiar with Ozark folklore first hand, in many cases. He stated that werewolves were once common in these mountains. He told me the legend of the Howler. The Howler was supposedly the last one of its kind. I believe it was the Howler that bit me. Detective Higdon killed him with the only thing that will end a werewolf's life . . . a silver bullet. If all this is true, I guess I'm the new Howler." He expected her to possibly react in fear.

Instead, she motioned Danny to sit next to her. She cupped his hand. Danny did not anticipate what she would say next. She whispered, "Bite me."

"What?" Danny was astonished.

"Bite me," she repeated seriously.

"Laura, I have no idea where this is all going. I have no idea what will happen to me when the full moon comes. If I did bite you, I have no clue what I am letting you in for. Although," he reasoned, "so far all I have experienced has been positive. At least, that is how I perceive it. Laura, I have no idea what comes next."

"Danny, being a wolf would be my dream. I have adored them from as far back as I can remember. They are strong, intelligent, family oriented, protect their young, and will defend their society to the death. They mate for life, only kill to survive, and even respect their elders. Bite me." Laura looked as serious as a heart attack.

"If I do this, I will have to break skin."

Laura stood and faced Danny. Reaching out, she pulled him near. She pulled her blouse down, exposing her left shoulder. "Here . . . . do it here."

As she exposed her shoulder, on her back was shamrock tattoo. Danny studied it and asked, "What is the meaning?"

Laura smiled. "Someday I will share that with you, but for now, let's say it brings me the luck of the Irish."

"Are you sure you want this?" Danny asked again.

She embraced him and softly kissed him lightly on the lips, whispering "Bite me."

* * * *

Wayne picked up Mike from the hotel. He confirmed Mike was unarmed. Mike was sure that Wayne did not have the slightest notion of what he was really dealing with.

"I hope you're not making a mistake," Mike cautioned.

"You saw what he did. He saved our lives. I think if he wanted us dead, he would've let Aaron finish what he started. As I see it, for some reason, he wants to remain in this area and he does not want us searching the caves looking to kill him. Should Christian and Katherine remove some of the bad seeds in this county remaining transparent, so what? Mike, I have had more than enough of our revolving door of justice. I don't have to tell you. I work my ass off arresting this scum, gathering evidence, and preparing a case, and bingo! It is all plea-bargained down to nothing. I just wish I could give this blood sucker a list of names he could have for dinner!"

"Wayne, you have not seen what I have. These things will tear your throat out in a heartbeat. My first exposure was to a lair in a drainage pipe that was littered with bodies. When these monsters get hungry, I don't think they care much about anything other than draining the life from some poor soul."

"Mike, what can I tell you? In this tri-county area, we literally have a thousand pedophiles registered. We probably have half that many not registered. As a father of a young daughter, what do you think I'm more afraid of, a vampire, or this hoard of incurables that we release to prey on our society? I am scared shitless of sending my girl to daycare. I can't let go of her hand at the damned mall in the daytime. If you could get rid of all the vampires in the world or all the pedophiles, which would you choose? Let me ask, what were your last three cases before coming down here to Branson?"

Mike had to think for a moment. "Well, I had an easy one where a drunken husband shot his wife to death. Other than they didn't get along, there was no rhyme or reason. The one before that was the Quick Stop robbery where the clerk was shot dead over $27. Let's see, my third was a coked out mother that drowned her 3 year old. She'll likely plead insanity, go to the mental hospital, and be out in a few years. That's my last three, and all were on the same day."

"Okay . . . before coming to Branson, when was the last time you had evidence or faced a vampire?"

"Well, I killed the last one I faced in Minneapolis, so, a little over a year ago."

"And vampires are a problem why?" Higdon asked rhetorically.

"Hey, it's not like we get to choose. It's all bad, regardless." Mike began. "We both went to a Christian College. Where do you think God fits in to all of this? You have always been the more religious one."

"Boy, did you touch on the wrong subject. I once believed in nothing but kindness and forgiveness, but this job has opened my eyes a great deal. I'm sure my minister would not like to hear this, but my belief goes far beyond an eye for an eye. I no longer believe that everyone is worthy of forgiveness. I would not like to picture my Lord Jesus in a negative way, so instead, I imagine Saint Michael, who is more of an enforcer. What would he do if he caught an adult abusing a child? What would he do if he caught a man selling addictive poisons to his brethren? He would simply strike them down. Mike, I truly believe that some people should just be eliminated, period."

"I hear you. Most times I feel like I'm on a treadmill. Every damned day the same shit. I have seen fathers killing their families and mothers killing their kids. Last month I had a 16 year old that killed his grandparents. Then we have the gangs. These kids don't even know each other and kill each other just because they wear different colors. But where does a vampire fit in? It's just an indiscriminate, damned killing machine," Mike responded.

"And a serial killer is not? Realistically, how many kids have been killed by drug dealers?"

Mike thought for a moment. "Wayne, I don't disagree and I have surely made compromises that I have had second thoughts about, but a vampire is scary anyway you cut it."

"Honestly, it was that thing that killed Jerry that seemed mindless and out of control. I never want to see anything like that again. With the vampires, they have to trust us not to hunt them down. We know they're vulnerable in daylight. We also know they are likely cave dwellers. Though I asked you to be unarmed, I have a squirt gun filled with holy water in my pocket. So we're not completely at their mercy."

They drove to a dock near the riverboat in the state park. There sat a small rowboat with an electric motor. The electric motor ran quietly as they glided over the water. As was usual, a thick foggy blanket fell over the warm water as the cool air rolled in. When they reached the shore of the island, they walked from the boat and stood on the shore, looking out at the surrounding waters. With the riverboat in the distance, the scene was serene. Mike looked over to Wayne. "What now? You send up the bat signal?"

"No, I will just concentrate and call to him."

Mike watched as Wayne closed his eyes and began 'summoning' Christian with his mind.

On the Boardwalk, Christian stopped and looked to the air. He turned to Katherine. "He is calling. Can you hear it?"

"Yes, we should go."

It would take a few minutes for Christian and Katherine to leave the Boardwalk and get to a spot where they could take to the air without notice. Mike was about to start kidding Wayne about his transmitter being broken when the vampires landed silently.

"You summoned?"

Chapter Eleven

Mike was speechless as Katherine and Christian stood in the darkness, waiting for Higdon to present his need. "I'll be damned," is all Mike could mumble. Even Wayne found it incredible. They all stood, silently staring at one another for an uncomfortable moment before Christian broke the silence.

"I hope that if you are not in need, that this will not become a habit."

Mike couldn't help but joke. "I suppose we interrupted you from doing vampire-type things?"

"We were enjoying our evening strolling along the boardwalk," Christian replied dryly.

"I need to explain some specific guidelines that I can live with," Wayne stated. Christian winced.

"I see no weapons, but feel a strong repulsion. Why is this?"

Wayne produced the squirt gun from his jacket.

"What is this?" Christian asked. "It seems harmful to us, but it does not resemble a traditional weapon."

Higdon aimed it behind himself and pulled the trigger. A stream of Holy water shot about twelve feet. "Holy water. This can be quite effective."

Besides being surprised at this weapon that could be harmful to him, he bristled as to why they would even bring it with them. To Christian, it represented mistrust. "Why would you bring such a weapon?"

"Unlike you, I have no protections. You are a weapon within your very being. Our trust will be built over time."

"And you?" Christian pointed to Mike.

"Tomorrow I will go home to Minneapolis. I'll be back in a few weeks for another visit," Mike replied.

"Remember that you will sleep nights and enjoy the sunrise only because of my intervention . . ." Christian reminded him.

Wayne asked. "Who have you . . . er . . . eliminated recently?"

Christian became angry. "I will not report our behavior to you. Not now or ever! All you need to know is that you will never hear of our activity. This is better for all our sakes. Katherine is aware of your contaminated society, and she will easily guide us to feed within your guidelines. You have no need for details. You are much for the better not knowing."

Katherine smiled. "I will offer you this and only this as an example that will settle your conscience. There is no longer a meth lab where there once was one. Of course, you had no knowledge of this anyway. There is an armed group of sociopathic radicals that have one less member. There is a violent motorcycle gang that has a few less members. This is all we will ever tell you, and I only share this to indicate our direction."

Immediately the 'undercover' cop came to Higdon's mind. 'Was he a victim?' Higdon wondered.

Mike saw an opportunity to ask. "Christian, I'm going home to Minneapolis. I must address the Professor's disappearance. I know Aaron killed him. Do you know where the Professor's body is? This would bring closure to all those that were close with him. Without the body, he will remain a missing person."

Christian could see no reason to divulge the whereabouts of the corpse. Plus, he understood that in showing them the location deep in the wilderness, he would expose more bodies, for it was likely Aaron's dumping ground, so he lied. "I wish I could help you, but Aaron made no mention of this incident. I had a certain respect for the old man. He left me with a profound thought that will always remain with me. I would say I am sorry, but I am incapable of feeling remorse. I find your sadness, at times, confusing."

"What is so confusing about missing someone?"

"Because it is inevitable. Life and death are simply a cycle. You are dying as we speak. Why should death be so surprising? The old man lived a long and full life and in fact, died pursuing his obsession. I understand missing his presence, but what is there to mourn?"

Mike found this a contradiction. "Did you not mourn Anne?"

Christian thought for a moment. "Our relationship spanned two lifetimes, something you can never comprehend . . . but point taken."

Mike spoke softly, but knew it was beyond a vampire's comprehension. "We will miss him, but it's all about closure. What if your Anne had merely disappeared?"

"I would mourn her essence, not her physical body. However, I can understand this closure you seek, but I would be seeking revenge. The killing of Aaron should have given you the satisfaction and closure you wish."

Christian was completely baffled as he felt that a dead body, in itself, had no value.

Higdon had to ask an important question. "Christian, if I can determine the habits of an '*undesirable*' individual and supply you with a point and time in which this person would be vulnerable to you, would you eliminate this person for me?"

Christian smiled knowingly and pointed to Katherine. "Take into account that it is a rare individual that would not invite Katherine in. So yes, provided this is not to become too frequent, it would be our pleasure." Christian looked to Mike. "Have a safe passage. It might be that we will meet again on your return. I would say it was a pleasure, but we both know that it was not so."

"Christian, I don't exactly approve of this collaboration; not because of moral reasons, but because I feel my friend's safety is in jeopardy. Should anything happen to Wayne, I will return with my own methods of vengeance."

For the first time, Christian sensed no fear in Mike as they stared eye to eye. "If Higdon is harmed, it will not be by Katherine or me. On this, you have my word." He stepped away. "It seems we are finished with our business. I hope this leaves you with a confidence that we can be summoned, and that we will present no threat to those in the common public. With this, we bid you good night."

As Wayne and Mike watched, Katherine and Christian slowly rose into the dark sky.

"A beer before bedtime?" Wayne asked.

"Why the hell not?"

* * * *

Danny sat back, watching Laura sleep. Given what he had experienced, he knew she would likely be asleep for a day. He counted all the cash he had robbed from the previous night and all totaled it was over $37,000 dollars. He stared at her and admired her beauty. Her eyes were dark and mysterious, and her thick hair fell like a crown, framing her beautiful face. He touched her hand, and even in her unconscious state, she squeezed back, as if it represented security. Danny brushed her hair back and kissed her forehead. He knew what a wondrous day she would soon face when she would awake within a whole new body. He knew she would not awaken soon, and he also knew she was safe, so he decided to go out and add to his cash and put a dent in Branson's criminal activity. As he walked outside and although it was night, to Danny, it was like the daytime. He could see as clearly as if the sun were shining.

Right in the midst of the Branson entertainment strip was a major hotel. Residing there was a pimp who ran a prostitution ring. His organization was all run by cell phones, as the girls that worked for him traveled to meet their customers elsewhere. Danny knew that in this hotel room besides the pimp, were two or more enforcers. These men were muscle to be used, should a girl call having trouble with a customer. This man did not look the role of a pimp. He dressed well and rarely allowed any activity to enter the hotel. All the business was done by cell phone, so nothing even came across the switchboard. To the hotel, he was a welcomed long-term guest who appeared to enjoy golf. Danny knew better. He had made food deliveries there. He also knew his muscle was also the pickup men for all the cash. Being late in the week, there would be a lot of it. So, Danny drove to Branson.

He parked his vehicle in a dark corner of the hotel's lot. He decided to carry a thermal bag to appear as though he was delivering a food order. No one took notice of Danny as he boarded the elevator. Arriving on the top floor, he proceeded to what was one of a few penthouse suites. He softly knocked on the door. "Who is it?" a voice called out.

"Room service," Danny answered. He waited for a moment and slowly, the door opened. Without warning, Danny pushed against it with great force, knocking the bodyguard down. A second one jumped to his feet and Danny could see him reaching behind his back for a gun. Danny moved forward quickly and kicked the man solidly in the chest, sending him backwards. Without a pause, Danny went to the pimp, who was fumbling through a drawer to get another gun when Danny grabbed him by the throat. Danny then stated, "No guns!" While holding the man with one hand, Danny produced a 9mm semi-automatic from the drawer. He pointed it at the two enforcers and waved them to the couch.

"Sit, muscle heads! Set all of the guns on the table."

Without saying anymore, Danny released the pimp and walked over, putting the weapons in his thermal bag. "Are there anymore guns here?" One of the men who just couldn't see Danny as that much of a threat rose up, attempting to grab him. "Get this little bastard!" he screamed. In a blur, Danny struck him square in the face and blood splattered everywhere.

Danny muttered, "Damn; I hoped it wouldn't go like this!"

The other two men took it as their cue to attack. Having superior peripheral vision, Danny could see the man in front and the pimp coming from his right. He turned and grabbed the pimp, using the pimp's forward motion, and threw him into the man in front of him. This sent the sofa completely backwards. Danny jumped the sofa and was on them both. A few solid punches and the men were holding their hands up in defeat. "No more!" the pimp yelled. "What the fuck is this? What do you want?"

Danny just stated, in almost a whisper, "Money. I want all the money."

The pimp just shook his head. "Look, kid. This is going to a drop that is destined for Bobby Raye. You can have my cut, but don't put a crimp in this pipeline. Bobby will hunt you down like a dog."

Danny just smiled. "Bobby Raye, blah, blah, blah. That's all I hear around here. You tell this Bobby Raye that I am one dog he doesn't want to fuck with. Now, I want the cash."

The pimp pointed to the desk as his cell phone rang. Danny picked it up and smashed it against the wall. He opened the drawer and it was full of cash, all neatly banded in bundles. While they watched, he filled his thermal bag.

The pimp just couldn't believe Danny was doing this. "Kid, we all know who you are. We all know you worked at Elmer's. Bobby will find you in a second."

Danny sneered. "Bobby won't find me. But you tell Bobby Raye that I will gladly meet with him. You tell him the night of the next full moon that I will be on the island on Table Rock Lake. He can bring a bodyguard if he likes. Remember, the night of the next full moon."

The pimp was confused. "Full moon? What the fuck is that? On the island? Bobby is going to think I'm fucking nuts!"

Danny casually walked over to him and grabbed him by the collar. "Maybe he will take you more seriously when you are talking from a hospital bed." Danny then slammed him against the wall and the pimp crumpled to the floor. He then turned to the other two. "You guys need anymore?" They both shook their heads an emphatic 'No!'

Danny picked up the thermal bag and walked out, slamming the door. No one but the doorman even noticed him leaving, who smiled an acknowledgement. Danny tossed the bag in the back of his vehicle and headed home to sleep next to his beloved Laura.

* * * *

The next day after seeing Mike off, Wayne decided to have a quiet lunch. He stepped into Elmer's and sat in the back, facing the door. In his mind, all was well except for letting the bad publicity run itself out. He laughed as he read the local paper that stated that the Chateau hotel was undergoing 'remodeling' and renovating the atrium. *'Remodeling, my ass!'* he thought. *'Branson! They can spin anything!'* He figured life would get back to normal. Mike was on his way home, Christian and Katherine would stay invisible, and he assumed the Howler was dead. Wayne hoped he would resume tending to minor robberies and domestic disputes. He was looking forward to his forthcoming boredom. Then, the door of Elmer's swung open.

In walked a little man that Higdon quickly recognized. It was a man he once met that he, or anyone else, was not likely to forget—Bobby Raye. He was a short man, who attempted to compensate by wearing cowboy boots with the highest heels possible. It gave him a walk like he was on stilts. He had blonde hair, but combed it into a huge pompadour—in the old fifties style, like a young Elvis. He thought he dressed fashionably, but he looked obnoxious, always wearing a colorful silk shirt with freshly ironed denim jeans. Until he opened his mouth, one might assume him to be gay, with his flashy jewelry. He walked into Elmer's with his two enormous bodyguards as if he owned the place. As he looked around surveying the interior and making sure he was well noticed, all Wayne could think was, *'Oh shit!'* Higdon was all too familiar with Bobby, and was not sure whether he was a psychopath or a sociopath . . . but knew him as bad news.

Seeing Higdon, he smiled and yelled, "Hey! Bobby Raye knows you! You used to be in Springfield!"

He walked back to Wayne's booth and slid in, leaving his two companions standing. In a tone of sarcasm, Wayne said "Why don't you have a seat?"

"So you're in Branson now?"

"Yeah. I got tired of Springfield. So are you here seeing an Elvis show, or jewelry shopping?" Wayne remained sarcastic, throwing an insult right over Bobby's head.

"Nah. Bobby Raye got problems here Wayne, and if Bobby Raye got problems, you got problems." Bobby reached over and grabbed one of Wayne's French fries.

"How do you figure?" Wayne asked.

"A number of my operations have been . . . let's say . . . interrupted. Bobby Raye don't like that." Bobby Raye then gave a grimace. "Bobby Raye don't like these fries either . . . too greasy."

Wayne smiled. "I did hear a few of your friends or associates were in the ER recently."

"No, Higdon, this is serious. About fifty-plus thousand serious," Bobby replied.

"What?" Wayne had no idea of the amount of money involved.

"Bobby Raye is told there is this young man named Danny, who has become a giant pain in Bobby Raye's ass. He busted up a number of my associate's businesses and robbed them. He is either one bold-ass mother fucker, or he has a death wish."

Wayne, in a flash of ill placed humor, asked "Did your associates report it to the police?"

Bobby's temper flared. "Higdon, Bobby Raye ain't screwing around here. Bobby Raye will turn this town upside down. Bobby Raye does all he can to keep everything on the down low. Never is my shit in the Branson news. We both know what the game is. If you can catch Bobby Raye's guys, good for you. We get our attorneys and go down that road. But this is different. This kid is acting like a damned vigilante thief bastard."

"So, Bobby Raye is willing to swear out a warrant?" Wayne asked in jest, not having a care about Bobby's operations.

"Funny, but not funny! Bobby Raye is taking this kid out when Bobby Raye finds him." Bobby whispered seriously.

"Well, I heard he skipped town and went to Florida a few days ago," Wayne offered.

"Higdon, he must have came back on the Red Eye, because three of Bobby Raye's guys and about twenty-thousand dollars say he was in town last night."

Wayne was shocked. "Off the record, what the hell are we talking about here? *Wayne* knows very little about this . . ." Wayne mocked Bobbie's third-person speak.

"So far, here is Bobby's list of damages. Bobby has a sidewalk salesman on the boardwalk—he hit him. Bobby has a little girlie operation—he hit that. Bobby has a little weed distribution—he hit that. He tried to get the drop on some Hell's Ravens, and a few days later a couple of them had an unfortunate motorcycle accident. Bobby has an escort service—he hit that. Bobby also has a small . . . let's say . . . chemical manufacturing company. It got blowed up. So far, I've got four dead and seven visiting the ER. All this within three fucking days! Now that's too much bad luck to be coincidence."

Bobby could see by Wayne's expression that this was a total revelation. "And you think Danny did all this?"

"Yeah. The little bastard wants to meet with Bobby Raye."

"Where? When?"

"Now if I tell you that, Bobby Raye would have to wade through police tape to get there. All I'll say is it's in the future."

"Well, if Danny really did all that, then he went completely off the deep end. Do what you have to do," Wayne replied seriously.

Bobby was surprised. "That don't sound like the Wayne Higdon I knew?"

"This Wayne Higdon has learned a few lessons. Wayne gives the devil his due." Again, mocking Bobby, but without notice.

"So you'll be looking the other way?"

"I want no trouble with you in Branson. This Danny can't possibly be walking, so I'm sure you have a contact at the DMV to get his license number and car description. Do what you have to do, but I hope I don't have to hear about it."

"When Bobby Raye finds him, all you will hear is a damned scream echoing these mountains! Wayne, you enjoy your lunch." Wayne watched as Bobby did his 'stilted' walk, followed by his bodyguards out the door.

"See you, Bobby." Wayne was really confused. Was it even possible that Danny could do all that damage? Why would he blow up a meth lab? How could timid, clean-cut Danny do any of this? Wayne began thinking of all the possibilities. Maybe Danny just snapped? Maybe he was on the pain killers that the doctor gave him? Whatever the reason, Wayne concluded that if Danny really did do all that damage, then Bobby deserved his revenge, as long as it did not become a public spectacle. Should he see Danny, he would surely tell him to leave town quick! What Wayne did not know was that the 'damage' was being done by both Christian and Danny!

* * * *

Laura awoke to find Danny watching over her. He knew exactly what she was feeling. He knew she would look around the room, realizing and then testing her new vision. He watched and could tell she was focusing on different objects and seeing things for the first time. She examined her hands, sensing they were stronger, and then her arms, which now had more muscle definition. She smiled at him and arose, moving toward him and sniffing at his neck, as if memorizing his scent. Her first words reflected the same feeling he had experienced. "I need to be outside. I need to run."

Behind their trailer was literally miles of open wilderness, and they took off like the wind. He watched the expression on her face as she became aware of her new speed and agility. Then she suddenly stopped and looked perplexed. "What?" he asked.

"So what is the downside?"

"So far, other than a change in my preferred diet, I haven't found any yet. However, only God knows what the full moon will bring. I understand that for three nights we really will become wolves. Old Jonah told me to bring a set of clothes and go out to the wilderness. I'm thinking we will go out to that island on Table Rock. It's deserted, and we will be away from the population, so we won't hurt anyone, except possibly one person who just may pay us a visit.

"Who? Why would you do that?"

"Hell, I have no idea if the guy will show up, but his name is Bobby Raye. He is the vice king in these parts."

"Why would you do that?"

"Well, for one thing, he wants to kill me. I'm guessing I should kill him first. I figure I'll let the Howler do it."

Laura smiled. "Not if I get to him first!"

"Oh, don't worry, because he certainly will not come alone. We will have plenty of toys to play with."

"I'm hungry, let's eat!" Laura suggested.

"I have food in the trailer. We should eat away from the public, because your appetite for rare meat will be conspicuous. I have plenty in the refrigerator."

"I'll race you!" Laura took off running. Danny just laughed, knowing she still had to discover her strength and night vision.

* * * *

The following week was rather routine for Wayne, as his life fell back into a 'normal' pace. Abby, his wife, was happy once again with her husband keeping regular hours. There seemed to be no 'unusual' events and Branson had returned to its wholesome atmosphere. If Danny was still out there creating havoc for Bobby Raye, the problems with these illegal activities were certainly not being reported to the police. All Wayne knew was that if Christian and Katherine were out there, they were truly invisible to the public and authorities. But something was bothering Wayne. He wanted to know if he could use them to eliminate certain problems. There was a known child molester that lived outside the city in an isolated area. This man had been convicted twice and accused and acquitted multiple times because of parents not allowing their children to face this molester and testify in court. Wayne knew it was only a matter of time before he would be putting handcuffs on him again. He wondered, '*Can I get Christian and Katherine to pay him a visit? Could they make this monster go away before he harmed another child?*' He decided to test this possibility. So he waited for the sun to set and headed for the wilderness. Driving to a deserted area outside the city, he sat and 'called' for Christian. As he stood leaning against his car, they startled him, appearing from behind.

"Is there a problem?" Christian asked.

"None whatsoever," Wayne replied. "I need a favor."

"How can we help you?" Christian asked, while Katherine remained quiet and only smiling.

"Near where we are is a house. It is isolated and is by the lake. Parked outside will be a white van. There is no garage or other buildings, and the house is also white and it is quite neglected. It sits far from the main highway. The address is 244 W. Farm Road S. In this house is a man that harms children. He has harmed many, and will surely repeat this behavior if he hasn't already. Until we have evidence, which will mean another child is harmed, the police can't touch him. Can you?"

"Do you have an image of this man?" Christian asked.

Wayne produced a photo. Christian studied it and handed it to Katherine, who also studied it and handed it back to Wayne. "He will no longer be your problem."

Wayne could say nothing more than "Thank you."

Christian focused on Wayne. "I sense no fear in you. I also sense you brought no weapons to defend from us."

"You are correct. In truth, I am beginning to view you more as an asset than a threat."

Christian smiled. "We have a trust."

"We do have something. In this last week, I realized that almost every day I feared man. I fear for my safety when I serve a warrant. I fear for my safety when I respond to any number of calls. I also fear for my daughter when she is at preschool. I live with a lot of fear. I don't exactly approve of who you are, but honestly, if I could get you to clean out a few prisons, it would make me very happy. Which begs the question; have you ever thought of lightening the prison population?"

"We have never had the need," Christian answered without emotion.

"Hey, it's a thought. Again, thank you."

"I will not report the result of this task, so you need not call. We have no reason to meet again."

Wayne watched as they both rose into the air and disappeared. He stood at his car, wondering if he was doing something that might doom his soul to hell. He wondered, *'Could Jesus tolerate a man who harms a child? Would Jesus stand by and do nothing? Literally, what would Jesus do?'* Wayne drove home and just felt the need to hug his wife and child, and hold them near.

* * * *

Wayne had no knowledge that Christian and Katherine had not yet eaten and needed to feed.

"Can we locate this man that Higdon wants removed?" Christian asked.

"Most easily," Katherine responded.

"Why not get it over with and be done with it?"

With night vision and from the air, they followed along the farm road and were easily able to focus on the house Higdon had described. What Higdon didn't know was that Christian and Katherine already knew the areas outside the city limits like the back of their hands. They landed in the yard.

"How will we proceed?"

Katherine smiled. "Leave it to me."

Christian watched as she walked to the door and knocked politely. When the door opened, there was no doubt that it was their soon-to-be victim.

"I'm sorry, but my car broke down. Can I come in and use your phone?" Katherine used her sweetest voice.

The man appeared agitated. "What, no cell phone?"

"In fact, yes, but it fails to get a signal out here, so I left it in the car."

The man grimaced. "Yeah, okay. Come on in. Make it quick."

Once inviting her in, he had sealed his fate. Katherine instantly morphed into her vampire presence. The man stepped back in horror. "Oh God!" he gasped.

She grabbed him by the shirt, pulling him outside. "God will not help you! In fact, even if he could, I believe he would look the other way," she growled.

Christian approached, also in his vampire presence. The man put his hands over his face, shielding his eyes from the horrific sight. He kept repeating, "Oh God, oh God, oh God!"

Christian grabbed him by the throat. "Is the pleasure yours or mine?"

Katherine hissed, "Enjoy!"

Christian bit into his neck as the man screamed in pain and horror. He then passed the man to Katherine, who also began her feeding. They passed him back and forth until his heart stopped beating.

"What now?" Christian asked.

"Well, to make things look as if he just left and possibly relocated I should get his personal effects and his wallet, and turn out the lights. Then we can dump the body in the mountains." She entered the house and picked up the man's wallet and keys, turning out all the lights and locking the door as she left.

"Nice and neat. Higdon should be pleased," she stated.

In seconds, they were gone. Having fed, they would enjoy going to Branson and strolling along the boardwalk.

* * * *

Weeks went by before Wayne was meeting the tour bus from Minneapolis and Mike Evans exited with a smile. "I see you're still alive," he laughed.

Entering the Chateau hotel, he marveled at the new atrium. The 'remodeling' was finished and it glistened. They proceeded to have lunch. At the top floor of the hotel was the restaurant that overlooked the beautiful lake and mountains in a spectacular view. After ordering, Wayne asked, "So? How you been?"

"Good! I've got some information for you. The squirt gun works!"

Wayne was surprised. "You actually used it?"

"I had to try, as it was killing me. So I went hunting. I found one in the storm drain under the city."

"You went alone?" Wayne was shocked.

"Yeah, who else could I ask? I took my miner's helmet and went where I knew we had encountered them before. I went in the daytime and found one sleeping, just hanging upside down. I had my crossbow, but decided I would see how one would react to being doused in holy water. I had gone out and bought a huge super shooter that held about a quart. So I blasted him. I doused that bastard with it. I had no idea whether he would take off and flee like a rocket or attack. Instead, he landed in front of me, writhing in pain and screaming like a banshee. Basically, I had a stationary target, and I put one right in his heart," Mike stated proudly. "So to answer the question, they are, for the most part, paralyzed in pain."

"You're kidding me?" Wayne was amazed.

"No buddy, I'm not."

"The Professor?" Wayne asked.

"I guess he will always be a missing person, at least for seven years. Expect the FBI down here sometime soon to ask you a few questions. Shame though, since I know he deserves a memorial service. How goes it with you?"

Wayne grinned. "Great! Everything has been quiet. I called for a favor a few weeks ago. I asked Christian to make a child molester disappear."

"Did he?"

"I assume so. The guy is gone. Reported missing by the person he was renting from. It appears he has skipped town."

"You think he did?"

"Permanently."

Mike wondered. "Do you meet with them on a regular basis?"

"Actually, only that once when I asked for the favor and other than that, I haven't heard a thing. Better yet, nothing unusual has been reported. They are literally invisible to the public."

"So, nothing out of the ordinary?" Mike wondered.

"I don't know if you remember that delivery guy who went through the window, but it seems he has turned into a vigilante and that he was cleaning out the drug dealers and brothels for awhile. The day you left I met with the Springfield vice king who was out to kill him."

"Did he?"

"Honestly, I have no clue. Obviously, if a drug dealer gets robbed he doesn't call us, but if Danny is still alive, he has not been seen. That's about it."

"And you?" Wayne asked.

"What's to say? It's Minneapolis. Big city, lots of urban crime, gang activity, and no shortage of homicides. What would be the chance of me getting on here in Branson?" Mike asked.

"Hell, I think we have an opening, so I would imagine great! The department would love having someone with your experience. Mike, I really need to get a few things done. How about if Abby and I come and get you around seven?" Wayne asked.

"What's the agenda?"

"What else? A ride on the riverboat!"

*   *   *   *

Like most late evenings in the Ozarks, the sky was clear and as the sun went down, the stars littered the sky so that the constellations appeared as a huge display. One could not ask for a more beautiful evening. Even though a month had gone by, Mike still got a chill crossing over the dock onto the boat, remembering standing in the water under it, having escaped Aaron. He glanced toward the island where he last saw the Professor. Boarding the vessel, they entered the main dining room and prepared for dinner. Mike could not help but scan the upper levels, checking if Christian might be there. Wayne caught him and stated, "Not to worry."

This time, Mike relaxed and enjoyed the band as it played a variety of upbeat dinner music. The last time they were there, he didn't eat a bite, but this time, he was amazed at how great the food was. Mike made polite conversation with Abby, as she was genuinely glad to see him. To Mike, it seemed unusual that hardly anyone greeted Wayne, but Abby appeared to be a social butterfly, as people seemed to go out of their way to say hello. At the dinner break before the main show, Abby left the table to talk with some friends. Mike looked to Wayne and asked, "Can we take a walk on the deck?"

"Sure, let's go up top."

The boat in mid-cruise was a fair distance from the dock and the island. By the time they reached the upper level, they were alone.

"So, Abby really doesn't know a thing?"

"Nope! I took your advice. Although, I'm glad you're here, because I needed someone to talk about it with. I never shared a thing with Abby."

"That's good. Believe me, she would be looking at you in whole different way. Telling my wife was the beginning of the end. To this day she thinks I'm insane."

As they talked, they never heard Christian and Katherine land on the deck behind them. Christian's voice startled them a bit.

"Mister Evans, Mister Higdon, good evening."

Mike and Wayne turned to Christian and Katherine, who were looking fresh and very, very human.

"I didn't call?" Wayne replied.

"No, we saw you here on the deck and felt it only polite to say hello."

Mike couldn't help his sarcasm. "I would ask how you were, but I guess you're still dead."

"Always in jest, despite your fear," Christian replied with a smile.

"I am told that your coexistence is going well," Mike stated.

"Higdon and I have achieved Détente. I hope you and I can achieve the same someday."

"Actually, it may come sooner than later. As a cop, the damage and carnage I face daily sometimes makes me feel that humans are the greatest monsters."

No sooner than Higdon looked upward to view a clear full moon, in the distance, a long, strong howl could be heard echoing the mountains. Higdon and Evans shared looks of concern.

"Impossible!" Higdon gasped.

"That's no ordinary sized wolf and being from Minnesota, I know what one sounds like," Evans replied.

They all listened as the Howl came again.

"OOOOOOOOOOOOooooooooooooooOOOOOOOOOOOOOO OOO!"

Christian immediately stated the obvious. "It is the Howler!"

Higdon was dumbfounded. "I killed the Howler! I shot six silver bullets into his heart!"

Then as they listened there came another surprise.

"O O O O O O O O O O O O o o o o o o o O O O O O O O O O,
OOOOOOOOOOoooooOOOOOOOOOOOOO!"

"There's two of them?"

Christian turned to Katherine and nodded, signaling their departure. "Gentlemen, we will take our leave." In a flash, they were gone.

Higdon and Evans just stood, confused.

"It can't be? It just can't be?" Higdon kept repeating as the howls continued.

"O O O O O O O O O O O O o o o o o o o O O O O O O O O O,
OOOOOOOOOOooooooOOOOOOOOOO!"

"Wayne, either you shot the wrong guy, which I doubt, or they multiplied. Either way, I'm guessing my vacation is ruined again! Higdon, I hope you have more of those silver bullets."

* * * *

At the dock from where the riverboat left, a long black limousine arrived. First, a huge bodyguard got out and looked around before nodding his approval. Then, out stepped Bobby Raye. He began yelling, "Get Bobby Raye's hardware!" Bobby was referring to his gun belt and a pair of Colt .45 revolvers. With him were four of the toughest men Missouri could offer.

"This little shit better show up! He is sure short a few marbles! Once he is on that island, he has nowhere to run to. Little bastard is right where Bobby Raye wants him!"

Obviously, Bobby Raye was in for a surprise!

* * * *

"OOOOOOOOOOOOOOOoooooooooooOOOOOOOOOOOOOOO
O," echoed the mountains.

Wayne could only repeat. "I don't believe it! Damn it, I don't believe it!"

Mike just shook his head in wonder. "Higdon, there should be a billboard. 'Welcome to Branson; home of the vampires, werewolves, and who knows what the hell else!'"

"O O O O O O O O O O O O O o o o o o o o O O O O O !
OOOOOOOoooOOOOOOOOO!"

Evans stated the inevitable. "Looks like we're going hunting!"

This saga will continue in the forthcoming DeathWalker III,
Night of the Howler. 2013

About the Author

Edwin F. Becker was born in Chicago, Illinois, a Baby Boomer. Coming from an abusive broken home, he spent a number of elementary years in Maryville, a Catholic children's institution. There, he learned Latin and became an altar boy. He went on to become a professional musician and spent his later teen years traveling the states with an R&B Show band. He worked with the Byrds, Temptations, and Chicago, to name a few groups. During his travels he met and married his wife of 45 years. Entering college, he studied the emerging field of computers and eventually progressed to a programmer, systems analyst, telecommunications specialist, operations manager and finally to a VP of MIS for a major health care corporation. He assisted the Department of

Defense in automating their procurement department in Philadelphia in the early 1980's. He became president of a software company that catered to the sales and development of health care inventory management. Suffering a near fatal heart attack, he retired to the Ozarks where he opened a collectible store for a number of years. He has been writing original stories for over two decades for pure enjoyment. He has two daughters that have given him four granddaughters which he considers

God's ultimate gifts. His youngest daughter is involved with fostering abused children and rescuing animals, including horses. He has a son-in-law involved in law enforcement. His life experience and interests run the gamut. During his life, he has enjoyed boating, martial arts, ballistics, comics, guitars, motorcycles, religion, and the paranormal, to name a few personal interests. Today he resides in Branson, where he enjoys the year around activity and entertainment. He is very opinionated and many of his works contain a strong social subtext. Missouri, the "Show Me" state, seems an appropriate place to reside. His personal philosophy? "Leave everything and everyone better than you found them."

Please visit Ed at www.EdwinBecker.com